The Marbeck Inn
A Novel

by

Harold Brighouse

The Marbeck Inn
A Novel
by Harold Brighouse

ISBN: 978-93-63051-11-9

Published by

DOUBLE 9 BOOKS

2/13-B, Ansari Road
Daryaganj, New Delhi – 110002
info@double9books.com
www.double9books.com
Tel. 011-40042856

ABOUT THE AUTHOR

Harold Brighouse was an English playwright and author whose most famous work is Hobson's Choice. He was a significant member of the Manchester School of Dramatists, which also included Allan Monkhouse and Stanley Houghton. Harold Brighouse was born in Eccles, Lancashire, the eldest child of John Southworth Brighouse, a cotton-spinning manager, and Charlotte Amelia née Harrison, a headmistress. Harold attended a local school before winning a scholarship to Manchester Grammar School. At the age of 17, he dropped out of school and began working as a textile buyer at a shipping merchant's office. In 1902, he traveled to London to open an office for his company. He met Emily Lynes there, and they married in Lillington, Leamington Spa, in 1907. He was promoted at work and moved back to Manchester, but in 1908 he became a full-time writer. Brighouse wrote his first play, Lonesome Like, but The Doorway was the first to be produced. Ben Iden Payne staged this performance, which took place in 1909 at Annie Horniman's Gaiety Theatre in Manchester. Horniman and Payne helped Brighouse in the early phases of his career.

CONTENTS

CHAPTER I
THE STARTING-POINT

IT falls to some to be born, as they say, with a silver spoon in their mouths, and the witty have made play with the thought that the wise child chooses rich parents.

Sam Branstone lacked the completeness of that wisdom. He was born in one of those disconsolate streets of Manchester down which the stranger, passing by tram along a main road, hardly more delectable than its offshoots, looks and shudders; but was born with this difference from the many— that he was son to Anne Branstone, a notable woman, and wisdom may be conceded him for the discrimination of his choice.

If, however, it was Anne who gave him birth and started him in life, it was Mr. Councillor Travers who set him on his way from the mean street of his birth and started his career, and the circumstance which led to the intervention of Mr. Travers was due, not to Anne, but to the occupation of Tom Branstone.

Sam's father, Tom, was a porter at Victoria Station, Manchester, and there was just time between morning and afternoon school for young Sam to snatch a meal himself and to carry his father's dinner to him in a basin tied up in a bandanna handkerchief. In those days Victoria was an open station and a favourite dinner-hour lounge with boys from the neighbouring Grammar School. The attractions were partly the trains, partly the large automatic machines which delivered a packet of sweet biscuits in return for a penny. First one lunched frugally on the biscuits and pocketed the balance of one's lunch allowance to buy knives and other essentials, then one savoured the romance of a large station from which trains went to Blackpool and to the Yorkshire moors. Often one saw sailors on the through trains from Liverpool to Newcastle. One found secluded ends of platforms and ran races with luggage trucks. One was rather a nuisance, especially when one wrestled hardily at the platform's giddy edge and a train came in.

Sam, as a porter's son, was on the other side of the fence. He did not lark at Victoria Station, and took his opinions of those who did from his father, adding, perhaps, a touch of jealousy against these chartered libertines who wore the silver owl upon their caps of dual blue.

That day he had delivered Tom's dinner to him in the porters' room and was retracing his steps down the platform when he saw two of the Grammar School boys emerge in a confused whirl of battle and sag, interlocked, towards the line, hopelessly unconscious in their struggle of an incoming train. They reached the edge, deaf to all warning cries, and long before help could reach them, fell over it in one entangled mass. One boy, aroused to a sense of their common danger, was on his feet nimbly enough and across the line to safety: the other, Lance Travers, stayed where he fell, with a leg broken against the rail. Wits left the first lad; he could only howl as the engine swept inexorably on, and adult help, though active, could not avail in time. Sam had no precise recollection of what followed, and certainly acted on impulse. He dived to the line and dragged the injured boy across, escaping death for both by the skin of his teeth.

After that, all was confusion: an ambulance; inquiries; names taken and so on; and Sam only came to himself when he discovered that he was being punished for arriving late at school. It struck him as unfair, but he did not realize that he was a hero till the evening paper told him so. He, Samuel Branstone, had his name in the paper! Glory could go no further, because those were the dark ages of journalism, before the photograph illustrated all, and to read one's name in print was then the apogee. We have moved since those dull days, when "heart interest" was still to be in vented.

What profound satisfaction Anne Branstone found in that sober paragraph her son was not to know. She did not think it good for him to know, but she went about her house with softened eyes, and Sam heard her singing more than once; so per haps he may have guessed that she was pleased with him.

It was more than she allowed Mr. Oscar Travers to guess, he was Lance's father, an estate agent with a good suburban practice, and Anne met him at the door in a way which would have marred Sam's future had Travers not known that Lancashire women are apt to be undemonstrative. She found a portly gentleman on the doorstep and thought he wore a patronizing air. They resent patronage in Lancashire.

As a matter of fact, Travers had come to see what he could do for the lad who had saved his boy's life. That may be patronage, but he was thinking of it as the barest decency.

"Good evening," he said; "my name is Travers."

"This is a nice upset," she said, without inviting him to come in. "How's your son?"

"He's doing very well, thank you."

"Oh? Well, it's more than he deserves."

He did not argue that. "I wonder," he said, "if you would allow me to come in, or would you prefer me to return when your husband is at home?"

"He's at home now. It's his early night. He's having his tea."

"Shall I return when he has finished?" asked Travers with a nice tactfulness. He knew the curious delicacy against being seen eating by one of a superior class, as if that natural function were a deed of shame. But Anne was for short cuts and she never considered Tom's feelings overmuch.

"If you've owt to say," she said, "you'd better come in and get it over."

"I have something to say," said Travers, entering. "Ah," he added, as he caught sight of Sam, "this is— —?"

"It's him," Anne interrupted. She might have been identifying a criminal.

"May I shake your hand?" he asked, and shook it heartily, ignoring Anne's muttered protest that the hand had not been washed for hours. "I think you're a very plucky lad." He could have, said more than that, and felt that as an expression of his gratitude it was hopelessly inadequate, but Anne's eyes forbade effusiveness, and he wanted to propitiate Anne. He had something to propose which he had thought they would agree to rapturously, but was not so sure about the rapture now. For some reason, he had imagined that Sam would be one of a large family and was disappointed to find no evidence of other children about the room A large family would have made his proposal more certain of acceptance.

"Any brothers and sisters, Sam?" he asked; but Sam was tongue-tied, while Anne was silently but unmistakably asking Travers what business of his that was. However, Tom knew his place. Travers belonged with the tipping public, whose questions one answered.

"He has an elder sister, sir. Our Madge. She works out." She was, in fact, a general servant.

Travers felt his confidence ebb fast, both at this information and at Anne's austere disapprobation of Tom's communicativeness. He felt it was suggested to him that his visit was irrelevant, that Anne, this small woman, not uncomely, with her hands on her hips, and her black hair tightly combed into a ridiculous knob at the back, was, in fact, a rock, and that the impulses and desires of the two hulking men, Travers and Tom Branstone, would break in ineffectual foam against her adamantine resolution.

She glared formidably, hating a "fuss," judging Travers, who had invaded her home for the purpose of making a fuss.

"Indeed," said Travers, marking time and hardly attempting to conceal his dismay. The longer he spent in Anne's presence, the more uneasy he became. She seemed to divine his purpose, and to be telling him silently what she thought of him for having such a purpose. He had, indeed, banked on a large family; porters, he had felt certain, were prolific, and you may subtract one child from a family of ten without much heart-burning, whereas an only son is a serious matter. But time brought no graciousness to Anne's attitude. She even ignored the sacred rites of hospitality; though tea was on the table, she had not asked him to have a cup. So he gave up temporizing and decided to broach his purpose at once, before Anne reduced him to complete incoherence.

"Of course," he said, "you know me already as Lance's father. I don't know whether you happen to have heard of me beyond that?" Anne admitted nothing, and as it was to her he spoke, it did not matter that Tom, who had naturally spent a gossipy afternoon, was trying to signify that he realized the importance of Travers. "I'm an estate agent, if you understand what that means."

Anne nodded grimly. "Rent-collector said big," she defined.

"Well," said Travers, intending to suggest an amended definition and then thinking better of it. "Well, yes. I'm in the Council, too, you know. Well, now, Mrs. Branstone, I happen to be a widower and Lance is my only son. He means a great deal to me, and when I think how near I came to losing him this afternoon, how certainly I had lost him hut for the splendid presence of mind of this young hero here, I feel I owe a debt which I can never hope to pay."

"Mr. Travers," said Anne, "least said is soonest mended, and debts that you can never hope to pay are best forgotten. It's a kindly thought of yours to come and look us up to-night, but I'm not in the Council, and I'm no great hand at listening to long speeches. By your leave, we'll take the rest as said."

"By all means, Mrs. Branstone, so far as expressing my thanks goes. But I have a suggestion to make. Lance, as I said, is my only son. He's a lonely boy, and he'd be the better for a companion of his own age about the house. I was wondering if you would allow Sam to come and live with us? I should send him with Lance to the Grammar School, and I think I can promise that his future will be secured."

Sam's heart gave a great leap. He, Sam Bran-stone, a Grammar School boy, one of the elect, the Olympians whose play he had envied from afar! He looked at Anne with glittering eyes, faint with hope.

"Sam," she said, "Mr. Travers wants you to leave us. He's offering to adopt you as his son. Tell him the answer."

Anne never doubted that she was mistress of her house, and perhaps she did not doubt it now, but, for Sam, a child with the dreadful sensibility of a child, this moment when she demanded calmly, implacably, in the interests of discipline, that he should himself pronounce sentence on his soaring hopes was of a pitiable bitterness which brought him near the breaking-point. At one moment, to be raised to the heavens of ecstasy, and at the next to be cast down to the blackest hell of despondency; to be promised all, and to be expected to refuse! He was not more callous than any other child, and Anne knew perfectly well that a Land of Heart's Desire had been opened to him. It was not fair, and she knew that it was not fair, to ask him to speak the word of refusal; but she thought that it was good for him, and once she had, by her tone, if not by her actual words, indicated the reply which she required, she knew that he would suppress his leaping hopes and answer, in effect, that home, be it ever so humble, was home, and parents, whatever their status, were parents. He had a wild impulse to defy her, to tell her that he would come to see her on Saturday afternoons, that to wear the cap with the silver owl was the dearest ambition of his life, but he knew that it was hopeless. Even at such a moment as this, and with such an ally as Mr. Travers, he dared not challenge Anne. Her ascendancy was what it had always been, absolute. He shuffled unhappily and tried to meet Mr. Travers' eye bravely, but succeeded only in looking up as far as the second button of his waistcoat.

"No," said Sam Branstone, hero, and fled, a heartbroken, tear-washed child, to hide his face and choke his sobs upon his pillow. And he was named for valour in the evening paper!

"No," repeated Anne, when he had gone, and added, anticipating argument, "I'm a woman of few words."

Travers knew he was fighting a losing engagement, but he had a shot in the locker yet, and a hardy determination not to be worsted by the likes of Anne Branstone. His pride was up, a pride which, over and above his benevolence and his sense of the fitness of things, would not allow him to regard the saving of his son's life lightly. Travers counted, the saviour of the son of Travers counted. He had offered to lift Sam Branstone in one way, and if they would not let him do it in that way, he would do it in another. Sam Branstone, willy nilly, was going to be lifted.

"I suppose," he said, covering the retreat from his first position, "that it is of no use pointing out to you the advantages which my proposal offers to your son?" She shook her head. "Come, Mrs. Branstone," he went on, conscious that it was no use and platitudinous at that, "we all have to make sacrifices for our children."

"I make them," said Anne curtly. It was true.

"Yet you will not make this?"

She was thoughtful for a moment, and Travers began to hope that he was making an impression. "I'm sure that it's Genesis twenty-two," she said, "but I disremember the verse."

"Genesis," he repeated, mystified.

"Abraham and Isaac," she explained her allusion. "Some sacrifices aren't looked for from us, and the Lord sent an angel to say so in those days, but I've to be my own angel in these."

"But Abraham," he said, "was going to sacrifice his son to the Lord."

"And I won't," she said, conveying her opinion of Travers, who had tried to "come God Almighty over her," as she expressed it later to Tom. But Travers was not to be rebuffed. He had come to play Providence to Sam (and so far granted that her allusion was apposite), but his providence could compromise. He wasn't an absolute Jehovah.

"If Sam may not be Lance's home companion," he said, "at least let them be school companions. Let me pay his fees at the Grammar School, and— —" He was going to add "for appropriate clothes," but something in Anne's attitude told him that he had gone far enough, and he stopped short with the completion of his sentence in mid air.

Anne believed in education. She wasn't convinced that a Grammar School education was superior, as education, to a Parish School, but its associations were. It gave a chance of "getting on" which transcended anything the Parish School could offer. It was a start in life which set one automatically above the lower rungs of the ladder.

"Yes," she said, but said it with a difficulty which Travers noted and, indeed, applauded. He was Lancastrian himself, and honoured her for her independence. He knew the mother-pride, the fierce individualism which she had subdued before she had consented to take a favour even for her son who earned it, and wasted no more words. "I'm glad," he said. "Good night," and, shaking hands, was gone.

"Finish your tea, Tom," she said to her husband who had suspended operations during the interview. "I want to clear away." She stood a moment pensively. "I'm a weak woman," she decided.

Tom Branstone ate his tea, reserving judgment.

CHAPTER II
WHERE THE SHOE PINCHED

WHEN Anne Branstone set her hand to the plough she ploughed deep, and it was not her fault if the harvest was not immense. But she did not misdirect her energy; she made certain that the seed was good seed before she harnessed her plough. To drop metaphor, she let young Sam prove that he was worth troubling over before she took trouble—trouble, that is, as Anne understood the word. Of course, she sent him "decent" to the Grammar School, and if that meant that she and Madge went without new spring hats that year, well, last year's hats must do. It was no great matter, and the greater pride swallowed up the less. Mr. Travers paid the fees, so that her son could associate with his, and Anne saw to it thoroughly that, in externals, Sam should be worthy to associate with Lance.

That was the beginning, and Sam, so far, was untried metal. Then, at the end of his first term, he came out top of his form at the July examinations, and, after that, Anne began to take things seriously.

It was not pure ability which brought Sam to that proud eminence so much as the fact that he had been put in a form whose standard was really too low for him, and he had not worked over hard at lessons, being naturally preoccupied, in a first term, with finding his feet. Nor had that been too difficult. The Manchester Grammar School was a democratic institution. Schoolboys, anyhow, are not all snobs, and, in this instance, the presence amongst the paying boys of a leaven of Foundation Scholars, often from homes as poor as Sam's, made acclimatization easy for him.

But his feat impressed Anne, though all she said, when the lists came out with the name of "Branstone, S." at the head of II. Alpha, was, "Of course!" as if any other place were impossible for a son of hers; and it decided her that Sam would "pay for" taking trouble. She proceeded to take trouble.

Tom Branstone's first real inkling of what was passing in Anne's mind came to that good, easy man when he mentioned that his holidays were due in a fortnight.

"You'll take a holiday at home this year, my lad," she informed him.

"But why's that, Anne?" he asked. "Blackpool's in the same place as it was, and I get privilege passes on the line."

"Sam's not in the same place, though," she said. "He's at the Grammar School. It's a place where other boys wear decent clothes, and I'll see that Sam shan't fall behind them."

Tom took a holiday at home, varied with trips on the foot-plates of friendly engine-drivers, and fortified his soul with the consolations of tobacco. They were consolations which were not to be vouchsafed to him much longer. Tobacco cost money, and Anne had need of it.

In spite of Travers' generosity—or of as much of it as she could bring herself to accept—it was not an easy thing for Anne to keep her son at the Grammar School. It was desperately difficult, but Anne was Anne. The boy had his foot on the educational ladder, and she meant him to go to the top, rung by rung and scholarship by scholarship. When Sam took his honours degree at Oxford, Anne would relax; till then, she was a crusader. She sacrificed all to that ambition. Sam should have his chance, at no matter what cost to her, to Tom and to Madge. The boy must be as well dressed as his fellows, and he must play their games. Games are an essential part of English education, and Anne, with her constant eye to the main chance, recognized the importance of the playing-fields in cementing friendships with boys who might be useful to Sam in after life. But games are expensive, and Tom gave, up smoking when Sam was put into his class eleven. Anne gave up nothing. She had nothing more to give.

Honestly, Sam was grateful. Anne did not boast to him of the sacrifices which they all made, but with the candour which distinguishes working-class homes where anything but bare necessity is exceptional, he was aware of every move, of all their deprivation, and did his best to square accounts. But it was not a brilliant best, and after that first term, Anne never repeated the satisfaction of seeing her son carry away a form prize on Speech Day at the Free Trade Hall. He was a worker, a safe plodding "swot," taking by sheer application a respectable place in the lists, but never heading them again, and especially he was weak at mathematics.

That troubled Anne distressingly. Mathematics appeared to her the corner-stone of education, though in truth they mattered little to Sam, who had followed Lance to the Classical side of the school, where mathematics were an unconsidered trifle. But Anne recked nothing of that. She had found the heel of her Achilles, and set herself to make that vulnerable place secure. You are to picture Anne, with her forty years of a working woman's life behind her, wrestling with algebra and trigonometry, blazing a trail for Sam to follow. It was heroic and, by some mental freak, successful. She taught herself, then tutored him, and it was not Sam who scraped through to an average place in the mathematics examinations, but Anne in Sam. Day after day, in the intervals of cook ing, cleaning, washing, she studied the text-books which so puzzled him, and at night explained their knotty points to him with a wonderful clarity. She had no education in particular, nothing but a general capacity and a monstrous will—a will that surmounted the obstacle of acquiring knowledge at an age when few can learn, and the greater obstacle of patient teaching to a boy who had a blind spot for mathematics. She illumined his darkness, but perhaps she hampered his classics and made her hopes of Oxford visionary.

Slowly and painfully, as the terms went by, with Branstone, S. rising steadily in the school, but keeping regularly to his mediocre place in class, Anne acknowledged to herself that her goose was not a swan. It made her the more eager to cultivate what she called the social side; and through that she met with a defeat.

From the beginning, Sam's rise in the world had borne heavily on Madge, his sister, who was of an age for gaiety and of a mind untouched by ambition, personal or vicarious. When Sam went to the Grammar School, Madge was in service and very content. Anne had her out of that at once; she wasn't going to run the risk of Madge being the servant in the house of one of Sands school companions. It was unusual, but Madge preferred service, where she was lucky in her employers, to the weaving-shed, where she had free evenings, but strenuous days with no gossiping callers at the back door to break their monotony. And it became a considerable question in Madge's mind whether she would now be able to outface Anne in the matter of George Chappie. Anne required a presentable brother-in-law for Sam.

Like Madge, George was unambitious, except that he wanted her, which was ambition of a kind. Madge was small, like her mother, but derived in most else from her father. She had freckles and carroty hair, and the makings of a querulous shrew, but George saw otherwise, and desired Madge to have and to hold, for better for worse, and didn't perceive that the odds were heavily against its being better. He was a wisp of a man himself, and thought he was enterprising because he was a window-cleaner; window-cleaning was a new trade then. But Anne did not concur with that opinion, and Madge was in no very sanguine frame of mind when George came in one night with an "It's now or never" look unmistakably in his eye. The trouble was that Anne was not the sort of mother one defied with impunity.

He came in shyly enough—a determined George was a contradiction in terms—but plucked up courage at once when he found that she was alone but for Sam. Sam's presence was inevitable, but need not be acknowledged. In a house, not, indeed, of one room, but of one fire and one gas-jet, Sam had grown apt at insulating himself when he sat with his books at the table. The business of the house went on, so did Sam's studies, and neither interfered with the other. Sam, absorbed in his construe of Cicero's *De Senectute* for the morrow, was absolutely unconscious of Madge and George.

It was not Sam who troubled George, but Madge had truth with her when she told her suitor that he looked worried. George jerked his thumb vaguely streetwards. "It's her again," he explained. "I can't think why God made landladies. I ask you, Madge, is another blanket in this weather a thing to fly into a temper about?"

"It's cold," said Madge. "Won't she give you another?"

"I don't know yet whether she'll give me one or not. But she's had my last word. Another blanket or I'll flit."

"You've threatened that so often."

He admitted it. "I know. It takes an earthquake to shift some folks, and I reckon I'm one of them. I stay where I'm set." And his tone implied that conservatism was an admirable virtue.

Madge did not think so. "That's what my mother says of you," she observed, a trifle tartly.

"It's no lie, either," he placidly agreed. "Seems to me," he went on, with a look, ardent but appealing, at Madge, "that there's only one thing will flit me from Mrs. Whitehead's. You couldn't give a guess at it, could you?"

"Yes, I could," said Madge brazenly. After all, she was Anne's daughter, and direct. Then, despite herself, she fenced coyly: "You're leaving the town, I reckon, Mr. Chappie."

He stood aghast at the revolutionary thought. "Nay," he said earnestly. "I'm set here and I'll not leave willing. There's something to keep me where I am."

"Your job's not worth so much," she said, misunderstanding wilfully.

"It's steady, though," he defended it, "and a growing trade. My master's getting a lot of window-cleaning contracts all over the town. But it's not my job that keeps me here. It's— — —" He dropped his cap and fumbled for it nervously, somehow finding a sort of courage in the act, so that when he rose he faced her with a spirit which was, for him, quite debonair. "Now, you'll not stop me, will you? I've come on purpose to get this off my chest and I've worked myself up to a point. I'm a bit slow at most things and I'm easily put off, so I'll ask you to give my humble request a patient hearing."

Madge looked at him acutely, and decided that his resolution was strong enough to survive something that she very much wanted to say. "I'd rather this didn't come straight on top of a row with your landlady," she said.

"Aye," he agreed, "I can see your meaning, but it's that that roused me to point. Love's like a pan of soup with me. It's got to seethe a while before it boils. But I'm boiling now, and I'm here to tell you so. I've loved you since I saw you, Madge. After Sunday School one day it was, with a wind on that blew the bonny curls across your eyes. I always fancied gold and you're gold twice over." Madge was deeply moved at this idealization of her hair. She had been made more peevishly conscious of its redness than ever by the unsparing comments of the weaving-shed, but she did not see wherein she was gold twice over until he explained it. "I didn't notice that the first day. I only saw your hair. I hadn't the nerve to come close enough to see the colour of your eyes. But when I did, and found them all gold-brown as well, that finished me. I was deep in love to the top of my head. Drowned in it, you might say."

"You're talking a lot of nonsense, George," said Madge, with a fond appreciation that belied her words.

"I'm telling you I love you," he said, "and I'm asking if there's anything that you could see your way to tell me in return. I know I'm not smart, Madge, but I'd work my fingers off to make you happy. Can't you say you love me, lass? Not," he added, "if it isn't true, of course. I wouldn't ask you to tell a lie even to oblige me."

"It might not be a lie," said Madge softly, "but——" She paused so that he was left to guess the rest.

"But," he suggested, "you don't care to go so far as to say it?"

He watched her timidly, with courage oozing out of him. She had all but given him to hope, but now it appeared she had no more to say. "Well, I can understand," he said, half turning towards the door. "I'm not much of a chap, and you might easily have put me down much harder than you did. It's soft letting now, by reason of your tactful ways. I'll... I'll go and see if Mrs. Whitehead has given me yon other blanket."

He was at the door before she stopped him. "George!" she said, "come back. You're getting this all wrong. You know about my brother." George nearly smiled. "It'ud not be your mother's fault if I didn't," he said.

"No," she said; "I suppose everybody knows about his going to the Grammar School. They don't all know what it means." Madge was trying to be loyal to the family ideal, she was trying not to be bitter, but it wasn't easy. It was one thing to go without new hats and the accustomed ways of service, but another to go without George.

"I'd like you to understand that this family puts itself about a bit for Sam's sake. We think he'll go a long way up in the world, and the rest of us aren't doing anything to keep him down. None of us, no matter how it hurts. Are you seeing what I mean?"

He saw. "I'm not class enough for you," he said.

It was a part, but not the whole, of her meaning, and Madge wanted no misapprehensions. "You're class enough for me," she said, "but I'm telling you where the doubt comes in. It's a habit we've got in this family. We think of Sam." That made the matter plain; she loved him, and while he granted there was a certain impediment through Anne's habit of subordinating everything to Sam's interests, he saw no just cause why he should not marry Madge. "I wouldn't knowingly do anything to upset your mother," he said, "but I've told you I'm boiling with my love for you. I'm easily put off my purpose as a rule. I mean to say, supposing I ask Mrs. Whitehead for a kipper for my tea, and she tells me eggs are cheap and she's got an egg instead, I don't make a song about it—so long as the egg's not extra stale. But I'll own I didn't think of Sam in this. I thought it was for you and me to settle by ourselves."

"Sam's in it," said Madge dully. "He's in everything in this house."

Then Anne came in and the disturbance of her entrance, together with the fact that he had finished his passage of *"De Senectute"* made Sam aware that something was toward. He kept his eyes discreetly on his book, but fluttered the pages of his dictionary no more. He found youth more arresting than old age.

Anne's quick comprehension took the situation in at once. She had been shopping, and as she put her parcels on the dresser she gave Madge the benefit of a wordless reproof. She could say a good deal without opening her mouth, and said it. But Madge was not going to be parted from her George without a fight. Sam apart, George was eligible, and Madge saw this as an unique occasion—the occasion for leaving Sam out. At least, she meant to try.

George was turned craven at sight of Anne and sidled to the door. "I'll be getting on home, I think," he said.

"You wait your hurry," said Madge hardily. "Mother, George has been asking me to wed him."

It was the gage of battle, for Anne knew the fact already. The statement of it was a challenge. She met it coolly. "Has he?" she said. "Well, I hope you told him gently."

And at that George found his second wind of courage, and intervened like a man. "She's told me nothing with her tongue. Nothing for certain. But a blind man on a galloping horse could read the thoughts of her. Mrs. Branstone, I love that girl as if she'd put a spell on me. It's the biggest feeling that's come into my life, and I'm full and bursting with it, or I'd not have the face to expose my inside thoughts to you like this. And if you'll only tell me I can take her, the Mayor in his carriage won't be happier than me."

"You know how steady George is, mother," Madge seconded him.

"He needs to be," said Anne dryly. "He's a window-cleaner."

"I'm steady by nature, Mrs. Branstone, as well as trade. I don't drink. Somehow one glass of ale is enough to make me whimsical, so I take none at all. I know I'm being bowdacious in my love, but I'm moved to plead with you. We'd not be standing in Sam's way. We'd live that quiet and snug you'd never know we're in the town at all." Anne looked at him with a faint trace of appreciation drenched in her profound contempt. A poor creature, but he had his thimbleful of spunk! "It would need to be quiet," she said, "with two to keep on your wage. Are you contented with it?"

Disastrously, he was. "It's a regular job," he said, voicing his pride at being above the ranks of casual workers. In Anne's view, a hopeless case.

"It's a regular rotten job," she retorted, but spoke more softly than her wont "I've Sam to consider, Madge. You might live quiet, but Sam's brother-in-law has got to make a better show of it than to be seen all over the place at the top of a ladder like a monkey on a stick. I'm not being hard on you, George Chappie, and I've nothing against you bar that you're not good enough. You better yourself and you'll do. Stay as you are, and Madge'ull do the same."

George opened his mouth to speak, but found that nothing came. It *was* a regular job, it satisfied his ambitions, and her objections were inexplicable. He had shot his bolt and, having no more to say, he went, relapsing to such invertebracy that when he found that Mrs. Whitehead had not added the other blanket to his bed he had nothing to say to her either, but spread a threadbare overcoat on the coverlet and shivered unhappily to sleep.

CHAPTER III
THE HELL-PIKE CLUB

TO a schoolboy of sixteen, love is an imbecile emotion, its victims harmless lunatics, and it is not to be supposed that Sam's interest in the affair of Madge and George was based on intimate understanding. His conspiratorial action came rather as a lark: behind, perhaps, was the recognition that adults did habitually make fools of themselves in this way, that his loyalty in such a case was to Madge who was of his generation, and that Anne in obstructing their marriage was outrunning the constable in her demands for self-sacrifice on his behalf.

Larking, defined as enjoyable interference with other people for motives either benevolent or purely egotistic, was a weakness of Samuel Branstone, and the boy was father to the man. He did not agree with Anne that the marriage was inimical to his interests. True, George cleaned windows and balanced hardily at the top of swaying ladders, a precarious trade, but his own. Apparently it suited the Georgian temperament, and that funambulist would not wear a placard on his back proclaiming that he was brother-in-law to Branstone of the Classical Fifth.

Branstone, who was going to rise in the world, would necessarily have poor relations, and it hardly mattered how poor. Indeed, the poorer they were the more cheaply he could afterwards play providence to them, since their standards would be low and their expectations small.

So it wasn't a nice, impulsive lark, but coldblooded and calculated, which is almost as objectionable in a lark as organization in Charity. It is prudent good intentions that pave the way to Hell.

He saw that there was a difference between this and the elopements of that romantic literature with which he busied his relaxed hours: sometimes the lady, but always the lover, was enterprising, while he knew that George could never instigate anything. But that made things more amusing for Sam, who could pull strings with absolute assurance that his puppets would never take to dancing on their own account, or to any tune but the one he piped; and it is not given to all of us to be Omnipotence at the price of a ten-pound note.

As always, Sam had luck. In the romantic elopements whose technique he began to study with new interest, money was never a difficulty, but the god in the machine of George Chappie's elopement must put money in his purse, or there could be no elopement.

Sam liked money, but he must have liked power more, for, coming miraculously into money at this time, he devoted it to this end. He came into money because journalism was swiftly on the up grade since the days, four years ago, when it couldn't show its readers a photograph of Sam Branstone, hero, in the evening paper, and had reached the civilized stage of picture competitions.

You bought a weekly paper which printed six crude wood-cuts supposed to disguise the names of (say) famous battles, and it did not strain your intellect to discover that the picture of a station with "Waterloo" beneath its clock was intended to represent the battle of that name. But pause: it was not all so easy as that. Inflamed by avarice and the childish ease of identifying the battles in the first series, you bought the next week's number, and the next, until the competition closed, and you found that the designs were increasingly baffling. It was not quite money for nothing. It called for some knowledge of history and a sort of knack in cheap wit to interpret the pictures. A garden syringe, and a stage Irishman brandishing something that might easily be a cudgel but wasn't, represented, in fact, the not very renowned battle of Seringapatam, and there were pictures which could bear two interpretations.

It was this last which led Sam to go into partnership with Lance Travers. Both partners admitted that Sam's wits were the sharper, so it was only fair that Lance should finance the partnership and buy the papers. And Sam, sanguine of winning, but desiring secrecy, preferred that the firm should be registered in Lance's name, so that if and when Sam became a capitalist, he and not Anne should control his wealth. His ideas of the uses of capital already went beyond the Post Office Savings Bank.

The weekly paper's object was to increase its circulation, so it allowed and encouraged competitors to send in numerous attempts, and printed ambiguous drawings to tempt to prodigality. It is to be feared that Classics suffered an eclipse at this period of journalistic enterprise. The partners had other and more serious objects in life. And they won! They won the second prize. It wasn't a house or a motor-car or any of the fantastic prizes with which still later journalism rewarded its intelligent readers, but they divided twenty pounds and, for them, ten pounds each was paradise enow. Lance bought a bicycle. Sam didn't. He bought a wedding-ring, and he had a talk with Sarah Pullen, who was so passionately Madge's bosom friend that she had gone into the mill with her.

Sarah received him coldly; she looked upon him as the cause of her friend's martyrdom and thought the cause unworthy.

Sam cleared the air at once. "I'm on Madge's side. I'm not going to see her made unhappy for my sake," he said, and Sarah relented so far as to absolve him of personal malignity.

"Much you can do to help it, though," she said. "I *can* do much," he replied, "but," he flattered her, "perhaps you can do more. You see, Sarah," he went on confidentially, "Madge trusts you and she doesn't trust me. Now, between ourselves, she needs a friend's advice. Put yourself in her place. Would you knuckle under to your mother?"

"I'd see her further first," said Sarah.

"I wonder," said Sam, "if you could see your way to communicating your views to Madge without mentioning that I suggested it?"

"You!" said Sarah. "You! It'ud take a dozen your size to suggest anything to me. Get off home and play marbles, or I'll give you a slap on th' earhole that you'll remember."

They didn't play marbles in the Classical Fifth, but Sam was content to put her allusion down to ignorance rather than deliberate insult. He had gained his point: the atmosphere he desired created was about to he created.

He left that pot to simmer and turned his mind to George, whom he judged less susceptible than Madge to the promptings of a friend. Besides, he knew no friend of George, and confessed himself at fault.

One day, shortly before the Whitsuntide holidays, he was staring gloomily out of the window at the top of the stairs outside the Fifth Form room, watching the boys of the Chetham's Hospital at play in that yard of theirs which the Grammar School pretends to scorn but secretly envies, when he heard behind him a conversation between Lance Travers and Dubby Stewart which set his brain awhirl. Yet it was not a distinguished conversation.

"Who ever heard of anyone in Manchester staying at home in Whit week?" asked Lance.

Sam had heard, often.

"It isn't done," said Dubby, who had earned that abiding name when he was in the Lower Third, and once read "dubious" aloud with a short "u."

"But I've to do it," said Lance. "My governor's too busy to get away. Bit damnable, isn't it?"

"Matter of fact," said Dubby, "we're not going, either."

And it presently appeared that out of the form of twenty-four boys there were as many as six who lived in Manchester and were not going away. "It will be hell," prophesied one of the unfortunates.

"It needn't," said Sam Branstone, turning from the window to the mournful group.

"You're used to it. We're not," said someone cruelly, and Lance smacked his head. Allusions to anybody's poverty were bad form.

"What's the prescription?" asked Dubby, and Sam was silent for a minute. "Watch him. Something's dawning," chaffed Dubby. It wasn't dawning, it had dawned; but at first it looked like a risk, and then much less like one, and Sam smiled beautifully as he realized that he, at least, had all to gain and nothing to lose. He drew the luckless five mysteriously aloof.

"The prescription," he said, "is to have a holiday in Manchester, in a holiday house." He let that soak for a minute, and then, "Our own house," he added. "There are six of us. We join together and we take a house. A small house, and I daresay some of you won't like the neighbours, but as the neighbours won't like us, that's as broad as it's long. Swagger neighbours wouldn't stand us anyhow, and the smaller the house the smaller the rent. Something like four-and-six a week is my idea. That's nine-pence a week for each of us, and we've a house of our own for that to do what we like in."

"By Jove!" said someone admiringly.

"What shall we call it?" said another, a trifle doubtfully.

"Call it?" said Lance. "That's obvious. The Hell-fire Club."

And, of course, if any doubt remained, that settled it. Who would regret the seaside if he could be a member of the Hell-fire Club? Lance was commissioned to negotiate with his father, the estate agent, but it was Sam who really chose their house. It was a house which in Sam's opinion excellently suited the requirements of a young married couple of the window-cleaning class. Mr. Travers told Lance that he would stop the value of any damage out of his pocket-money, and on those conditions let them the house. But he need not have made that cautionary threat; Sam saw that there was no damage.

The Hell fire Club assembled for its initiatory debauch on the first day of the holidays, and by eleven a.m. three inexpert cigarette-smokers had had occasion to use the slopstone as a vomitorium. It left them feeling chilly, and Dubby suggested that a house-warming without a fire was a solecism, even on a hot day, so a lavish plutocrat brought in two sacks of coal and a supply of chips. Firelighting is a sport out of which a certain excitement can be derived, but only for a short time, and the same evanescent quality attaches to the pleasure of sitting on bare boards.

"I'm too stiff to be happy," said Lance. "I vote we furnish this club."

Carried, *nem. com.* "I'm afraid, though," said Sam, "that I shall not be able to contribute much."

"Wait till you're asked, my son," said Dubby. "By the time we five have finished looting our homes, this place will be a little palace."

Loot is a brave word, suggestive of the treasures of the purple East, but it was, in most instances, a case of permitted loot, the offscourings of lumber rooms. Sandy Reed, however, was the sort of boy who is happiest with a hammer in his hand, and Dubby had an eye for chintz. To repair the veteran furniture which they brought struck Sandy as work for a man. Behind him was his infantile past of fret-work and model yachts; before him the foremanship of the Hell-fire Club repair-shop. He worked and was the cause of work in others. And it was willing work, partly because it was for an idea, partly because that first day had threatened boredom and here was something definite to do, mostly because it was making a noise.

The ill-assorted chairs, tables and sofas which they collected under their roof had this in common at the end, that they were strong; and having by their own efforts made them strong, the boys did not by their rioting make them weak again. They respected their handiwork, and Dubby's chintz procured a sort of uniformity.

A club, of course, must eat and drink, and kitchen utensils, mostly odd but all practicable, were gathered together that they might precede the pleasures of eating with the pleasures of cooking. It was camp-life in town, except that they went home to sleep, and so long as the activities of "settling in" endured, they relished it abundantly.

About a fortnight was what Sam had mentally set as the life of the Hell-fire Club, and he had no intentions of paying the rent by himself for more than a week or so. They had decided that Sunday was not a club-day—there were difficulties at home—and Sam took George Chappie for a walk. "I like this street," he said as they turned the corner. "Madge always fancied this district."

"Did she?" said George gloomily.

"We'll go in here," and Sam produced the key and introduced George to the Club premises. "What do you think of it?"

The chintz took George's eye at once. "By gum!" he said.

"Sit down," said Sam. "This is where you're going to live when you're married to Madge. It isn't your furniture yet, but it's going to be. I'm going to give it you for a wedding present. There isn't a bed in, as you see, but there will be, and I ask you, George, is it or is it not better than Mrs. Whitehead's?"

"Aye," said George, "but you're going ahead a bit too fast for me."

"Not at all," said Sam. "Yours is the pace that kills. The slow pace, not the quick. Now, this place isn't at your disposal yet, but if you'll put up the banns next Sunday and get married as soon as you can after the three Sundays, you can walk in here and hang your hat up on that hook. It's a brass hook, George. We don't approve of nails in this house. I might mention that it will be all right about the banns. Mother has dinner to cook on Sundays and doesn't go to morning service, and to-day is father's Sunday off from the station and lie's on duty for the next three Sundays. So," he concluded, "there you are."

"You're promising a lot. Is this house yours?"

"The rent is four-and-six," said Sam, "which isn't more than you can afford to pay. And you bind yourself to nothing by putting up the banns. If I fail to deliver you this house and all that's in it, you needn't get married. But I've a word of advice for you, George. Let Madge hear of it first from the parson's lips in church. She won't scream and she won't faint. We don't, in our family, and it saves you the trouble of asking her. Is it a bet?"

George hesitated. "Come upstairs and see the other room," said Sam. George saw, and marvelled. "I'll come round with you now to church," said Sam. "We've just nice time to catch the clerk after service."

"By gum!" said George Chappie. "I'll do it. They can't hang me. But," he added as he cast a last look at the household gods which Sam Bran-stone promised should be his, "they may hang you."

Sam grinned blandly.

CHAPTER IV
THE COMPLEAT ANGLER

HE had succeeded with George beyond expectations, but that easy victory did not deceive him into thinking that his battle was won. Madge, he had said, would neither scream nor faint on hearing her banns announced and he wished he was as confident about it as he had sounded. Much, in his view too much, depended on the vigour of Sarah Pullen's advice.

He was taking risks all round, but found he rather liked it. There was the risk that the Hell-fire Club would not tire of its toy in time. An encouraging increase in absenteeism amongst the members elated him, but the steadfast faith of an enthusiastic pair depressed him sadly. He hoped, however, to find a way out of that wood.

And there was the risk that some acquaintance of Anne's would mention the banns to her. He saw no way to counter that. It was a risk he had to take. Fortunately, his father's best friend, Terry O'Rourke, was a Catholic.

As things stood, he saw Madge as the weakest link in his chain. She collapsed before the will of Anne like an opera hat, and he was candidly afraid of her making a scene in church, either from pleasure or from anger, when the banns were read. Not that he shrank on principle from scenes, only that word of it would undoubtedly be carried to Anne and the fat be in the fire.

Rummaging one day that week at a second-hand bookstall in Withy Grove, without the slightest intention of buying, he was attracted by a title and recklessly planked his tuppence down. Intrigue, he felt, was punishing his finances, but this title gave him too good an opening with Madge to be the subject of economy. The title was "The Clandestine Marriage," and he knew that Sarah Pullen would be in that night to see Madge.

He was reading the play very earnestly when she called, though it rather bored him and he thought its plot elementary compared with his own. Sarah was no reader, but she noticed the cover because the word "marriage" was an unfailing lure.

"Whatever has the boy got hold of now?" She inquired, taking his bait sweetly.

He showed her. "Do you know what it means?" he asked.

"I know what marriage means," she said.

"By hearsay," he told the virgin pungently. "But I meant the middle word."

She eyed it closely. "You're always bragging your knowledge. I'm not at the Grammar myself and Greek is Greek to me. Fat lot of good it'ud be in a weaving-shed, and all." She had a practical mind.

"This isn't Greek," he said, "it's English."

"It's not the sort of English we talk in Manchester, choose how."

"I'll tell you what it means."

"Wait till you're asked, cheeky."

He didn't wait. "It means surreptitious."

"I'm a grand sight the wiser for that. It'll mean a thick ear for you if you don't stop coming the schoolmaster over me. I'm here to talk to Madge, not to you."

He winked at Sarah with the eye which was hidden from Madge. "The Secret Marriage, Sarah. That's what it means."

Sarah was interested now. "Does it tell you how to work it?"

"I might do that myself," he said.

"Don't talk so foolish, Sam," said his sister. "Are you coming for a walk, Sarah?"

"When I'm ready," said Sarah. "Now then, young Sam, spit it out."

"Oh," said Sam. "It isn't much. Only I happened to be out for a walk with George Chappie the other day and we went into a house that's pretty full of furniture."

"George Chappie with a house of furniture!" cried Madge.

"I suppose he's getting married," said Sam. "He courted you at one time, didn't he, Madge? I rather liked his taste in furniture."

"Taste!" cried Madge with spirit. "I'll taste him. I'll eat him raw for this. After all he said to me no more than a month ago, to take up with another wench! What's the hussy's name?"

"Her name?" said Sam. "Let's see. Sunday to-morrow, isn't it? The banns might be up. If I were you I'd go and find out."

"As true as I'm alive I'll tear every hair from her head," said Madge.

"I wouldn't," said Sam. "You have red hair, but better red than bald."

"Her!" said Sarah. "Do you mean— —?"

"Look here, Sarah," Sam interrupted, and used a formula which he had thought out rather carefully. "Do you imagine I'd be giving you a message like this if he hadn't sent it?"

"Message! What message?"

Then Anne came in.

"Yes, Sarah," she heard Sam saying with a pedagogic air. "The word clandestine means secret." He resumed with zest the reading of his play and, though theirs was a small house, managed to avoid being alone with Madge up to church time on the morrow. He had business out that Saturday night—to make sure of George, whom he found full of panting resolution to catch the clerk and cancel the banns. The glamour of that furniture had lasted this long with George, but the awful hazard of the Sunday morning eclipsed the glow as it came nearer. George wilted at the thought of Madge rising in her place with a firm, irrevocable "I forbid the banns" upon her lips.

There had begun, too, to be a quality too much like that of an Arabian night about his visit to the Club. Sam was a wonderful boy and George granted his high superiority; but even George, the humble, did not quite see Sam as a miracle-worker. He even began to doubt the existence of the enchanted Palace which Sam had shown him, and that it was within Sam's competence to hand over that house to him appeared now ridiculous. Sam came just in time.

"Would you care," he said, "to have another look at your house?"

George would, but he hadn't time then: he was going; to see the clerk, and till he saw the clerk he was a man obsessed with an idea. "I suppose," he said sceptically, "that it's still there?"

"Of course," said Sam, "and has a few more things in since you saw it."

"Well," said George, "it's a nice house, but I'm going to see yon clerk to tell him not to put up banns."

Sam smiled, relieved to know that he was not too late. "Don't do that," he said. "Madge is pleased."

"What!" said George. "Say that again."

"Madge is pleased," repeated Sam brazenly. He was sure she was. He trusted Sarah Pullen now.

"Did she tell you so?" asked George.

"Do you imagine I'd be giving you a message like this if she hadn't sent it?"

George took his cap off. "If that's so— —" he said.

"It's so," said Sam, not defining what was so.

The banns went up, and Sam was able to devote his undivided attention to Club affairs, as to which he had an idea arising out of the boredom he suffered while reading "The Clandestine Marriage." That tuppence was a fruitful investment.

A wet day came and with it, what was now rare, a full attendance at the Club. But, since their repairs and decorations were complete, there was nothing to do except to sit on their reliable chairs and admire their reliability.

"For a Hell-fire Club," said Sandy, "we lack hellishness."

"Lance named us," said Dubby. "He ought to make suggestions."

"Of a new name?" asked Sandy. "Call it the Eviscerated Emasculates."

"Call it a damned failure," said another, and was sat upon. They welcomed the diversion, but the thought had reached home.

"What's the matter," said Sam, when order was restored, "is that we aren't serious enough."

"Oh, hell!" said Lance.

"I mean it, Lance. We're not a set of kids from the Lower School. If we were, we might sit round and read Chums and the Boy's Own Paper." Two men of the Classical Fifth and the Hell-fire Club looked guiltily at him, but decided that he was not making personal allusions. "As it is, we have higher interests. Now, there are six of us here and that's enough, with doubling, to take parts in a Shakesperian play. I vote we read a play. In fact, I brought some down."

This suited Lance, who had aspirations towards the stage. "Bags I Romeo," he said.

Sandy was less fired to enthusiasm, but, "All right," he said, "if you choose a play with lots of thick bits in it."

"We certainly," said Sam, "shall not read an edition prepared for the use of girls' schoofs."

"*Merry Wives of Windsor*, then," said Dubby. "Lance can spout Romeo out of his bedroom window to stop a cat-fight."

Sam would have preferred a tragedy; he feared they would enjoy reading The Merry Wives and so, on the whole, they did, but there were only five promises to turn up next day and two of those were conditional upon its being wet. Sam wasn't dissatisfied, and as a comedy was postulated chose *Much Ado about Nothing*, because he thought that it was dull in patches and also for a reason of his own. He wanted to make certain that he had nothing to learn as an intriguer from a famous case of match-making. He found he had.

Although it rained, *Much Ado* had only four readers at the opening and only two at the close. Lance sent postcards that night to the members announcing *Hamlet* for the morrow. He wanted to read Hamlet's part, but if you can't have *Hamlet* without the Prince, neither can you read it satisfactorily with one other participant.

Lance and Sam struggled through an act, then Lance gave in. "I'm getting tired of this Club," he said. "The members have no brain."

"It isn't raining," said Sam.

"No. Lancashire's batting, too. Let's go and see Albert Ward and Frank Sugg at Old Tafford."

Next day, the Club was uninhabited, except by the ghost of Sam's broadest smile, its only tenant for a week. The freeze-out was accomplished, and its engineer had confidence enough to spend three pounds of his capital on a bed and bedding, "to await instructions before delivering." Then he saw Lance Travers and pointed out to him that there were better uses to be made of ninepence a week than to waste it on a club which nobody used.

"Nuisance, though, about the chairs and stuff," said Lance, implying his agreement that the Club had failed.

"I can't have them back here, because I'm turning our attic into an aviary. That's why I've had no time to go to the Club," he explained with a faint apology, and took Sam up to see his birds.

"What shall we do about all that furniture at the Club? Pity the fifth of November is so far off."

"I'll try to think of something," said Sam, rather terrified at Lance's incendiary suggestion. "In any case it must be discussed at a full meeting. Let's call the members together."

An urgent whip resulted in a full and slightly shame-faced attendance. Nobody tried to dispute that the Club was a corpse: the only question was what to do with its bones. "Well," said Sam, "if none of you has a suggestion to make, I'll make one. Nobody's aching to take the stuff back where it came from. Now," he went on candidly, "we *could* sell it to a dealer, but I'm against that because dealers are thieves and they'd give us about thirty bob for the lot. But my sister's getting married and I don't mind offering the Club five pounds for its property. That," he indicated, "is a pound each for the five of you."

"Cash on the nail?" asked Dubby, whose forebears came from Scotland. He distrusted Sam in the character of capitalist.

"Oh, yes," explained the candid Sam. "You see, when I met Lance yesterday I said I'd think of a way out of the difficulty and I came prepared."

"I vote we take it," said Sandy. "I can buy a lot of tools with a pound."

"I don't see why we should pander to your vices," said Lance. "We're still a Club and this is club money."

"The Club is dead."

"Not yet. Not till we've killed it gloriously on Sam's sister's fiver. There's a hell of a bust in five pounds and we have to drink the bride's health. Champagne's my drink."

It wasn't, but it was rather too often his father's, and Lance was emulous, and, frightened a little of his own suggestion, carried things now with a rush. "We're the Hell-Fire Club," he said, "and champagne is the dew of Hell. Any member shirking will be held under the tap for half an hour." They braved it out, most of them conscience-stricken, and the Hell-fire Club almost deserved its name in the hour of its extinction. Things might have been serious had not Sam, by a well-timed push, caused Lance to shatter a full magnum on the floor.

As it was, five hangdog members reached home late, but presentable. But they were most unhappy boys. The sixth boy was happy. He had consumed a sober and interesting meal at other people's expense, encountering several delectable sorts of food for the first time and experiencing that human but reprehensible thrill which results from feeling that one is a clever fellow.

Distance of course lent enchantment to the Hell-fire Club. When school reassembled and boys fresh from the seaside tried to excite the jealousy of the stay-at-homes with tales of land and sea, they were loftily put in their places and struck to dumb admiration by legends of the dashing vice of the Hell-fire Club. It lived in story as it had never lived in fact.

Sam visited the premises, on the day after the Club died, to wipe up the mess, thriftily to salve some untouched edibles for a coming wedding-feast, and by receiving and installing the bed to dedicate the house to better uses. Then he put the key in his pocket and took it to George. He had kept his bargain and now it was for George to keep his.

There remained the question of Anne, and as a preliminary to its solution Sam had recommended Madge to look peaked. Madge, naturally inclined to that condition, had no difficulty in accentuating its appearance by recourse to the vinegar bottle until even Anne, intolerant as she was of small weaknesses, had to own that Madge looked unhappy and unwell.

On the night before her wedding, Madge shut herself up in her bedroom whence the sounds as of a very ecstasy of woe penetrated to the kitchen. Yet her woe was not ecstatic and hardly woe at all. She wept because she was going to be married next day, because when one is going to be married next day one weeps. One brims with undefinable emotion and overflows into tears.

But Anne, listening from the kitchen, where she sat with Sam, was moved to unaccustomed softness. "That girl is fretting sadly," she said. "It's a mort of trouble to be taking over a wastrel like George Chappie."

"Mother," said Sam speculatively, "I wonder whether you have ever considered the influence of matter over mind?"

"I'm considering the influence of something that does not matter," she replied. "The influence of George Chappie."

"Suppose," said Sam, "suppose that George Chappie lived in a decent house of his own, with furniture that he took a pride in, instead of in those awful lodgings of his. Don't you think that he would live up to his surroundings? Don't you think that it would make a man of him?"

"George Chappie is as far from having a decent house as he is from wedding our Madge."

"That's true," said Sam, "as far—and as near."

"As near?" asked Anne suspiciously. "Sithee, Sam, have you been up to something?"

"Will you hear me out if I tell you a story?" he asked.

"Am I going to like it?" she fenced cautiously. "I am hoping," he said piously, "to have your forgiveness. It's a matter of happiness."

He told her what he had done and how and why he had done it. "The wedding's to-morrow," he ended, "and I hope you'll go." He told his exploit without arrogance and without extenuation, and it is not to be supposed that Anne was unaware that a nice moralist would have found much in it to criticize, but Sam had come out on top and that, for Anne, almost excused his methods. It almost excused his coming out on top of her.

"I'll go to the wedding," she said, "and I'll forgive them. They are no more than a pair of naturals in the hands of a schemer." Sam grinned appreciatively. "But I'll not let you down so easy," she went on, and the grin faded. "You're clever, my lad, but you're a schoolboy, and the place for showing your cleverness is at school. It's too long since you brought me home a prize, and if you want my forgiveness for letting you rap my knuckles like this, you'll bring me a prize this Midsummer. Is that a bargain, Sam?"

"I always try," he said, which was true.

"Try harder," said Anne Branstone dryly.

CHAPTER V
LAST SCHOOL-DAYS

SAM had not a dog's chance of winning the form prize of the Classical Fifth, and knew it. He learnt with difficulty, retaining what he learnt; but the process was slow and his form was overshadowed by the brilliance of two boys who learnt easily and rapidly.

It annoyed Sam to know that he had no chance against these two. Poetic justice cried out that he, the railway porter's son, should defeat Bull, whose father was a professor at the University, and Adams, son of a merchant prince whose "Hong" was as familiar in the godowns of Shanghai as his name in Princess Street and on 'Change; but it was hopeless. The prize lay inevitably between these two who took to classics like ducks to water and read Homer for (they said) pleasure, whilst their form-mates struggled with Euripides in acknowledged agony. They were both unpopular, both prigs, but unassailably pre-eminent; and they were two. Had it been a case of Bull alone, or Adams alone, Sam might have worked heroically on the off-chance, that his rival would be ill at examination time, but it was too far-fetched to hope that both would simultaneously ail.

He had long passed beyond Anne's powers of tuition. It was not a "sound commercial education" that one got on the Classical side, and mathematics had ceased to figure in his course. He went to the Classical side because Lance was there and stayed because of Anne's golden dream of Oxford. The gold, she knew, was tarnished now, but if she no longer saw in Sam the winner of an open scholarship at Balliol, she had not abandoned hope that he might carry off one of the close scholarships which the School commanded. Sam himself was sceptical about even that qualified ambition.

But he had to win a prize to satisfy Anne, and if he could not win the prize of which she was thinking, he would try to win one of which she did not think. It was certainly a prize, and a handsome prize, open not only to a form but to the whole school—a prize for reading.

He had a secondary spur, too, in the fact that Lance, that ardent elocutionist, looked on this prize as his own, and the thought of beating Lance on his chosen ground tickled Sam's fancy. Not that he was cocksure.

He knew his handicap too well for that, but he had always known it, and from the first day of his school life studied to correct his accent. He did not, even now, even at the price of being thought pedantic, indulge in slang. Lance, perhaps because he came from a motherless home, perhaps from a stupid bravado, larded his speech with silly blasphemies and the current vulgarisms, and, in fact, he did it with an air; but Sam had to guard his tongue. There is a difference, too easily detected, between correct slang and incorrect English: one must first speak correctly before one can dare successfully to be incorrect, and Sam's handicap was that he came from a home where they used, in Sarah Pullen's words, "the sort of English we speak in Manchester;" the other sort was an alien tongue and held to be an affectation of the insincere.

There was a set piece—the opening speech in *Comus*—the inefficients were weeded out, and the elect tested on "unseens." It was the "unseens" that frightened Sam: he rehearsed *Comus* till a misplaced aitch was a physical impossibility, and he was sure of his rhythm and the intelligence of his rendering; but he knew that aitches were elusive when he was nervous. "Then don't be nervous," was counsel of perfection: the ordeal of the "unseen" test intimidated him.

But he practised, and did not spare himself. If sweat and blood would win that prize, Sam would spend both. He read aloud by the hour—classics of course suffering—with a pin in his hand with which he resolutely drew blood at every aitch he dropped; and in his reading he was fortunate. He read *The Spectator* which he had borrowed by pure chance from the school library, and the judges handed him a passage from *The Spectator* to read at the unseen test, and one of the great speeches of Marlowe's *Tamburlaine*, whose thundering music had so much attracted Sam that he knew the purple patch by heart.

He won the prize; staggered across the platform of the Free Trade Hall with a Gibbon in six sumptuous volumes, calf-bound, stamped with the school arms; he rode "in triumph through Persepolis," and thought that it was "sweet and full of pomp;" then, when it was over and the last "Gaudeamus" of that Speech Day had been sung and the last cheers for the holidays (always the heartiest) been given, he sought his mother in the crowd.

"Well?" said Sam, who had kept this glory as a surprise for her.

"Aye," said Anne, "but it might be better. You've won a prize and you're forgiven, but you know well enough that you've diddled me. I wanted a prize to show that you'd the gift of learning, and you've won one to show that you've the gift of the gab. I knew it already," she ended dryly, "and you're nobbut tenth out of the twenty-four in your class. Will they move you up?"

She dissembled the genuine pride with which she had seen him cross that platform and take his bulky prize, because she felt inly that the chief talent Sam had proved was a talent for deception. This was a prize, but she thought it too barely within the meaning of the act: it observed the letter of his bargain and eluded the spirit.

She did him less than justice. The average hoy came to school knowing English; Sam had had to learn it, and here was proof, in a prize won against the whole school and not merely against a form, that he had learned his lesson well.

Her disparagement depressed him. He had not reached, and with a mother like Anne he could not at his age reach, the healthy younger generation's contempt for the opinions of its elders. He felt weakened in his belief in the social and economical value of a decent accent and grew careless in preserving it. His Gibbon lay upon his shelf unread, an empty glory, and, in the event, his prize was to lead to a calamity. It was to lead, indirectly, to Tom Branstone's death.

Sam found himself, after the holidays, moved up to the Transitus, the last boy to be moved there from the Fifth. He was not sure that it pleased him. Left in the Fifth he might have been a Triton among the minnows: in the Transitus he was incurably a minnow. But he discovered there an atmosphere to which he might have responded better than he did. Discipline was slacker; one had reached the ante-room to the Sixth and was assumed to be serious; one had the privilege of a form-room which was open in the lunch-hour so that one had not to wait with smaller fry in the corridors; and, above all, the form-master was a gentleman as well as a scholar.

He was not blind to these advantages, but he did not, somehow, "come on" with his classics. The terrible facility of Bull and Adams was a constant discouragement: mere perseverance was outvied by natural ability and dragged its leaden weight behind. He knew himself incapable of shining in this company, and gave up a losing fight the more readily because the half-term brought a new diversion, and a chance to coruscate.

He was cast, as winner of the reading prize, for the Christmas play. He, Sam Branstone, was to act Shylock at the Conversazione, whilst Lance Travers was given Bassanio—salt on the still bleeding wound of his defeat. Greek Tragedy interested Sam no more. He saw Irving's Shylock from the gallery of the Theatre Royal, and, for comparative purposes, Benson's. He haunted Cheetham Hill, observing Jewish "types." He came to the first rehearsal, like any other novice, knowing every line of his part—and had painfully to unlearn and relearn under the direction of the brisk little mathematics master who took the play-in hand.

Anne screened her pride in this distinction. Play-acting was, in any case, questionable, too newly come to respectable estate to be accepted unreservedly. But, in secret, she determined that she would be one of Sam's audience and Tom another.

Parents were invited to the Conversazione—that was what conversaziones were for—but Anne and Tom had never accepted the invitation before. It implied evening dress.

She decided that she could "manage" with her Sunday dress and two yards of lace; but Tom, too, must be there, and Tom must not shame Sam. She thought she saw a way.

"Nay, nay," said Tom, "I couldn't do it, lass. I'd never dare."

"You should have thought of that before you became Sam's father," she replied. "I'm going to see him and I'll none go alone. You're coming with me. I reckon Mr. O'Rourke will be in to-night as usual."

"Aye," said Tom, suspecting nothing.

One basis of his friendship with O'Rourke was that their evenings off happened to coincide, Tom's from Victoria Station and Terry's from the old-fashioned commercial hotel in Mosley Street, where he was an institution. Terry was a waiter, but Tom had not yet seen the connection between his friend's profession and the Grammar School Conversazione. He was never very bright.

Terry had a hard head and a professional style, rather like a successful doctor's bed-side manner, which wheedled more tips from commercial travellers than they gave at any other hotel in their rounds, but he had a sunken vein of poetic superstition and, when Anne interrupted them, he was explaining to Tom that he tolerated the Royal Hotel because he could see from its window the green of the grass outside the Infirmary. Manchester was Manchester because it lacked grass. The "good folk" couldn't dance on granite sets: only on grass did one find fairy-rings and only where grass abounded were people blessed.

"You'll not be wanting your dress-clothes next Wednesday night, I reckon," said Anne, breaking in without apology.

"Why, no, Mrs. Branstone," he said. "Wednesday's the night when I dress like the public. I've gone into a strange hotel and been mistaken for an ordinary customer on a Wednesday night."

"Then you'll maybe not object to lending Tom your clothes next week. I want him to be mistaken for a swell."

"There's a shine on them," objected Terry, "that you can see your face in."

"Dress-clothes," pronounced Anne, "are dressy when they shine. If you'll put studs and a clean shirt in with them, I'll be obliged, and I'll send the shirt back washed."

"But, Anne——" protested Tom.

"You hold your hush," she said. "It's settled. Go on about the fairies, Terry."

Fairies seemed to Anne entirely suitable as a subject of conversation for those children, men.

Terry brought the clothes himself and personally assisted at Tom's transformation from a railway porter into a "swell." His tie, at any rate, was nicely tied, but "I feel the awkwardest fool alive," said Tom, as well he might, with clothes which fitted where they touched; Anne, had she confessed her inward sinking, must have admitted that she was in no better case herself, but confession was far from her: she had to be brazen for two. Yet even Anne's high courage failed her in the ladies' dressing-room: she emerged so humbled by the splendours which she had seen unveiled that, at a word from Tom, she would have turned tail and fled.

But Tom had found countenance. Mr. Travers, meeting him on the stair, had taken charge of him, and now added Anne to his convoy. It was kindly tact increased to the power of heroism: he talked hard and sheltered his waifs from feeling the curious glances which, even in that mixed company, were directed embarrassingly at them. He ignored a quiet, well-known alderman, who obviously wanted to speak to him. He shepherded them to their places in the Lecture Theatre, sat with them and accomplished the incredible feat of putting Tom Branstone at his ease in the midst of the tipping public.

Travers acquired more merit that night than by all his payments of Sam's school-fees: and Sam himself did nobly, not only on the stage whence he acted at Anne and bowed to Anne, but afterwards when, still in his costume, he paraded with her, drank coffee with her, and met with Shylockian hatred any eye which seemed to hint that he had not tremendous reason to be proud of his little mother. And what he did for her, Lance and Mr. Travers did for Tom.

Undoubtedly, a huge success: a night of nights, carved on the tablets of memory in letters of gold: never, not by so much as a dubious hint, to be associated with the illness of Tom Branstone. That was, of course, caused by overwork at Christmas at the station. It had and could have nothing to do with the fact that Tom, coming in ecstasy from the heated school into the cold December night, presently threw off his overcoat and danced exulting on the pavement: conduct so utterly unprecedented, so wholly un-Tom-like, that he had footed it merrily for ten minutes before Anne recovered enough command of him to put an end to the discreditable performance. Besides, for five of the ten minutes, she had danced hand in hand with him. She, too, exulted, but neither of them ever referred to their pagan capering again.

Poor Tom! He had not had so many nights of triumph in his life that this should be his last, but he was soon to start upon a journey from which even Anne's imperious will was powerless to call him back. She helping him, he struggled hard against pneumonia and made a better fight with death than he had ever made with life, but his course was run and the school had not reopened after the holidays when Tom Branstone ceased to fight. It seemed that, on the night of the Conversazione, he had had his hour, and

"men must endure
Their going hence even as their coming hither:
Ripeness is all."

It did not come to Sam as the shattering of his world—only the death of Anne could have done that—but certainly as a stunning blow. It was the first time that he had come intimately close to death and he missed death's beauty and its peace. He saw too well its ugliness and the detail of a burial. It hurt, not because Tom Branstone had had but little joy in life, but because he died too soon to see the glory of his son. In after years, Sam Branstone would have liked to recall how Tom's death softened him, how he melted to tears before that waxen face and lovingly bought flowers to put inside the coffin.

It wouldn't do. It didn't fit the facts. He knew that, honestly, he had been angry with his father for dying, especially for dying in the holidays. It spoiled the holidays and it robbed Sam of the day's holiday he would have had for the funeral had Tom had the gumption to die in termtime. He resented his father's death as he would have resented an unjust thrashing from him—if Tom Branstone ever thrashed anybody. Tom had died prematurely, while he was still useful to Sam. He had bilked Sam, and Sam was angry.

Not only had Tom died too soon to see the glory of his son, but his son's glory was seriously jeopardized by the breadwinner's death. Sam had, in his innermost soul, given up the idea of Oxford; he was not apt enough at classics, but he was far from admitting it now. It was Tom's death, and that alone, which deprived him of that crown.

Anne felt it deeply. She had loved Tom with something like mother-love as well as wife's. If she had been hard with him, it was for his good, and he as well as she had known that her hardness was like the hardness of a crab's shell, hiding a tender place inside. Now that he was dead she could hide her grief as she had hidden her love, and went about her business soberly. Soberly she drew her money from the Sick and Burial Society and soberly she spent it on "black" for Sam, for George, Madge and herself, doing those things which Tom would have expected to be done to dignify his death, but adding nothing that would make his funeral a neighbours' raree-show.

She came back from the cemetery with dry eyes and soberly presided at the inevitable meal (where she had to comfort a lachrymose O'Rourke) and, on the morrow, soberly set out to visit Mr. Travers, and to tell him that, of course, she could not now keep Sam at school. It was little that Travers was allowed to guess from this stoic that this was the end of her dream for Sam, that with Tom's death the underpinnings of her world had flopped. And her pride stood where it stood five years ago: no more now than then would she accept from Travers money to pay expenses.

She shook her head defiantly. "The lad'ull have to work," she said.

Travers knew adamant when he saw it. "Then, at least, let him come here and work in my office." Anne almost glared. "I want a fair field and no favour. He'll have to start as office-boy, with the wages of an office-boy."

"Oh, hardly that, Mrs. Branstone. Remember, he comes to me from the Classical Transitus."

"Yes," she said, "and much use that is to an estate agent. He can't add up a row of figures."

She had no delusions about the practical value of a public school education.

"I think, though, that we must let it count for something," he replied, and Anne, compromising against the grain, consented to let it count for fifteen shillings a week "until we see," added Mr. Travers, "how he shapes." He intended to see very soon.

Anne nodded grimly. "I'll see he shapes," she said, and Sam, silent witness of this pregnant interview, was hardly surprised by Anne's first words on reaching home. "Get out those old arithmetic text-books of yours," she said, "and look up mensuration. I've not forgotten it, if you have."

CHAPTER VI
THE NEST-EGG

TOM Branstone had drawn a wage of a pound a week, and tips may have averaged ten shillings but more probably did not; your sixpenny tipper is a rare bird in Manchester.

Yet Anne had saved steadily, and she had not allowed a life-long habit to be interrupted by a little thing like the necessity of providing Sam with Grammar School books and clothes. I do not say that it was admirable in her, but merely that it was heroic. It was an incredible feat, but it can be done: it is done every day by people for whom the word "thrift" has meaning. Perhaps they are often unlovely in their lives or perhaps they have the robust satisfaction of those who live for an idea: opinion has always differed as to whether what they do is worth doing, and modern opinion inclines strongly to the belief that it is not. Life to these iconoclasts seems more important than the means of life.

To Anne it seemed abundantly worth while, and the proof was here now when she found that the interest on her savings amounted to three and four-pence weekly. They could live on Sam's earnings and Anne's "means" without pinching. Her forethought made all the difference now between too little and enough.

It was, of course, only to Anne that this seemed enough: Sam took a larger view, but found his vision cramped for some time to come by the conditions he met with in Mr. Travers' office. Certainly that generous soul did not mean to humiliate Sam; he did not mean Sam to begin as office-boy; but, whatever his intentions, the clerks in his office defeated them. Sam was a newcomer, the latest arrival, in a minority of one against the old inhabitants; was there, moreover, obviously to do as he was told. He was told to sweep the floor in the morning, to copy letters and to lick stamps. He did these things rebelliously, bitter at heart that such menial service should be required of an ex-member of the Classical Transitus, certain that there was some mistake, that he had only to catch Mr. Travers' eye when he was so shamefully occupied for that gentleman to take instant and drastic measures with the clerks who misemployed him.

Mr. Travers' eye, even though caught at what Sam thought an opportune moment, While Sam copied letters, unexpectedly failed to disapprove. He seemed less preoccupied with Sam's affairs than Sam was. As a matter of fact, he took a long distance view of Sam, and took it, unfortunately, rather muggily. Travers had the defect of his quality. A generous man, he was generous in the worst way to himself, and Sam soon learnt the meaning of a euphemism, current in the office, "Mr. Travers is attending a property auction." Property auctions are, it is true, usually held on licensed premises, and whether Mr. Travers was or was not attending an auction he was certainly on licensed premises more often than was good for either his business or himself.

And it was bad for Sam, not because it left him to find his own feet in the office and to fight unbacked with his superiors (wherein, indeed, it was good), but because he had figured Travers from afar as a princely gentleman, without reproach, and the discovery of his failing took Sam a long way on the road to cynicism. In youth one's faith dies hard, and, being dead, turns rapidly corrupt.

The business was an excellent one, rotting slowly from the top, and Sam found the office a notable place in which to pick up knowledge of the world; especially, since he lacked good direction, of the shadier ways of the world. He felt that he had declined in status: his school-friends, there his equals, had gone either to the Universities or, with influence behind them, to the professions. If they went to business, it was as their fathers' sons. They were not scratch men, and Sam felt that he was starting at the scratch-line.

Travers had really no intentions that Sam should feel himself misprized. The boy had to learn the business, and the way to understanding lay from the bottom upwards. But Sam contrasted himself bitterly with Lance, first at school and then at Cambridge. In that, indeed, he found a minimum of consolation. It wasn't rational, but to Anne and consequently to Sam, university had meant Oxford, and he won a hardy solace from the thought that Lance was, after all, "only" at Cambridge.

Meantime, he grew in knowledge of his world, and education came to Sam, not in the cloistered freedom of the Isis, but where, in Manchester, he went collecting rents: in country courts where hard laws operated hardly: and in the office, where men did not greet each other with a friendly smile, but gave instead the "competition glare." It was not a kindly school in which he spent the developing years, but one where it was taught that self's the man, and magnanimity is a mistake. "Get on or get out," and Sam got on with a sort of choleric zeal which gave no quarter and expected none.

But he did not get on fast enough to please himself. He had, he thought, stepped down from the days of the Grammar School where he belonged with the caste that rules or, at any rate, administers, the caste that sits on velvet and overlooks the mob. Now he was in the cockpit, with the mob that struggles to ascend, and, to Sam, a wage of thirty shillings a week at the age of twenty was a derisory ascension. Anne thought it satisfying, and it was her contentment with his rate of progress which first made him begin to think of her as, after all, a limited person. You didn't bribe Sam Branstone to be meekly satisfied with thirty shillings a week.

"The trouble is," he said to the only man in the office with whom he was in the least confidential, "that you don't begin to get on till you've got a bit of capital together. Money breeds money."

His friend suggested betting as a means to affluence, and offered to tell him of a dead certainty.

Sam assumed his cunningest air of a superman of the world. "The best row of houses where I go for the rents," he said, "belongs to Jack Elsworth, the bookie. I don't see why I should help him to buy another house."

"Bookies don't always win," said the optimist.

"No," said Sam. "It's possible to make money out of betting and it's possible to get a baby by a harlot, but that isn't what the harlot's for, and it isn't what the bookie's for."

At this time, harlots were the pegs on which Sam hung his wit. He had no other use for them, but had discovered that a coarse turn of phrase was an asset in his world and therefore wielded it. But the effect of this little conversation was to crystallize his aim. He wanted that "bit of capital" badly, and did not intend that, if opportunity presented, a nice regard for scruple should hold him back from taking anything the gods might send. He had no ultimate design, but fortune came to the fortunate and money to the moneyed, so that the first move was, obviously, to get money. He wanted a jumping-off place; then he would soar.

Opportunity walked into the office in the person of Joseph of Arimathea Minnifie. That was his full baptismal name: analogous with the styles of certain limited companies, such as John Smith (of Newcastle) Limited, to distinguish that Smith from other Smiths. Minnifie's mother had explained to the parson that she was a New Testament woman. To her intimates she had put it that she chose the name Joseph because she liked it, but she also liked a man to be a man. It was deduced that she supposed the third Joseph in the Bible would have acted differently from the first in the affair of Potiphar's wife.

Sam's accent had degenerated since the days of Shylock and the reading prize. It had kept bad company, and might be known by the company it kept to-day rather than by that which it used to keep at school; but he could still, without too great an effort, assume a well-bred speech and was often sent with a prospective buyer to show off any likely houses on Mr. Travers' list. Because it was usual for him to go on such errands, and not because anyone supposed that niceties of speech could or would have any effect on Mr. Minnifie, he was sent with him in a cab to tour the suburbs where Travers had property in charge.

A coarse accent was not likely to offend Joseph Minnifie, who a fortnight earlier had been a market porter at Shude Hill, but had now come into money, well invested in the best Brewery securities, from his uncle, a publican. Minnifie had sold out some of the shares because he could now satisfy a long ambition and live in his own house. He proposed, he told Mr. Travers, to retire to the country.

"The country?" asked Travers, whose practice was suburban.

"Well," said Minnifie, "summat quiet and homely. I'd like a change from Rochdale Road. I thought," he went on rather shyly, "of Whalley Range. It's a good neighbourhood."

Travers refrained from pointing out that Whalley Range was not usually regarded as the country, but was, in fact, of the inner ring of suburbs, a penny tram fare from the centre of Manchester. "Oh, yes, Mr. Minnifie," he said. "I think I can satisfy you in W'halley Range. I have several available houses on my books in that district."

"I'll pay three hundred pound for what I like," said Minnifie, quite fiercely. "I've got it in my pocket now." He was fierce because he was not yet quite sure that his legacy was not phantom gold, and he pulled out a bundle of notes as much to assure himself that they were still where he had put them as with the idea of proving his good faith to Travers.

Travers concealed a smile. After all, commission on three hundred pounds is not to be sneezed at, but neither was this the sort of client for whom Traver's disturbed his habits. "I have myself," he said, "a large property auction to attend in the city, but Mr. Branstone will go with you to inspect the houses." He smiled kindly on Sam, and added, lest Minnifie should think his affair, so important to him, underrated by the agent: "Mr. Branstone is my confidential man. When Mr. Branstone tells you anything about the houses you are going to see, it is as if I spoke myself."

"I see," said Minnifie. "He's your foreman, and you needn't tell me you'll back him up. I know foremen."

"Well, his word is certainly as good as mine. I leave you in safe hands, Mr. Minnifie." And Travers went out to attend his first auction of the day, which usually happened at eleven o'clock in the morning.

Sam and the client took a cab to Whalley Range, where Minnifie inspected several houses which were to be had at about his price. But he was hard to satisfy, and, what was worse, apparently unable to define his reasons for dissatisfaction. As Sam praised this and that about a house, Minnifie admitted that such things were praiseworthy, but he would, please, see another house. Sam was a little piqued and tried his best to be genial, suspecting that Minnifie resented being fobbed off with a "foreman"; and Sam's best was very good, so that presently the ice was thawed.

Minnifle stood at the bow-window of a dining-room and looked up and down the street. It was empty save for a tradesman's boy. From somewhere round the corner came the diminished rattle of a milk-cart. Minnifle shook his head sadly.

"It's quiet," he said. "See that road. Nothing stirring. What is there for the missus to look at when she sits in the window?"

"It's morning," said Sam. "Things will be brisker in the afternoon." But his tone lacked conviction, and he could not resist the temptation to add: "There's a cat crossing the road now."

"Come out," said Minnifle. "This'ull none do," and when they stood upon the door-step he sniffed the air of Whalley Range with disapproval. "I don't like it and it's no use pretending that I do. It's got a cold smell to me. It isn't homely."

"I know what you mean," said Sam, diagnosing the trouble. "Wait a bit." He gave the cabman an address and was careful to leave the window open. They came to other streets where the scent of yesterday's fried fish still lingered in the air and the nose of Mr. Minnifle inhaled it greedily. "This is better," he pronounced.

They had come to Greenheys, which, when De Quincey's father built a country house there in 1791, was "separated from the last outskirts of Manchester by an entire mile." It is by no means separated now, and good houses of the mid-Victorian period are to be had cheaply because good tenants dislike bad neighbours. Travers had one of these survivals from an urbane past on his books and Sam hugged himself for thinking of it now: that house had proved itself the whitest of white elephants.

Mr. Minnifie, exhilarated by the spicy smells of Greenheys, was no longer a timid excursionist looking only where his guide bade him, but a house hunter hot upon the trail, with eyes that spied on each side of their route.

"Ah!" he called suddenly. "Stop!"

The cabman stopped. "But we're not there," said Sam, rather blankly.

"I think we are," said Minnifie, and got out of the cab.

Sam followed, in that leaden state of mind which often precedes inspiration. What had attracted Minnifie was a semi-detached house at a corner, which the trams passed. Opposite were shops, and there was a lively stir in the street. Certainly, Mrs. Minnifie would have something to see here when she looked out of the window.

Sam knew that pair of houses, and what he knew made him fear that he would not, this time, rid Mr. Travers of the white elephant on his books. They were good houses enough, but the people who had furniture to fill them were not the sort of people who welcomed shops opposite their windows and trams past their gate, so that both had been long empty. Now, however, they were for sale, under a will, and a quick sale was wanted that the estate might be wound up. They would certainly go cheaply on that account, and the more so since two attempted auctions had proved abortive. There had been no offers.

And here was Mr. Minnilie plainly delighted, and those houses not in Travers' charge, but in that of a rival agency! Sam felt depressed, then as dawn follows darkness, lie thought of what Travers had said, that Sam's word was as good as his own. It was going to be, and Mr. Minnifie's money as good in Sam's hands as in those of Calverts', the legitimate agents for this pair of houses. He stepped out briskly now, the ardent salesman.

"One moment, Mr. Minnifie. I haven't the key of this house with me, but it is at the shop opposite. I will get it." His quick eye had read so much on Calverts' notice board, but by the time he returned, Minnifie had also seen that rival name on the board and mentioned the fact.

"I know," said Sam. "The board has not been altered, but this property is in my hands now."

Which was true.

The house enchanted Minnifie, who had made up his mind in advance to be enchanted. And, of course, rooms may be in need of decoration, but good proportions tell, even on a Mr. Minnifie. This house was very different from the jerry-built villas of Whalley Range.

"What's price?" he asked.

"Three hundred and fifteen pounds," said Sam.

"I said three hundred and I'll none budge."

"If you will come to the office at six, I shall be able to tell you," said Sam, naming a queer hour, seeing that the office closed at half-past five.

"All right," said Minnifie. "It's a firm offer at three hundred, and I'm a man of my word."

Sam devoutly hoped so. He was taking a considerable gamble on it. They parted, and Sam, as usual, went home for lunch, but, not as usual, returned with his cheque-book in his pocket. His accumulated savings were five pounds, but he possessed a cheque-book. He waited rather carefully until the banks had closed, then he walked into Calverts' offices and offered them two hundred and fifty pounds for the pair of semi-detached houses in Greenheys. They accepted two hundred and seventy-five; and Sam drew a cheque for that amount, and received the title-deeds in exchange. Then he palpitated, but it was, in any case, safely after banking hours. Calverts could not present his cheque that day.

He was busy at five-thirty, when the clerks left, and proposed to work late for a while, "to clear things up," he said. At six Minnifie arrived, true to his word, and Sam could have kissed him. He had spent the longest half hour of his life. He took Minnifie by the private door into Travers' office, so that he should not see the empty general office, and put him in the client's chair, himself usurping Travers' seat.

"Well, Mr. Minnifie," he said, "suppose I told you that the price is still three fifteen, what would you say?"

"I'd say 'Good-day,'" and Minnifie showed that he meant it by rising to his feet. Sam went on hurriedly.

"Ah! Then it's as well that I've succeeded. It has been an infinitude of trouble—-"

"I reckon," said Minnifie, "that you're here to take trouble. Leastways, if it's easy money in your line, it's the only line that's made that way."

"Oh, we have our troubles, like everybody else. This document," he went on, "conveys the house to you. The price is three hundred pounds."

"It's a bargain," said Mr. Minnifie, producing his notes, "count'em." Sam counted feverishly, then made out a receipt. Nothing short of murder would have induced him to part with that money now.

"If you will meet me to-morrow at twelve at that address—a lawyer's—we will have the conveyance put in proper form."

"I've seen a bit of lawyers lately over this brass of mine," said Minnifie, "and I don't like'em. They eat money."

"But in this case," said Sam magnanimously, "I pay the lawyer's fees."

"Then I'll be there," said Minnifie.

Sam was waiting next day for the doors of his bank to open, and breathed colossal relief when his three hundred pounds were safely in to meet his cheque. He had a net profit of some twenty pounds, after settling for the conveyancing, and he had a house to sell. Not long afterwards, he sold it for one hundred and seventy-five pounds.

The fact that one of the pair had been thought desirable by somebody caused somebody else to desire the other: and Sam could only hope that the new neighbours would not compare notes. If they did, it did not matter; he had only obeyed the axiom of commerce, "Buy cheap, sell dear," and it was not his fault that in the one case he had had to sell less dearly than in the other.

His bank credit was two hundred pounds.

CHAPTER VII
THE FLEDGLING CAPITALIST

IN Sam's opinion, nobody had suffered. Mr. Travers lost nothing, because the corner house had conquered Minnifie at sight, and he would not in any case have bought the white elephant which Travers had for sale. Calverts had got as much as they expected to get for the houses, or they would not have sold, while the beneficiary under the late owner's will was a charity, and Sam hoped that charity was charitable enough not to look a gift-horse in the mouth: if it wasn't, it ought to be. As to the purchasers, who had certainly paid more for the property than they need have done, that was what purchasers were for. Why did smart business men exist if not to exploit purchasers?

All this was highly comforting, but to confess the need for comfort was to admit to disquiet, and he found that it was one thing to argue in this strain with his conscience, and another to boast to Anne of his achievement. Women don't understand business, and he had an uneasy feeling that the ethics of the transaction would not satisfy Anne. He decided that he had better not tell her, that he must resist his impulse of surprising her with the gift of a seal-skin coat, and remained a capitalist under the rose. There was no hurry, and perhaps his next stroke, when it came, would be under conditions that would bear the limelight of her scrutiny.

But repression was not all. Justify himself as he would, chuckle over his gains as he did, the matter searched him deeply and reacted sharply in two ways, of which the first began as that old expedient of sinners, conscience-money. There are defaulters who find absolution for themselves by sending notes, under initials, to the Chancellor of the Exchequer, and by having them acknowledged with impressiveness in the personal columns of the *Times*. That was not Sam's way: he did not do good deeds by stealth, and his conscience-money did not go out of the family. He used it philanthropically, but it was philanthropy and ten per cent, to begin with, and in the end it was very much more than ten per cent. It was the Chappie Bill Posting and Window-Cleaning Company.

He thought that he could, without exciting Anne's suspicions, tell her that his savings had reached ten pounds, and proposed to spend that sum for the benefit of George Chappie.

Inspired, perhaps, by his household gods, George was facing life bravely, and won a minor place in Anne's good graces when he and Madge produced a firstborn son, who had the remarkable quality of looking exactly like the infant Samuel, whose name he bore. But George had not, in her opinion, deserved Sam's generosity to this extent.

"You're over-good to them," she said. "You've made a man and woman of a pair of wastrels, and I'd let them alone to make their own way now."

"Do you think it will be much of a way?" asked Sam. "They're the sort that need help."

"Aye," she said, "they'll lean on you all right. They're good at leaning."

"Well," said Sam, drawing himself up. "Let them lean."

"Sam," said Anne, "I'm not fond, but if I told you what I think of you for this, you'd have the right to call me fond and foolish. I like you very well, my son. You're the strong man helping and supporting the weak."

She finished suddenly and a thought shamefacedly. She had praised him openly and considered it a weakness in her. Sam put a hand on her shoulder. It was not demonstrative, but his gesture was full of understanding, and Anne turned rapidly away, shaking him off almost with rudeness, taking very earnestly to her business of clearing away their tea-things.

Sam watched appreciatively through the corner of his eye. He relished praise from Anne, even when, as now, it was not strictly merited. The strong in Sam's philosophy did not support the weak, but the weak the strong. He was confirmed in his belief that women could not understand business. This, however, he reminded himself, was not pure business, it was conscience-money, which ought not to be unconscionably reproductive: so he bought George a hand-cart, ladder, bucket and leathers, and exacted from him not more than ten per cent, on his capital expenditure. In Travers' business Sam found opportunities of pushing George. A client took a house, and Sam would suggest with a nicely casual air that the windows needed cleaning. He would, to save the client trouble, then offer to send a man round, so that George's connection waxed, and he prospered to the tune of two amazing pounds a week, till the restless Sam began to widen his view of George's potentialities.

His eye for the main chance had always a useful squint which could see money round the corner as well as in the straight high road, and he thought that George, with his outfit of ladders, could see his talent for height in other ways than window cleaning. There was, for example, bill-posting, a trade whose mysteries Sam deemed it not beyond George's capabilities to learn.

The thing grew by degrees, from the first builder's hoarding which Sam rented venturously for advertising space, to a comfortable little business that ran itself by its own momentum long after he tired of its comparative insignificance. With George, the start was all: he could always plod where Sam had led, and as Sam had time to set the ball rolling, and money enough to spoon-feed the infant business with capital, George kept the thing in being by careful, steady management. He hadn't boasted when he told Anne he was steady.

Of course, Sam was impatient and deplored his active partner's inactivity. He grew tired of the gradual increase, but, all the same, the business was unquestionably successful, and he relished hugely his sense of being the power behind the throne, if only behind a small, conservative, so lamentably unambitious throne. Sam also was among the king makers.

The other, greater sequel to his reaction led to more pyrotechnical results, and eventually to Sam's launch on his career. Nothing happened at first, and indeed for so long that he was feeling himself between the devil of the estate office and the deep sea of George's persistent carefulness. The Chappie Bill-Posting Company was good enough for George, but not for Sam: there were too many com petitors with too great resources, while the estate office routine bored him, and opportunities for piratical enterprise did not recur.

He felt, at twenty-four years of age, and at two pounds ten a week, that he was growing old in service, he who was not meant to serve but to be served.

But then—desolating thought—was he meant to be served? Had he lost, or was he, at any rate, not losing the accent of speech and mind of those who are served? He knew that his accent had touched pitch and been defiled: those bawdy stories of his were told in the tongue of his hearers, and there had been clients lately who had spoken to him, when inspecting property, as if he were a clerk, and not a pleasant, gentlemanly youth of obvious superiority to his present, no doubt temporary, job. He had a sudden fear that the job might not be temporary after all, and there followed a time when he was wholly bent on self-improvement, when he abjured the narrow way of professional text-books and read that he might become well-read, that he might bandy allusions with those old school-fellows of his who had gone to Universities, that he might, if he could not hope to shine, at least be not outshone.

It wasn't *pour le bon motif,* and he did not even pretend to like the greater part of what he read. He crammed against the grain, and a growing row of the "World's Classics" figured on his shelf as trophies of his perseverance. Industriously he rubbed away the rust which had accumulated on his mind since it took its not very brilliant polish of the Grammar School. He took down the dust-stained Gibbon he had won for reading, and ploughed heroically through it.

That reminded him of another chink in his armour. A man of the world must have the knack of speaking to the world, and Sam became a member of the Concentrics. As Anne once told him, he had the gift of the gab, but, except for his present fluent recommendations of houses to prospective tenants, it was a talent he had buried. Now, however, he proposed to dig it up and did it in (he thought) the ambitious surroundings of the Concentrics, who were indeed as mixed a company as he could have found anywhere, and on that account the better for his purpose.

The common centre which was supposed to hold the Concentrics together was a love of literature, but they tended to drop literature for politics on the slightest pretext. There were literary enthusiasts amongst them, but it rarely happened that one man's enthusiasm coincided with another's. It did less than coincide. A member would read a laborious paper on some man of letters, and the subsequent discussion would be conducted by men who began their intelligent speeches by admitting that they had not read a word of, say, Henry James or Lafcadio Hearn, but that their opinion was nevertheless so and so. Whereas, of course, nobody ever confessed to ignorance of politics. Politics is like law, only more so. One is presumed by the law to know the law, which is highly presumptuous of the law, because not even the lawyers know the law, and they must often go to judges, at their client's expense, to find out what the law is: and the "more so," as applied to politics, is that while laymen hesitate to argue a point of law, and go to an expert, they never hesitate to argue a point of politics, and *are* the expert.

Political discussions amongst the Concentrics were real and passionate, literary discussions unreal and frigid; and as "social reform" became a favourite shibboleth about this time, literature took a back seat in favour of subjects about which men could grow emotional and their oratory rhetorical. It was all one to Sam, who was here to speak, and did his reading at home.

He spoke often, so that he soon improved, and he practised the literary allusiveness which was the purpose of his reading to such effect that he attracted the attention of the chairman, who was the Rev. Peter Struggles.

It is not, strictly, fair to say that a man is handicapped through life by a name like Struggles, because the legal process by which one can change an undesirable name is inexpensive, but Peter had never thought of such a move, and wore his handicap without being aware of it. In any case, he failed in life. He had a round face, red hair, side-whiskers: took snuff and messed his coat: was perfectly futile in practical affairs and absolutely "a dear." His scholarship was not profound, but he loved letters genuinely, He had failed steadily for thirty years to run a private school for boys in a suburb which was degenerating to industrialism, and late in life had taken orders, quite sincerely, not in the least with the idea of helping his school with a new respectability. It was, anyhow, beyond help, and a man who offered tradesmen's sons a sound commercial education was presently to buy him out.

Peter Struggles, well in his fifties, became curate to a vicar of forty, in the large, rough-and-tumble parish of St. Mary's. One says that he had failed in life, and, by Sam's standards, he had, and even by the working standards of his church. A man at fifty-six should not be a curate with an income of some hundred and twenty pounds a year. But if a man is happy at fifty-six to be a curate with that income? If he find satisfaction in it? Snuff was his indulgence, and the chairmanship of the Concentrics, who were not sectarian, his dissipation. For the rest, Peter had made harbour. To the pushing educationist who had bought him out, for a song, and now profaned his old school buildings with shorthand and the rudiments of bookkeeping, Peter was a failure and a pathetic failure. He was not conscious of failure himself, nor of anything but a serene contentment that he had found, if late, the work that he was fit to do. Through sheer single-minded, inoffensive, unobtrusive goodness he came to be a figure in that parish, and a power. Undignified in bearing, and careless in dress, he had a dignity of mind and soul.

Sam Branstone despised a worldly failure, here was a man of more than twice Sam's years, with less money than Sam had, and, by all his canons, Sam should have despised Peter. But he didn't. It was partly, no doubt, other people's opinions that influenced Sam—the universal esteem which Peter Struggles won—but it was by much more the innate nobility of the old curate. Sam began his speaking at the Concentrics to impress his fellow members, he ended by caring only for the appreciation of the quaint, slovenly figure who occupied the chair.

He got the appreciation he craved. Peter was shrewd enough to discount Sam's rhetorics, and the flashy tricks of apt quotation: he saw Sam as a misguided, self-seeking thruster who read only for veneer and spoke only to impress. But, at least, Sam tried, and Peter could admire perseverance.

The thing was to direct Sam's perseverance well, and Peter asked him to supper.

Our man of the world was prodigiously thrilled. The honour was exceptional, for Peter could not afford to be a host often, and Sam was aware not only of its rarity, but of Peter's unique standing in the parish: and, more than that, of Peter's worth. To be singled out by Peter Struggles, and asked to sup, was, socially, a triumph. It sounds absurd, and perhaps it is absurd that one good man should shine so brightly by contrast with the fifteen thousand others of an over-crowded parish, but that was why Peter was a colossus amongst the pigmies, and why Sam Branstone was egregiously excited by an invitation to sup at Peter's little house.

Peter did not invite Sam to preach at him. It was the boy's mind rather than his soul that was the target of his aim, and Peter's select library to which he trusted for influence. Certainly the little meal of cold beef and cocoa was not calculated to impress, nor the old, worn furniture, with the gaping rents in its horse-hair coverings, through which the stuffing poured. He handled books with reverence, and spoke of them, but Sam was hardly listening. He was under fire from another battery.

Ada Struggles met young men at church functions, and spoke with them at Sunday School, but she had few opportunities of greater intimacy, and was not the lady to waste so rare a chance as this. Peter droned on amongst his books and presently was lost in reading one. Ada lost herself in nothing except a burning desire, to monopolize Sam. Books did not interest Ada: getting married did.

The trouble was that in the days of his school's comparative prosperity, Peter had done Ada rather well. Perhaps as a schoolmaster himself, he got special consideration over terms, but at any rate he had sent her to a good boarding school. She had received the education of a lady, and it wasn't fair, it didn't chime with the fitness of things that she should now be the daughter of an impractical curate. Her case, to some extent, was parallel with Sam's: the past of both had augured well, and the future depended on their wits.

There, however, the parallel ceased, for Ada had few wits, but she had moods, and the reverse side of the moping discontent, which was endemic with her, was the meretricious brilliance she now paraded for Sam's entanglement. Ada was "all out" after her prey, in her best clothes and her best, that is, her most captivatingly genial manners.

Sam thought that she illuminated that dingy book-surrounded room. They were not gay books with gilded bindings, but solid, well-worn volumes of ponderous aspect. The books repelled and Ada invited. Youth called to youth: youth answered to the call.

He was obsessed with his idea of accent, and the worldly value of superiority in speech. Ada's first appeal to him, though she did not know it, was that she spoke well; her second was that she was her father's daughter; her third, as she knew perfectly, was the helplessness which she used cunningly to flatter his masculine importance. She told him without a word that he was a strong, powerful man, and she a flower which he might pluck and wear. And she did the anemone business quite effectively.

There was not much of Ada, and what there was was not remarkable, but she was fluffy and frilly and feminine in the feebler way. She had on something that was not silk but suggested the rustle of silk. After all, it was not Ada's fault that it was not silk, or that her intimate underclothing was of flannelette; she could only use the opportunities she had, and they were few.

But she had the prettiness, the rather silly and never lasting prettiness, which accompanies anæmia.

It would not wear, and she knew that it would not wear. She was becoming desperate. Sam was sent by heaven.

He thought so, too. Old Struggles read "Marcus Aurelius," standing by his book-shelf, utterly forgetful of his guest, and the guest thought that Peter's preoccupation was also instructed by heaven. It left him free for Ada.

What he said to Ada and what Ada said to him were things of no importance: their serious conversation was not conducted by their tongues, but by their eyes.

This is the sort of thing:

Ada (her voice): Of course, I remember seeing you quite often in church, Mr. Branstone.

(Her eyes): And you found favour in my sight.

Sam (his voice): Naturally, I always saw you whenever I went.

(His eyes): It was for you I went to church.

Ada (her voice): I'm glad that you were able to come in to-night. I am often lonely in the evenings. Father is so wrapped up in his books.

(Her eyes): Meeting you is the great moment of my life. I'm an unhappy princess in an ogre's tower. Rescue me. Rescue me.

Sam (his voice): It was most kind of Mr. Struggles to ask me in for a talk about books.

(His eyes): Books be damned. I'm fascinated by the sensuous rustle of your skirts, and I'm a hero sent to kiss the wistful look away from your pleading eyes.

And so on. By the end of the evening, had the unsaid speeches or half of them been written down, Ada had evidence enough to have brought a breach of promise action against a recalcitrant Sam. Only Sam was not recalcitrant, but, on the contrary, ardent. It was, Ada congratulated herself, uncommonly good going for a first meeting.

Peter emerged from "Marcus Aurelius" with a gentle smile which lighted up his undistinguished face. "Yes. Pagan but grand," he said, quite unaware that half an hour had passed since he last spoke. "I'll lend you this book, Branstone, and now".—he glanced at the clock—"I'm afraid that I must turn you out. I'd no idea it was so late. How rapidly the time passes when one is talking about one's books!"

CHAPTER VIII
ADA STRUGGLES

THERE were moments during that night when Sam imagined that he was in the stranglehold of a grand passion: times when he quite successfully deceived himself that he burned for Ada.

And certainly the experience, unique for him, of a sleepless night lent colour to the belief that he was passionately in love, whereas he was, in fact, merely attracted by a girl who had spared no pains to attract; and what kept Sam awake was not passion but calculation. The affair, indeed, was as broad as it was long: it had a slender basis of mutual attraction, and a monstrous superstructure on each side of self-interest.

He did not "see through" Ada to the point of being prophetic about her, but he did even from the beginning perceive that Anne was not likely to be enthusiastic. But would Anne greet any daughter-in-law with open arms? Was there born the daughter of Eve whom Anne would think the peer of her Sam? He did not want to cross his mother, but a man must be a man, and a mother's fondness and her jealousy of the intending wife were things about which one had to be callous. The world, as Benedick said, must be peopled.

Anne would see eye to eye with him as to the practical advantages of Ada. Ada was Peter's daughter.

That parentage had, by way of discount, the defect of its quality. Socially it was a great thing to be Peter's son-in-law, and not only socially but ideally. Sam's admiration for the curate was genuine enough, and he knew that Anne shared it. But there was the question of money, and Peter had none. Sam kept his mother, and would have to keep his wife. He saw in Ada an asset which he could ultimately exploit, but, in the meantime, until there came into his mind the scheme which should turn his association with Peter into money, he must reckon on a tight period. Anne would see the tight period, but not the unborn, fruitful plan on which he counted for their future. And he could not hurry that plan to birth. His schemes came to him when he least expected them, spontaneously. They were not to be forced by worry.

Again, he reminded himself, there was no hurry. He had only just met Ada, and was planning as if his engagement ring were on her finger. Not that he had any serious doubts about that ring and Ada's willingness to wear it, but she did not wear it yet, and there was time in hand, and to spare, for consideration of these practical affairs.

Meantime, he loved her, and love, according to the authors, was the most wonderful thing in the world. He told himself very firmly that he loved Ada, and that love was wonderful. Reiteration is so potent that before morning he believed what he wished to believe. He recalled the soft pressure of her hand when she said "Good night," the froufrou of her skirt, her melting eye; and persuaded himself that Ada Struggles was a pearl beyond price.

He was perfectly sure that he loved her, and for proof there was his sleeplessness. It occurred to him that as he could not sleep, and was only thinking in circles, he might as well do something to hasten the time when he could see Ada again. He could not return "Marcus Aurelius" to Peter until he had read it, and if he returned it with unexpected promptitude, he must be ready to face a stiff examination in it; therefore he lit the gas and read "Marcus Aurelius" by way of serving Ada, whom he loved.

Hard service, too, for there was not much in Sam's philosophy which agreed with the Emperor's, but two nights later he was ringing Peter's bell with the book under his arm, an ordered précis of it in his mind, and some selected passages from it on his tongue. They were not selected because Sam liked them, but because he thought Peter liked them.

Peter was out, but Ada was in, and, curiously enough for one who was not an optimist either by nature or experience, dressed again in her Sunday clothes.

She opened the door to him. "Father is out, Mr. Branstone," she said.

"I only called to return him this book."

"I do not think he will be long," said Ada promptly, who knew very well that Peter would certainly be late. "Will you not come in and wait for him?"

He came, crossing his Rubicon. The unchaperoned intimacy of that night struck both of them as a daring short cut to a position to which they were not entitled—a thing properly done only by the engaged and the maturely and securely engaged. Luck fought for Ada.

"I'm afraid I can't stay very long," he hedged desperately.

Ada sat down and crossed her knees. A neat ankle was effectively on exhibition. "That chair of father's," she said, "is fairly comfortable." Also, it faced Ada's, and he drew up another, less inviting, chair, and placed it flush with the fire. Except by a side-glance, he could not see her ankle now, and evaded that aphrodisiac, while Peter's chair, though empty, completed the semi-circle, and seemed to give a sort of countenance to their interview. Sam drew much comfort from that chair, and tried to guide their conversation into literary paths of which the chair would have approved. He discoursed of "Marcus Aurelius," and he was very dull, but felt virtuous.

Ada did not believe that it was virtuous to be dull, and mentally cursed that *tertium quid*, the ghost of Peter Struggles, whom Sam had so firmly established in his chair; but she saw that the pace was not to be quickened here, under Peter's roof.

"I think your knowledge of books is wonderful, Mr. Branstone," she said, when Sam had exhausted his ideas about "Marcus Aurelius."

"I never find time to read, myself. Whenever I have the opportunity of recreation, I go out for exercise." The statement lacked the merit of truth She never took exercise, but was adept at sitting in front of a fire doing exactly nothing. The point was that in this house of the good Peter, Sam's enterprise was burked, and she wanted him where he could race without a handicap. "Do you ever go to Heaton Park?" she asked conversationally. "I shall probably be going there on Saturday."

"With—with your father?" asked Sam.

"Oh, no," she answered brightly. "Saturday is sermon day. That is why I am in the way here, although," she added pathetically, "I fear he often finds me in the way. I am not bookish like you and him." She gave that explanation suddenly, and it satisfied him.

"I am not really bookish, either," he said. "Of course you won't be going alone to Heaton Park."

She hoped not. "I expect so," she said.

Sam took the plunge. "Could I have the honour of accompanying you, Miss Struggles?"

"Oh, but you are so busy. I must not waste your time."

"It couldn't be wasted with you," said Sam, and glanced guiltily at Peter's chair, as if he had exceeded the limits of propriety, but he had never seen Peter with anything but a benevolent smile, on his face, and was unable to see him imaginatively now in any other mood. He took fresh courage. "May I call for you?"

"That," said Ada, "would never do. It would disturb father at his sermon. I shall go by tram at about three o'clock." She rose. There was nothing to be done with Sam in that house, but she pinned her faith to Heaton Park: and not in vain.

Allow for the difference in size, distance and the general scale of things, and Heaton Park may be regarded as the Manchester equivalent to Richmond Park.

Once upon a time the Manchester Town Council had a magnificent opportunity, and lost it. There are legends that they did not mean to lose it, and that they did not lose it through any fault of theirs. But they lost it. They lost the chance of buying Trafford Park, which lies along the banks of the Manchester Ship Canal, and was bought by Mr. Ernest Terah Hooley. It is said that Trafford Park, now a flourishing and rather American-look-ing industrial town (even the streets in its residential area are numbered, and not named, after the American plan, and railways stray about the roads, *more Americano*), is the one successful enterprise associated with the name of Hooley. That may or may not be true: at any rate the Manchester Town Council missed its chance at Trafford Park, and when Heaton Park, another old estate, came into the market, the Council did not repeat their mistake.

One goes, ascending all the way, through Cheetham Hill, the Ghetto, to the heights of Crumpsall and the Park by a municipal tram, which is admirably cheap or criminally cheap (according to one's views on municipal trams), and, in any case, magnificently efficient: and at the end of the ride, one finds beauty. One may find tea at Heaton Hall, and pictures that overflow from the meagre Art Gallery in Mosley Street, and municipal golf-links, but one finds also beauty.

It is a rolling country, raised above the smoke, dotted with wood and lake. Old gardens cling about the Hall, with rhododendron glades where there are sculpture and pools, and the Park rolls free in open air that is as clean as any air can be within five miles of Manchester Town Hall. It, lacks of Paradise, and if one can see green hills from Heaton Park, one cannot kelp but see the factory stacks that crown them or rise up from the valleys, but beauty lingers here on the outskirts of an ugly city secure against the jerry-builder and the ultimate defilement.

Ada was going to Heaton Park. Lovers have gone to Heaton Park before Ada and they will go when Ada has crumbled to dust. Ada went, and Sam went with her.

He went with her, not she with him: but if she led, he was very, very far from admitting it, though it may have been his obscure, subconscious knowledge of her leadership which made him outwardly assume the mien and the gestures of a leader. He asserted, every inch of him, that he was man, the conqueror, and she permitted the assertion and flattered it. Leading, indeed, was not a habit of Ada's, who was born to be led, but it is given to all of us to outstrip our nature on occasion, and this was Ada's chance. A subtle skill was granted her that she might be cunning with her opportunity. She was all calculation now, while Sam forgot to calculate, and walked with Ada on his arm along the main drive of Heaton Park.

Romance kept step with him and put a radiant veil between his sober senses and this witching hour: through glamour he beheld his Ada, and saw that she was good. He soared to high ambition, either to die or to possess the nymph, and now, that heady hour, to put all to the test amongst the rhododendron bushes behind the Hall.

There, by a patch of ancient turf, he halted her, and found a seat near the pool where water-lilies thrive: a lovers' nook, love haunted. Who knows what ardours of the old régime, when lords and ladies trod that turf, had passed upon the now decaying stone of that comely seat? What ghostly lovers in satin and brocade stood round to bless them or to mock? Wood pigeons cooed above them, calling the tune, and Sam danced to it in an ecstasy of hot desire.

She had the sleek self-satisfaction of a cat, the same unhurried certainty that the mouse was hers to gobble when she chose. Ada was very happy.

But apprehension gripped him now. He had not known her for a week, and she was Ada. Peter's daughter. He stood aghast at his precipitance, then, with the feeling that it was after all a "stroke" (though a larger one than ever before), and that he believed in acting promptly, cleared his throat and plunged into speech.

"Miss Struggles," he said, "I know that I have only made your acquaintance during the current week, but I seem to have known you all my life. It's because I used to see you in church, I daresay. I mean we were not strangers when we met, and, anyhow," he continued recklessly, "I don't care if we were. I'm not the hesitating sort. I mean, show me a thing, and I can tell you right off whether it's good or bad. My mind's made up in a jiffy: that's the kind of fellow I am. And when my mind's made up, I act."

Ada had given a little gasp at the phrasing of his opening—that "during the current week," an idiom from his business correspondence slipping in here to mark his nervousness—but he was fairly launched now, and she purred gently like a cat well lubricated with butter.

"Yes, Mr. Branstone," she said, "I think men ought to be resolute."

"So do I," he replied. "And so I am. Quite resolute and quite determined about you."

"About me?" She turned innocent eyes wonderingly at him. "I didn't know you were being personal."

"Well," he said, "I am. I am," he repeated, and took her hand.

"Mr. Branstone," she murmured, as one who sees a vision splendid in a dream, and let her hand lie limp in his.

He bent to her. "Can't you," he asked hoarsely, "can't you call me Sam?"

She called him Sam, and he kissed her.

"Ada!" He spoke her name like a caress. "Ada!" Her name was wonderful; she was a miracle; Sam was triumphant love. At that moment he was passionately in love, and he had conquered. He had pressed the lips of his divinity, shyly, with a revealing inexpertness which should have charmed her, who, being a woman, knew all about love while Sam was in short trousers. It didn't charm Ada, it touched no deeper chord than satisfaction at a good job well done. This was his first, his freshest love, but she cared only that the fish was on her line, securely hooked. He saw her face, idealized her face and gloried in her face: she saw a wedding-ring, she was to be Mrs., she was to escape the book-ridden home of Peter Struggles. Both had their moment then, but Sam, in his, loved Ada, and Ada only loved herself.

"Darling," he said, and sought her lips again She saw the thirst of him—and used it.

She drew back. "I do not think you ought to kiss me again until we have mentioned this to father," said Ada Struggles, digging the hook more deeply in her fish. "Not," she went on, as she saw him flinch, "that I do not want you to. Only——"

"Yes," he said, as she left it at the "only," and allowed him to appreciate her infinite delicacy. "Yes. Of course. Shall we have tea at the Hall?"

"Oh," said Ada, "ought we to?" She was seen to tremble on the brink of a delicious temptation, and with difficulty to resist. "I'm afraid," she decided, "not yet. But father will have finished his sermon by now, and if you came and saw him at once, then... then, Sam..." She eyed him, languishing, and opened up for him the golden vista of a jocund courtship—once Peter had been "seen." He came, obediently, to see Peter, and she relaxed her standard so far as to take his arm down the drive of Heaton Park. Indeed, just at the corner by the copse, where they were hidden, he had an arm round her waist: his feet trod air, and his head was with the stars.

Ada was thinking, "If he gets the engagement ring to-night, I can show it after church to-morrow."

CHAPTER IX
ADA AND A MAD TRAM-CAR

ON general grounds—on the grounds, for instance, of anything so out-of-date and out of reason as filial piety—Ada was quite indifferent to Peter's "consent," and wanted it only to shackle Sam more firmly. She had not much doubt that Peter would consent, as in fact he did, though not so readily as she had anticipated. She did not exhibit an engagement ring at church next day for the reason that she had none to exhibit. Peter kept Sam too late for that.

Of course Ada was wrong about Peter: she thought him a good man and consequently a perfect fool, whereas his foolishness was imperfect, and he was subject, like most unworldly people, to streaks of acumen about worldly affairs. They come sometimes, these disconcerting fits of perception, as if a dam had burst, and usually the times are inconvenient to those who have reckoned on the unworldliness.

Peter answered her expectation so far as to say, "Bless my soul," and so far only. After that, he began an elaborate and skilful catechism of Sam, which pretended to be a friendly talk about books, but was really an examination of Sam Branstone, his character and disposition. At the beginning Peter knew little of Sam beyond what his observations at the Concentrics had told him, and Sam's volunteered remarks about his salary and his prospects interested Peter to a very slight extent. At the end Peter decided that Sam was to be trusted to make things easy for Ada on the material side, and that spiritually he was not beyond hope.

But he had not, spiritually, been touched as yet. Would Ada touch him? That was the question for Peter, who knew his Ada. Ada could be led. He admitted that he himself had failed with her, but he was not a strong man. A strong man, with love as his ally, could lead Ada, could form her, and Sam had strength, and, Peter thought, love. It depended, then, on whether Sam's love for Ada, reacting on him, would quicken his latent spirituality so that the lead he gave to Ada would be good. And on the whole Peter thought there was a reasonable chance. He believed in the power of love, he believed that love is God and God is love, and confronted with his pair of self-confessed lovers he read their future optimistically in the light of his belief. What else could Peter do? They said they were in love, they appeared to be in love, they had the symptoms of the state of love. He could only judge the case on the evidence before the court.

He could not know that with Sam the symptoms, though real, were temporary, and with Ada an intelligent mimicry. He gave his assent to their engagement formally and very solemnly.

Sam left the house late, thrilling with Ada's "Good-night" kiss, but the glow was quick to fade, and he found himself thinking rather of Peter than of Ada, whom of course, he loved. If ever probe was gentle, it was Peter's: nevertheless, Sam had felt the probe antagonistically. He had shivered naked before Peter's inquisition, he had understood that he was under examination, and resented it. It was, however disguisedly, opposition, and the thought of that kindly opponent led him to think of one from whom, also, opposition was to be expected, and, probably, less tactfully. It led to Anne.

Well, that was the fate of lovers: it was the way to deepen love and, perhaps already a little doubtful of his love, he welcomed the idea of Anne in opposition. It was curious that, while he thought of Ada as the one woman in the world, he should expect Anne to be hostile not merely to the idea of his marriage in general, but to marriage with Ada in particular. It was hardly loyal to Ada, who should have reigned unchallengably queen; and he could offer Anne the argument of the advantages of being Peter Struggles' son-in-law. But, with it all, he looked for friction, and Anne was not to disappoint him there, although at first she took it with a calmness which disarmed him.

He came in, of course, late, and ate his supper, silently hoping that she would give him an opening, but Anne asked no questions, though she had not seen him since early morning, and Sam was not often out for meals. She asked no questions because she wanted to watch him first. It was clear to her at a glance that he was in one of two conditions: he was drunk or he was in love, and she wanted to make no mistake. If it was drink she would move very promptly and directly: if love, cannily and by devious ways. She found quickly that it was not drink. It was more serious.

Her silence awed him. "Mother," he asked by way of breaking it, "aren't you well?"

"Aye," she said grimly, "I'm well. Are you?"

"I've eaten a good supper."

"I noticed that. I'll clear away now."

"Wait a bit. I've something to tell you."

"I reckon it'll keep till morning. You mayn't have known it, but you came in late. It's bed-time and beyond."

"Still," he said, "I'd like you to hear this tonight."

"You sound serious," said Anne, and sat. "What is it, Sam?"

"It's something rather wonderful, mother."

"It would be," said Anne. "What's her name?"

Sam rose, astonished at her perspicacity. "You guessed!"

"I'm none in my dotage yet." Anne was grim.

"Mother, I hope you're pleased. You must be pleased. It's all so wonderful to me."

"I asked you her name," said Anne.

"It's Ada Struggles. You know," he went on hurriedly, "how much we all admire her father."

"I know, but I don't know Ada."

"You will soon," said Sam enthusiastically.

"I will that," said Anne, and there was menace in her voice. She took her candle. "Good-night, my son," she said, kissing him, which was not habitual.

"Is that all?" he asked. "All that you have to say?"

"I don't know Ada yet," she said, and so was gone to bed.

Peter and Anne went opposite ways in their search to know whether this marriage was the right thing for their children's happiness. Peter ignored the bread and butter problem, or took it for granted: and his was the higher wisdom. He knew that Sam was not made of the stuff that starves for bread; not in his body but in his soul was Sam likely to be pinched.

Anne took the earthlier view that happiness resulted from home comforts. Ada, as she knew, was no shining beauty, and the better for that. Beauty is skin-deep. But she looked frail, only so, for the matter of that, did some of the toughest girls, and she took it that Sam had had the horse-sense to make some preliminary inquiries before he committed himself. Sam, it appeared, had not.

Was Ada strong and healthy? Was she economical? Could she cook? Was she her own dressmaker? And when she found that Sam could answer none of these questions, she said ironically: "Well, at least, you've eyes in your head. Is their house clean?"

Sam could only say that he supposed so, and Anne looked witheringly at him. "Yes, you're in love all right," she said. "They say love's blind. You're leaving a lot to me."

"Mother," he said, alarmed, "what are you going to do?"

"I'm going to get acquainted with Ada," she said. "One of us must know her, and you don't."

"If you'll be fair to her," said Sam. "I'm not afraid."

"I'll be fair," said Anne, and meant to be; but is a mother ever fair to the prospective wife of her only son? Perhaps, and in that case Anne went to Ada with an open mind. "After all," she reflected, "I daresay Tom Branstone's mother didn't think much of me, though Tom was one of ten and it makes a difference. It oughtn't to, though" — —she pulled herself up. "Anne, you'll be fair to the girl." She looked indulgently at Ada's curtains and rang Ada's bell.

But Ada was wearing silver bangles on her wrists and her shoes were made for show. Anne had the sort of pleasure which comes from having one's worst fears realized. She may have generalized too sweepingly, but she held that only shallow people wear silver bangles and shoes whose aim is daintiness and not durability.

First impressions, at any rate, went heavily against Ada, but Anne remembered her promise to be fair. It was possible that when Tom Branstone took Anne to see his mother, that lady did not like Anne's way of doing her hair. To each generation the symbols of its youth and perhaps bangles on Ada were not more skittish than a cairngorm brooch had been on Anne.

"I have tea ready, Mrs. Branstone," said Ada. "Sam told me you were coming."

"Did he?" Anne was surprised into saying. She had not told Sam of her intention and his guess at it and his warning of Ada had spoilt her plan of coming upon Ada unawares. She wanted Ada unprepared and unadorned: Ada at home, not Ada "at home." And Ada was very much "at home." The room had been "turned out" — and so had Peter that it might be — company manners and the company tea-pot were on exhibition, and everything was formal and obviously thought out. And, as Anne had to admit, not badly thought out either. Ada had not been to that expensive boarding school for nothing; she had an air to awe a porter's widow. Anne didn't like her trick of putting the milk in the cup before she poured the tea, nor her dogmatic way of asserting that it improved the flavour and that "everybody did it now." Everybody, did not do it, Anne did not do it; but, again, perhaps this was the modern touch, and Anne had come to be fair.

She made her first score when Ada left the room for hot water. "This room's been dusted to-day," thought Anne. "I'll see what her dusting is worth." She put it to the test by running her finger along the top of the books on one of the shelves, and her finger was very black.

The only way to keep books clean in Manchester is the way taken by nine out of ten people: they have no books. Some of the others put books behind glass, like orchids, the rest have the habit of blowing hard at a book when they take it from its shelf, and of washing their hands before opening it.

Anne did not know that. She kept Sam's few books clean by daily elbow-grease, and now furtively wiped her dirty finger on her stocking with the feeling that she had found out Ada. The dust on the books (and certainly it was thick) confirmed the impression left by the bangles, and Anne was not in the least ashamed of her spying. Sam had stolen a march on her by warning Ada and she paid him in his own coin.

And from then onwards the score rose steadily against Ada. There were cakes for tea. Now the only excuse for cakes was that one baked them oneself and Ada confessed that they came from Mrs. Stubbins and made the further mistake of showing an expert's knowledge in the productions of Mrs. Stubbins' confectionery shop. "Frivolous in food as well as dress," was Anne's comment. Her dress, Anne learnt, had been made by Madame Robinson.

"She's dear," said Ada, "but quite French. And, of course, she comes to church."

No Nonconformists need apply; but Anne was thinking not of Madame's religion but her bills. The employer of a quite French dressmaker called Robinson, born Duff, was no wife for Sam Branstone.

And by way of making Anne's assurance doubly sure, Ada let slip something about being under the doctor.

But Anne was not sanguine. She saw clearly enough that it was precisely Ada's weakness which was her strength with Sam. Sam had been leant upon by Madge and George, and liked it, as Anne herself, in that case, had liked it. But that was a different case from this. Madge had the claim of sisterhood; Anne could see nothing in Ada and Ada's weakness to give her the claim to lean on Sam: and the leaning in marriage should not be one-sided. Ada could give Sam nothing except herself, and Anne did not think that gift worth having.

Sam, unfortunately, did and Anne doubted her power of changing his mind. Her first attempt, at all events, must be with Ada, and she felt cramped in Ada's house, for the reason, perhaps, that it was Peter's house, the shrine of his simplicity. She wanted Ada cut off from the defences of the tea-table and her own familiar surroundings, and saying something about the warmth of the evening, suggested a ride on the top of a tram-car.

"I often do it myself," said Anne. "It blows the cobwebs away."

She did it as a matter of fact not often, for so it would have lost its quality of a dissipation, but with a wise irregularity she escaped the thraldom of her house on a tram-car. Tram rides were her romance, her safety-valve, her glimpse at life. Six-pennyworth of tram is cheaper in the long run than fourpennyworth of gin: both carry one away, but the tram-car brings one safely back.

Anne's lip tightened when she saw that Ada did not change the flimsy shoes and that her hat eclipsed their flimsiness. A "baby" hat, of imitation lace, from which her face peeped out like a drooping, sapless flower. "Yes," thought Anne. "Men being men, that hat is clever. It's a trap for fools and it caught my fool. Ada Struggles, you're dangerous."

They took the front seat on the tram and aloud she said, using purposely her roughest accent: "It's queer to think of our Sam marrying a lady. I'm not saying he doesn't deserve it, but his father were a railway porter and mine were a policeman. His sister was in service."

"Sam wall get on," said Ada, with conviction.

"I'm none doubting it," said Anne. "But he's had luck and it's a question if the luck'll hold. Mr. Travers took him up and sent him to Grammar School, and Sam didn't do too well there. He disappointed me and he's not gone on as he might have done. The fight's ahead of him yet and he'll need a fighter by his side. I've done my share for him this long while and I'm getting old. I shall be glad of a rest, Ada. Sam's an early riser and it's weary work getting up on a winter's morning to light the fire and get his breakfast ready. Only that won't trouble you. You're young."

"Of course," said Ada, "we shall have a servant."

"What!" exclaimed Anne, "on two pounds ten a week, with me to keep and all? I wouldn't reckon on that, if I were you. Later on, perhaps. But I know it can't be done at present, or Sam would have done it for me." The idea of Anne Branstone with a wench about her house struck her as humorous. Anne might have help some day—when she was bed-ridden: till then, her house was her house. "No," she went on, "you can take it from me that it'll not run to a servant. I don't know what his idea is about me, whether he will want me to live with you or not. Likely not. A man doesn't want his mother about when he's wed."

"No," agreed Ada hopefully. Anne oppressed her.

"No. And I can get on with a pound a week from him. That'll leave you thirty shillings. Well, I've done it, so I know it can be done, though mind you, it's a struggle all the time and double tides when the babies begin to come. But of course I'll help you—with advice. I'm not for forcing myself on you, but naturally I know Sam's ways and his likings about food. He's a bit difficult at times, too, but that's nothing. All men are and you'll know that, having had your father to do for. I don't say Sam's finicky, but he likes what he likes and I hope you're fond of the same things. It always turned me up to clean a rabbit, and I never liked the smell of onions, but that's a favourite dish of Sam's and so I'd just to grin and bear it. And I know you'll do the same for Sam."

Ada squirmed helplessly. She could have screamed. Anne sat at the outside of the seat and pinned her to it. The tram seemed a Juggernaut car which drove implacably over her dreams: a prison where she was tortured by a coarse old woman with work-roughened hands and an endless flow of vitriol. She wanted to tell Anne that she lied, that the more she deprecated Sam the more desirable Ada knew him to be, that her grapes were neither sour nor to be soured by Anne's insane jealousy; and she could not do it. The ride secmed more of a nightmare with every moment that passed. The tram was a mad wheeled cage with a mad driver and a mad guard. It left the lines and careered wildly into desolation, and she was fettered in it to an avenging fury who would not stop talking, but with ruthless common sense pricked all the bubbles of her hopes. She shut her eyes and abandoned herself to misery. Each minute seemed an hour. She thought that somebody was throttling her, that the flying cage was her tomb, that vampires sucked her blood, and her naked, drained body was shackled to her seat until the car, driving inevitably through black space, bumped finally against a star in one consuming smash. She opened her eyes to find that the tram had stopped at its suburban terminus and that Anne was asking: "Shall we get down for a walk or shall we go back by the same car?"

So she was still in the living world, and with the consciousness of it courage returned to her. For a minute she was silent, fighting her demons off, catching at facts and weighing them. Anne was not a vampire, but an old worn woman who had, curiously, the right to call Sam Branstone son—

Ada's future mother-in-law, and a quaint one too; one to be put firmly and haughtily in her place and kept there.

"We'll stay on this car," she replied. Its madness had departed. It was a tram, quite eminently sane and usual. "I think," she went on, "that you exaggerate the difficulties. I've no doubt that Sam will have more money by the time we're married. You see, he has me to work for now."

Not a simper with it either. Pure matter-of-fact statement, and the truth of it hit Anne, the cool assumption that Ada as a spur to effort was more competent than Anne. And this to Anne who had learnt algebra for Sam, to Anne who had underfed herself that he might wear the clothes a Grammar School boy ought to wear, to Anne who—oh, it was ineffable, but it defeated her because she knew, bitterly, gallingly, but undeniably, that it was true. This baby-faced chit, this fool in petticoats was more to Sam than the mother who bore him. Queen Anne was dead and Ada Struggles reigned in place of her.

CHAPTER X
GERALD ADAMS, SOCIOLOGIST

ANNE called at Madge's on her way home. Madge's, in spite of George's progress, was still the house which had been the premises of the Hell-fire Club. Anne did not often go there and never without reason, but Madge was at a loss to know the reason of this visit, nor did she guess it when Anne unobtrusively dovetailed into The conversation about young Sam Chappie a question which might have seemed irrelevant. "Have you done anything yet with that spare room of yours upstairs?" she asked.

"No," said Madge. "Nor likely to, I fancy." That was the reason of the visit. Anne was safeguarding her retreat, though she by no means admitted that it would come to a retreat. Engagements do not invariably lead to marriage. Meantime, hers was the waiting game and a rupture with Sam at this stage was to be avoided.

When he asked her, not too confidently, if she did not agree with him about the wonder of Ada, she exercised a noble self-restraint, and all she said was: "She's not the wife for a poor man, Sam."

"No," said Sam thoughtfully. "I'd tumbled to that. And I don't mean to be poor either," and so went out to open the dark chapter of his bright success. He went to the Concentrics, not knowing that he was going to his fate. He went because it was the night of their weekly meeting and he had to go somewhere to avoid Anne's eye, but his mood was not concentric. "I must get rich for Ada, rich for Ada," was the burden of his thought—so early did he justify Ada's words to Anne—and it was not a timely thought for a Concentrics evening.

He had even forgotten that he had a special interest in this meeting, where the lecturer was to be Adams, once Sam's pet aversion and unbeatable rival at the Grammar School. He was reminded of it when he found himself accosted by a young man whom he could not at first identify.

"Jove! If it isn't Sammy Branstone! Are you a member of these fossils?"

"Dubby Stewart!" said Sam, as recognition dawned on him.

"Reed's here as well, somewhere," said Stewart. "It's a gathering of the clan."

Reed and Stewart, it seemed, were both members, which is to say that they had come once or twice some time ago and continued to keep up the small subscription from force of habit or through sheer weakness to stop paying it. Few societies indeed could exist were it not for the enthusiasm of the attending nucleus and the subscriptions of the nonattending mass.

"We came to hear Gerald Adams make an ass of himself," Stewart explained. "What a subject!"

Sam had even forgotten what the subject was. "Rich for Ada, rich for Ada," was still ringing in his ears.

The subject was "Social Purity."

"Which accounts," said Stewart, "for the size of the audience. They've all come hoping for the worst. I know I have."

The worst did not happen, or, rather, if it did, it was so skilfully disguised that nobody recognized it as the worst. It was easy to mistake it for the best.

Adams was one part in earnest and two parts impish in the manner of the superior person who is out for an intellectual lark. He had a constant preoccupation with that which is known above all other questions as *the* social question. It was not a nice preoccupation for a young man: it was, for instance, remote from the healthy exuberance of Sam's Rabelaisianism. And, of course, Adams was wily: he wasn't the stuff of martyrdom. He enjoyed, as an intellectual gymnastic, the treatment of his subject so that it should at once shock his audience and win him their approval as an honest man doing an unpleasant job from conviction.

Sam agreed with Stewart. His old prejudice against Adams was strong within him and he hoped Adams would come a cropper. That was at the beginning, when Adams, with an egregious affectation of superiority, began to read his lecture; but soon, quite soon, Sam changed his mind and hoped for nothing but that the skilful skater would keep his balance, on the thin ice.

"Rich for Ada," and here, as Sam saw it, was a "stroke" indeed if Adams were successful to the end and if at the end he would listen sensibly to Sam.

Adams was in little danger. He was of Oxford, London, the world, and his audience of Manchester. And he stooped to conquer with a lecture that was a mosaic of advances and retreats, of blazing indiscretions and smug apologies, of audacities and diffidence.

Sam watched the audience keenly, and it would not be unjust to say that the audience gloated. Not all of them gloated, but as a whole, as an audience, they lapped up Adams' lecture like mother's milk. He called it frankness and gave unnecessary detail, he had an appearance of honest indignation and a reality of bathing in mud with relish. It was abominable but diabolically clever; indecent to the core, it artfully evaded anything to warrant a police court charge of indecency; it was foulness cloaked in piety, marching under the banner of Reform. He was a crusader in masquerade, flashing beneath their guard of British reticence a rapier whose hilt was a cross.

Adams found a curious satisfaction in standing there, like a penitent at a Salvation Army meeting, pretending to an immense personal knowledge of evil which was, happily, impossible, and he delighted in the presence of a cleric in the chair. The thing developed, for him, into an exciting game, a contest of his wits with Peter's. He had carried his audience, but the chairman sat aloof and dubious. If Peter saw through him, he had lost; if not, he won. For Peter he read the condemnatory passages with vibrant earnestness, and for Peter he read as if reluctantly, conscience-impelled, the details of his evidence.

Sam caught the infection, too, but hardly as a game. He hung on Peter's judgment with a deep anxiety, watched Peter flush and shuffle in his chair, saw him take snuff nervously, trembled at the moment when Peter seemed about to interrupt, sighed with relief when Peter sat back silently again and waited feverishly for the chairman's speech.

There would probably have been little doubt about Peter's verdict had Adams been an ordinary Concentric, lecturer and a member of the Society. But he was neither, and was there by invitation. And he was not only of Oxford, Peter's University, but brilliantly of Oxford, of Balliol, with academic honours thick upon him. If Peter thought, as Adams spoke, that he ought to call him to order, he remembered that Adams was a Double First, and desisted. He couldn't be a hypocrite—because he had won the Ireland. He was terribly in earnest now—because he had won the Greek Verse Prize. He was single-minded, chivalrous, braving the misapprehension of the scurrilous, open and honest—because he was a Fellow of Balliol.

It did not matter to Peter that Adams' father was the richest parishioner in St. Mary's; it mattered even less that Adams was exquisitely dressed in exactly the shade of grey appropriate to an ardent crusader. ("Look at his damned clothes," Reed had whispered to Stewart. "Hasn't he thought it out?" He had: his clothes were chaste if his lecture wasn't.) But scholarship did matter to Peter, whose other name was Charity, and once he had decided that Gerald was sincere, that all he said was subordinate to and justified by high purpose, he was generous, and the more generous because he had doubted.

"The subject of Mr. Adams' lecture," he said, "is like nettles: if it is not handled boldly, it stings. I have nothing but praise for the courage, the down rightness, the earnestness of his treatment of this distressing evil. I think that we have all been deeply stirred by his instances of man's inhumanity to women. As a churchman I feel a special responsibility and, may I say, a special gratitude to Mr. Adams for his study of this subject. Medicine, as we all know, has its martyrs, its research workers who sacrifice themselves for the health of their fellowmen. Mr. Adams, who has examined this social sore so thoroughly, at what cost in pain to himself only the most sensitive amongst us can guess, deserves to be ranked with the martyrs of science...." And so on, doubly handsome because he felt ashamed of himself for doubting Gerald's honesty, and made amends.

Adams had won his game, hands down. He thought the old boy gloriously funny and he thought Sam Branstone, who rose when Peter sat down, funnier still. Sam believed in striking while the iron was hot: he didn't want Peter to have the opportunity of changing his mind when he came to think things over coolly.

Sam began by congratulating himself on the good fortune that had been his in having been the school-fellow of the distinguished Mr. Adams. Adams gazed hard at Sam through his austere pince-nez and was observed perceptibly to start. "Gad," he was thinking, "it's that lout, the porter's son." But he liked Sam's flattery very well. Sam, it appeared, had been so deeply impressed by Mr. Adams' admirable, indeed eloquent and moving address, and by the chairman's very just eulogy of it, that he thought it would be a tremendous pity if so arresting, so well-written a paper failed to reach a wider audience than that before which it had been read. They had been waiting for this paper; its appeal was wide; the urgency of its need, instinct in every word of it, was emphasized by the chairman's remarks. He had, therefore, a practical proposal to make. The paper ought to be printed, and if Mr. Adams could spare him a few moments after the meeting, Sam hoped that he would let him arrange the matter.

He sat down amongst great applause. Under its cover Stewart whispered: "You inimitable ass!" Sam looked at him in pained surprise. "I want to see that paper in print," he declared indignantly.

The debate meandered in the usual futile way. Few had anything to say, but many liked the sound of their own voices and indulged their preference at length, till both speakers and talkers had taken their innings and Sam was able to go up to the platform. Peter had not changed his mind and was complimenting Adams in his simple, charming way.

It ought, no doubt, to have made Adams thoroughly ashamed of himself, but it did not. It hardened his cynicism so that, when Sam came up, all he was thinking was: "I've gulled the parson. Now to bounce the porter's son."

"How are you, Branstone?" he asked. "Glad to meet you again."

"And I you," said Sam. They shook hands. "Have you had time to think of what I proposed?"

"As a matter of fact," said Adams, which is the usual way of beginning a lie, "I'd thought of sending my little paper to one of the Reviews—the *Fortnightly* or the *Contemporary*."

"Excellent," said Peter.

Sam could have kicked him. "I venture to differ," he said. "The chief object should be to reach as wide a public as possible. My own idea was to do it by itself in the form of a——" he was going to say "pamphlet," but altered it to "brochure." He thought it sounded more attractive. "In the heavy reviews it would be read by comparatively few, and it would not stand alone as in a brochure. It would take its place along with other articles. And I have heard that contributors to the reviews are not paid highly."

Adams had not thought of payment at all, but he thought of it now, with zest. He was rich, but the idea of despoiling the porter's son, who had had the assurance to go to school with him, struck him as the crowning move in a jolly game. This was, transcendently, his night for winning.

"Oh, I don't know," he said, which was true. "I suppose I should get about twenty pounds for it."

"I will give you twenty-five," said Sam.

"Sam!" protested Peter. He approached the motive (as he understood it), but considered the offer reckless from a young man who contemplated matrimony.

"Twenty-five pounds," repeated Sam firmly.

"Well," laughed Gerald, quite unable not to laugh at the idiot's persistence, "if you're as keen on doing good as all that, I'll take the offer."

"Right," said Sam. "I'll settle it at once."

He went to the chairman's table and made out a form of assignment of copyright. He had a little knowledge of the law, and it was a dangerous thin—for the other fellow. But both Sam and Adams went home that night in a state of cherubic self-satisfaction.

"What a game?" thought Adams. "And what an ass!"

Curiously, the thoughts of Sammy Branstone were not dissimilar. He had this advantage over Adams: that Adams had read his paper and had not watched his audience all the time. Sam had watched the audience and thought twenty-five pounds a cheap price for that paper.

He slept on it, and awoke next day with confidence in his investment undisturbed, but the news which awaited him at the office shook him at first. It was one thing to see a profitable side-line in the publication of Adams' address and another to be suddenly obliged to regard the copyright of that paper as his one sound asset. He feared, in cold daylight, that it was not quite sound enough for that.

Yet what had happened did not come as a complete surprise. Sam knew Travers' habits and knew that men of his habits are liable to die suddenly. Travers had died in the night, and Sam was very angry.

He told himself that he had no luck with people's deaths. His father had died too soon for Sam, and now Travers was dead just when Sam had become engaged, and when he had undertaken a speculation which, however high his hopes of it, was after all speculative.

An estate agent's business is largely personal and, if there is no obvious successor, no heir apparent already in training for the succession, is apt to fall to pieces when its head dies. The process of disintegration in this case had set in long ago; drink had begun what death now ended; and there was no heir. Lance Travers had decided for medicine and was, on the material side, little affected by his father's death, since Travers had bought him a practice a year earlier somewhere in the South, and the neighbourhood was proving healthily valetudinarian.

The office was not a cheerful place that day. Men estimated their savings and balanced them against the probable weeks of unemployment before they found new places. A few of them, no doubt, might hope to "go with" the business to whomever bought it; and they wondered who would buy and which of them would be engaged by the purchaser.

They fancied Branstone's chances, and so, in fact, did Sam, but it was all in the air and exceedingly disturbing just when he had given himself so much else to think about. Even if he did move with the business, it could only be as a clerk. He lost the advantage of Travers' friendliness and, besides, he was not sure that anybody would think the business worth buying. Travers had no right to die.

Then the thought struck him that he was taking it lying down. He, a lad of mettle, was whining like these gutless clerks in the office. He was betraying his lucky star. Death, even Tom Branstone's, had not been forbiddingly unkind to him. Tom's death had led him indirectly to the office, to Minnifie, the Concentrics, Ada, and he began to see in Travers' death the possibilities of good. It might be the finger of fate, pointing him away from the office which had served its turn to a new dispensation to be arranged by the collaborators, Sam and Providence, upon the rock of Adams' paper.

They carried on the routine work of the office as men under sentence of death do little, ordinary things and find a solace in them. Then, late that afternoon, Lance Travers came. He had travelled since early morning, had been home, seen his father's doctor and his father's solicitor and was now come to see Sam. They sat in Travers' private office, where the blinds were drawn, and in the presence of Travers' son, who owed his life to him, Sam was conscious of a deeper feeling than he had ever known before, he was no longer angry because Travers had died, but mourned him honestly.

"By the way," said Lance presently, "did my father ever tell you about his will?"

"His will!" said Sam. "No. Why should he?"

"I thought he might have done," said Lance. "He made it last year after he bought me my practice. He thought then that he ought to do something for you, but he didn't expect to live long and he put it in his will. There's a thousand pounds for you."

Sam took it nicely. "I'd rather," he said, "that he were still alive;" and, at the moment, he meant it.

But he had been right. It was the finger of fate.

CHAPTER XI
UNDER WAY

AS a simple matter of course, Lance offered Sam the first refusal of his father's business, but was not surprised when Sam declined to think of it.

Sam was far more surprised at himself than Lance at Sam. Lance had never looked upon estate agency as a desirable profession, whereas Sam had been bored with its routine without losing his respect for its utility, and only yesterday he would have jumped at the chance of owning the business. He heard with astonishment the sound of his own voice politely refusing the offer, but having refused he did not tamper with his swift decision.

The fact is, one supposes, that what might be called the quick-firing part of his intelligence had absorbed and reacted to the fact of his thousand pounds before the whole of him was properly aware of it. At any rate, he refused, and, on reflection, approved his refusal.

His speculation in Gerald Adams wore a different aspect now that he was a capitalist. "Money," as he had remembered once before, "breeds money," and he doubted if Travers' business, robbed of Travers' genial personality, were fecund enough for the pace of money-breeding he anticipated. Perhaps, too, there was something in the thought that the Travers' agency was dead man's shoes, while, win or lose, the idea of publishing Adams' lecture was his own invention.

Another thing that happened to him with his legacy was the feeling that he had regained caste; he belonged again with his old school-fellows. "How many of them," he thought, "can lay hands at a moment's notice on a thousand pounds?" and walked erectly through the street where, naturally, since he had not met him in eight years until last night, he encountered Stewart.

"Hullo," said Stewart, "how's the patron of letters? And would a drink be any use to you?"

Sam hesitated. Did the way to the society of the Olympians lie through the doors of the public-house? Stewart was undeniably Olympian: he had the air, the manner, the clothes of well-assured success. He had a lightness and a poise that excited Sam's envy. He had style, this youth who might be anything, but who, Sam cynically thought, had probably not paid for his distinguished clothes, while Sam was the owner of a thousand pounds. He was, thereby, Olympian in quiet fact, which need not be shrieked from the house-tops, as Stewart had, apparently, to shriek. Sam *was*, and there was the possibility that Stewart only appeared to be. It gave him strength to refuse. Not from principle, but from economical prejudice Sam was a teetotaller.

"I don't take alcohol," he said.

"It's never too late to mend," said Stewart. "Still, there's a café here, and we'll drink coffee. It's bad for our hearts, but Balzac wrote the 'Comédie Humaine' on black coffee, so there may be something in the vice, though it isn't a habit of mine. Two black coffees, Sophie," he ordered from the waitress.

"If it isn't a habit of yours," asked Sam, "how do you come to know the waitress by name?"

"'My dear ass!" said Stewart pityingly.

"Do you call them all Sophie?"

"Only when it's their name. Your name is Sophie, isn't it?" he said as the girl returned with their coffee.

"Yes, sir."

Stewart appreciated Sam's astonishment. "I know I'm showing off, but I like it. If you see a girl with an idiotic silver brooch made up of the letters SOPHIE you can assume that it's her name, and not the name of her best boy. Simple, when you know how it's done, like all first-rate conjuring."

"I hadn't noticed her brooch," said Sam.

"I had. That's the difference. Still, it isn't fair to blame you. I'm a professional observer." Sam took Stewart to mean that he was a detective, but hadn't time to ask for confirmation, because Stewart asked instead: "And what, by the way, are you?" And threw him into some embarrassment by the question. What, indeed, at the moment was he?

"Doesn't your observation tell you?" he fenced.

"It told me last night that you're a considerable lunatic. Did you buy that stuff of Adams'?"

"Yes, I did."

"Thought I saw you in the act as I went out. Obviously, then, you're a tripe merchant."

"I wonder," said Sam, "whether you could help me, Stewart. Seriously, I mean."

"In the tripe trade?"

"I want very much to meet a journalist." He thought a detective ought to know journalists.

"But, my dear fellow, this is a café. It isn't a bar. What do you want a journalist for?"

"I will tell that to the journalist."

"If you want to start a paper and you're looking for an editor, you needn't look further than me. There have been candid moments in my life when I have called myself a journalist. At present, I edit the *Manchester Warden*, but I'm open to conviction." He didn't quite edit that paper—yet, but reported for it at six pounds a week. He did not know shorthand, but he quoted Joseph Conrad and Henry James, correctly and incongruously, when he wrote a notice of a music-hall performance.

"I'm afraid," said Sam astutely, "that when I said a journalist, I meant something very different from you, but I will tell you how I stand and perhaps you will advise me. Last night, as you know, I bought Adams' paper. I gave him twenty-five pounds for it."

"Lunacy," said Stewart, "is a mild word for your complaint. Twenty-five shillings would be a top price for it in a friendly market."

"To-day I reached the office to learn that my employer had died suddenly. You remember Lance Travers? It was his father, and with his death, for all practical purposes the business comes to an end. Well, you see my position."

Stewart quoted Sheridan: "'The Spanish Fleet thou canst not see, because it is not yet in sight.' And much the same applies to your position, my lad. Its postal address is the Womb of Time."

"That is true," said Sam. "And I may add that I am engaged to be married."

"I can admire thoroughness," said Stewart. "You omit none of the essentials."

"Now, with it all," said Sam, "I'm still too proud to go to Adams and ask him to let me off my bargain."

"And it wouldn't be any use if you did," said Stewart. "He'd laugh at you."

"I can believe it of him. But I'm landed with his paper. It has cost me twenty-live pounds. I meant to print it, and I mean to print it, but I mean now to sell it when it is printed." Sam left Stewart to suppose that, had Travers not died, he would have distributed that pamphlet free. "Money," he added, "is a necessity."

He had taken the right line. Stewart's instinctive generosity was touched, and he meant to give this lame dog a lift over the stile. "I see where your journalist comes in. All right, Branstone, you can count on me."

"On you?" said Sam. "Oh, I couldn't ask it of you."

"You didn't ask," replied Stewart naively. "I offer. I may edit the *Manchester Warden*, but Zeus nods sometimes, 'busmen have been known to take a holiday, and there is a paper called the *Sunday Judge* in whose chaste columns I have written under the name of Percy Persiflage. Send me a proof of that pamphlet and Percy shall stamp upon it. He will say that no decent person could read it without being revolted, and the pamphlet will boom. It's the Sunday-paper public that you want, and... No, Percy shall not stamp. Percy shall bless. He will be moved to admiration of Mr. Adams' earnestness, he will applaud the high moral purpose, and will do the rest by correspondence. Get your sisters and your cousins and your aunts to pitch in letters on either side, and I'll see they get printed. I make this alteration because of the bookstalls."

"The bookstalls?" asked Sam vaguely.

"This problem of distribution," said Stewart impressively, "is the most difficult question of modern life. The producer is here, you; the consumer (we hope) is everywhere, and the problem is to bring your pamphlet to the thirsting consumer. The answer is the bookstall, but the bookstalls are cautious. When I say bookstalls I mean the right bookstalls. You will never see your money back if the only bookstalls which will exhibit your pamphlet are those which sell atrociously printed paperbacked editions of 'Nana' and 'Fanny Hill.' You must flourish on *the* bookstalls, and they banned 'Esther Waters.' The bookstalls, Branstone, are going to call for tact, and tact shall begin with Percy's appreciation."

"Or earlier," said Sam.

"Earlier?"

"I hadn't thought of the bookstalls, but this may help there, as well as in other ways. I mean, as far as Manchester is concerned, and if we get it on the stalls here, they can't very well refuse it in other places."

"Manchester being Manchester, it isn't likely," said Stewart. "What's your idea?"

"Only this," said Sam, and showed him his proposed cover for the pamphlet.

THE SOCIAL EVIL

Being an Address

By Gerald Adams, M.A.,

Fellow of Balliol College, Oxford.

As Read before the Concentric Society with The Rev. Peter Struggles in the Chair.

Stewart looked at it, then he looked at Sam, and Sam seemed to him very little like a lame dog now. He whistled loudly. "You'll get your money back, my lad," he said. "But this is rough on Peter."

"Mr. Struggles approved of the lecture."

"I wonder if he will approve of this?" said Stewart.

"He can't go back on his word," said Sam. "Besides, I'm engaged to his daughter."

"The thing that troubles me," said Stewart admiringly, "is that I took you for a harmless lunatic. I'm only a journalist myself, with one foot in the *Manchester Warden* and the other in the *Sunday Judge*. I'm a Tory on Sundays and a Liberal on weekdays. I gave up honesty when I gave up being young, and I thought I knew the ropes by this time. But when I think that I took you for a guileless innocent, I want to go into a corner and kick myself hard."

Sam found this rather alarming he knew that his use, or misuse, of Peter's name was cunning, but began to regret that he had shown Stewart his pro posed cover. "But I get my review in the *Judge*?" he asked hardily.

"My son," said Stewart, "you do. I've spent sixpence on coffee and half an hour on you. There's good copy in this and I can't afford to waste it. I've my living to earn, and Gerald Adams deserves the worst he's going to get. At the same time, I'll allow myself the luxury of telling you that yours is a lowdown game."

"We didn't make the world what it is, did we?" said Sam.

"And neither you nor I will leave it any better than we found it," said Stewart, prophesying rashly with the boundless cynicism of his twenty-five years. "The worst of coffee," he went on, finishing his cup, "is that it makes you thirsty. I'm going across the road for a drink. Do you have one with me?"

"No, thanks," said Sam. "I have to see a printer."

"Oh, yes. Well, why not the Judge Press? I daresay I could get you in there on the ground floor."

"But they are not quite the right people for this. They print sporting papers, and— —"

"You'll die from overheated bearings in your brain-box," said Stewart. "You think of everything."

Sam had, at least, thought that a printer (however obscure by comparison was the Judge Press, whose works were a small town in themselves) who issued a religious paper was better for his purpose than the printers of the *Sunday Judge, Sporting Notions and the Football Times*. He went to Carter, Meadowbank & Co., who were on the verge of bankruptcy, but had the advantage of printing *Christian Comfort* and the *Church Child's Weekly*, and arranged with them to print five thousand copies of Adams' paper. Carter, who was the whole firm, looked askance at the title, but when Sam pointed out that the Rev. Mr. Struggles had approved of the contents, Carter succumbed at once, and did not even attempt a protest when Sam instructed him to print on the whole five thousand:

"This first edition of one thousand copies is issued at sixpence. The price for future editions will be one shilling. Samuel Branstone, Publisher."

Carter's dingy office was decorated with the chief products of his firm, texts, the stock-in-trade of commercialized religiosity. Well handled, there was money in texts, but Carter was an old man with declining powers and a conservative mind. Meadowbank, who had looked after the distributive side of the business, was lately dead, and Carter's nightly prayer was that the concern might last his time. As things were promising, it seemed unlikely, but here was Sam with an order for him and no disposition to beat him down in price. Carter did not like the instruction to describe five thousand copies as one thousand, and he didn't like the subject of the pamphlet, but he wanted business, and he couldn't conceive of a pirate sailing under the flag of Mr. Struggles.

Sam rammed that home, feeling the man's hesitation. "I think it probable," he said, "that Mr. Struggles will preach a sermon on this pamphlet. Perhaps I might tell you that I am going to be his son-in-law."

That settled Carter, and he took the order. He knew, and was sensitive to, the influence of Peter Struggles, curate. He knew that in the parish of. St. Mary's, Peter's smile counted for more than the vicar's weightiest word, and that while the vicar was unknown outside his parish, Peter had authority throughout Manchester—an authority which had lately growm through Peter's refusal of preferment to an easy living in the country. It hadn't, of course, been Peter who had told of that refusal, he had not told Ada. But it had leaked out, and Manchester, which despises selflessness in men, honoured it in the curate; Mancunians were flattered by his loyalty to St. Mary's and by the thought that they were fellow citizens to saintliness.

Emphatically, the name of Peter Struggles on the pamphlet was a *clou*, but Sam had not told Peter of it yet, and he must do it. He could not afford an accident, and Peter, he considered, was manageable.

Ada met him at the door with a bright smile, and raised expectant lips, but he shook his head, touch ing her shoulder tenderly, and passed in front of her into the room so that, when she followed, her face expressed the anxiety he desired. He entered himself as a man crushed by grief.

"What is it, Sam?" she asked. "What's the matter?"

Peter closed "Plotinus" reluctantly: he never found time enough for reading, and here was one of his few evenings interrupted. He had the thought, feeling it ungenerous, that interruptions of this kind would end when Ada was married.

"I've had sad news to-day. Mr. Travers died in the night. It's... it's rather a blow."

Peter disdained priestly conventionalities. "He was a good friend to you, Sam."

"A second father," said Sam carefully, not taking the opportunity of telling that Travers' friendship had lasted beyond death. Perhaps he thought this moment too sacred for the intrusion of a legacy. "Of course," he went on, "I've had all day to think of it, and of the difference this will make to me—to us, that is, Ada, for you and me."

"What difference, Sam?" she asked sharply.

"It comes to this," he said dejectedly, "that I am out of work and competition is so desperate. While he lived, I had his friendship behind me.

Now—I don't say that I'm afraid to stand alone. No doubt it will be good for me eventually, but, Ada, you see how it may postpone our hopes."

Ada saw it. "Plotinus" took that opportunity of slipping from Peter's knee, and Peter saw it, too, and sighed. "Oh, Sam!" said Ada.

"And," said Sam, looking at Peter with a fine affectation of guilt, "there is my recklessness of last night. In my then circumstances, it was extravagant. To-day it looks worse than that."

"You couldn't know," said Peter kindly.

"No," Sam agreed. "I couldn't know, and I have the feeling now that I must abide by what I did."

"Very proper, Sam, but Mr. Adams is not poor and I should think that if you were to go to him———"

"Oh, please," said Sam, "please don't press me to do that. A bargain, I feel so strongly, is a bargain and should be kept at all costs."

Peter felt silently ashamed of himself. "You are perfectly right," he said.

"Well," said Sam, "that's how I feel, but in a sense I'm landed with the thing and I propose to go on with it. As I see it—and I know there's a certain amount of inappropriateness in thinking at all of these practical affairs with my benefactor so recently dead, but I must, I must——" he looked at Ada and it was understood that his thought for her excused all—"As I see it, it's a case for going on and trying to pull the chestnuts out of the fire, so to speak. I shall print that paper, and the good that I hoped to do will not be lost because my circumstances have altered, but I shall make a small charge for it to cover expenses as far as possible. And as I naturally want it to sell well, I had the idea of stating on the cover that it was first read at the Concentrics under your chairmanship. The point of that is that all the members were not there last night; it will call their attention to it; and they will, I hope, buy. It makes certain of a few reliable purchasers."

"Quite, quite," said Peter. "It's an excellent idea. Though I can hardly suppose that mention of my name has any value, the name of the society should certainly help."

His modesty was quite incurable. He had not the faintest notion of the wide-spread influence of Peter Struggles. "I have thought of little else all day but Mr. Adams' paper. I wondered if it was my duty to speak of this terrible subject from the pulpit. The Church ought not to be silent or it may be thought to acquiesce."

Sam felt his heart leap within him. "Adams thought frankness best," he said.

"Yes, yes, at the Concentrics. But there are difficulties for me, and perhaps I shall speak only to the Young Men's Class at the-Sunday School. Though that," he reflected, "is perilously near to compromise."

"But what is it?" asked Ada. "What are you talking about?"

Sam was silent. So was Peter, and the silence grew till he felt it a reproach. He looked at Sam. "You see?" he said. "That is the dilemma of the Church. I shall speak to the young men, and, after that perhaps, perhaps——" He glanced at Ada.

"No," he finished decidedly, "I must leave it at that." He was fifty-six, and most of his life had been lived under Victoria the Good.

CHAPTER XII
DROPPING THE PILOT

ANNE lived for Sam: and if she rarely showed it, if, for instance, it appeared sometimes that she lived to make her house the cleanest in the row, that was no more than a symptom of her stoicism. She lived for Sam, and he knew it. She belonged to a race which hates ostentation like the devil and keeps its feelings veiled behind a grim reserve. It conceals emotion as a hidden treasure and wears a mask which strangers take to indicate a want of sensibility. She had not the habit of caressing Sam; she chastened whom she loved; and Sam was very well aware of the strength of Anne's love.

She was ready, at the proper time, to give him to the proper woman, but she held that Ada was not the woman nor this the time. She was ready to go her ways from Sam, and from life itself, when he made a marriage of which she could approve, but she was not ready to leave him to Ada Struggles of whom she disapproved. She was not ready to die for the likes of Ada Struggles. Let Sam marry Ada, and Anne, meant to live, because some day he would have need of her and, when the day came, she would be there.

Now, Sam would have been pleased if he could have told Anne about the pamphlet and the legacy. He had hoped after the Minnilie affair that his next "stroke" would be one of which he could tell Anne, but he did not see this as tellable. She would naturally ask what the pamphlet was about, and if Peter could not speak of it to his daughter, Sam could speak of it even less to his mother. And as to the legacy, what was the use of mentioning that to a woman who would point out that security was only to be had with two and a half per cent? Which wasn't at all Sam's notion of the uses of a thousand pounds.

After all, he was grown up and a man does not tell his mother everything. But unless he is a fool, he tells her the things which she is bound in any case to find out, and if he had foreseen the certainty of her finding out he would, not being a fool, have told her these. He did not foresee, because Anne did not read newspapers, but she had neighbours who did and who told her, with comments, of the storm which presently broke out in the columns of the *Sunday Judge*, and of Mr. Travers' will, which received a small paragraph in the paper when it was proved.

"There was a time when you and me didn't go in for secrets," she said to him. "You've not had much to say to me of late and I've not seen much of you, either, with the hours you're keeping, but I'd put it down to love. I know a man's not rational when he's courting, but it seems there's a lot about my son that I've to learn. Why didn't you tell me about Mr. Travers? Did you think I'd steal the money off you?"

"Of course not, mother, but I meant to come to you with a finished tale, not one that's only just begun. I'm engaged in a business affair of which I was going to tell you when it was complete."

"*Yes*," she said, "I see. You're risking your money. If you came out on the right side, you'd tell me about it, and if you lost you'd forget to tell me. Are you losing?"

"It's early days to say."

"Then maybe I'm still in time to nip this in the bud. What's this about the *Sunday Judge*?"

"I Have you seen it?" he asked.

"Aye. You're the talk of the street."

"That's splendid," he let slip before he was aware of it.

"Splendid! There's a gentleman writing to the paper to say that you're trading in immorality."

"I wrote that letter myself," grinned Sam.

"You did what?"

"I'm afraid I shall never make you understand."

"I doubt you won't. Lying to me like that. Expecting me to believe you write to the paper about yourself and call yourself hard names. And the letter's signed 'Truth-teller,' too. It's printed in the paper that my son has lifted the lid from the cesspool and let loose a smell to make decent people vomit."

"Yes. I know. Advertising is a coarse art."

"Your name's blackened for ever. And it's my name, Sam, and the name your father gave me. It's the name of honest folk and— —"

"Mother, mother, don't I tell you that it's all advertisement?"

"What you tell me and what I can believe are coming to be two different things. I know what an advertisement in the paper is and I know what a letter is. This is a letter."

Sam felt the hopelessness of further argument.

She had a simple-minded faith in the integrity of newspapers and the printed word, but he could at least show that the word could contradict itself. "Very well," he said, "it's a letter, and so is this." He took a copy of the paper from his pocket. Stewart had kept his word, no great feat since he had a good idea of what his editor supposed the Sunday public to want, and a column of fervent correspondence flared under the heading of "The Social Evil.—Is the Pamphlet Justified?" Sam chose a letter which described Adams as a crusader and Branstone, his publisher, as a high-souled social reformer courageously risking misapprehension for principle and the right, calling the endorsement of the Rev. Peter Struggles to witness in proof of his irreproachable motives. "Well," said Sam, "am I to be misapprehended after all, and by you?"

"You told me you wrote the other letter," she said. "Don't you mean that you wrote this one?"

"I don't," he said truthfully. He wrote his, attacking himself, on one side of Stewart's desk, while Stewart at the other defended him. It had been great fun.

"And what," she asked, "is the business affair you say you're engaged on?"

"Why," he said unguardedly, "it's this."

"Then I don't misapprehend at all, my son. I apprehend very well. And you've worked Peter Struggles into it. Was that why you got engaged to Ada?"

"Mother!" he protested. "Doubt me if you like, but you must not doubt Mr. Struggles. He surely is above suspicion."

"He's keeping bad company just now," said Anne, "and I doubt you've been too clever for him."

Sam chose to be offended. "Is that what you think of me?" he asked.

"That you're clever. Aye. I think that all right. I've known it since the time when you tricked a parcel of schoolboys out of a house of furniture and put George Chappie into it. You're clever in the wrong places, Sam. When you were at school, you were clever out of school. You're at business now and you ought; to be clever in honesty, and I've the notion that you're being clever in dishonesty."

"Of course," he said, "this only shows how right I was not to tell you. It's the old story. Women don't understand business."

"I know. Business is a pair of spectacles that makes black into white, but I don't wear spectacles myself. Are you going to tell me what you're doing with that thousand pounds?"

"I told you it isn't decided yet. But if the sales of that pamphlet go up this week as they did last, I'm going into the publishing business with it."

"So that you can publish more of the same sort?"

"If I can get them. There's a lot of money in it."

"Sam," she said earnestly, "is that all you're caring about?"

"You told me yourself that Ada was not the wife for a poor man." He considered that a very neat score, to seem to make Anne responsible, but Anne was not to be deceived by any such seeming. As she saw it, Ada had corrupted Sam, Ada was the motive of this misuse of his cleverness; and the bitterness for Anne was doubly poignant. She believed in Sam, with a faith which had never swerved in spite of her disappointment in his school career; but she realized now that he had been marking time in Travers' office, that it was Ada and not she who had quickened his energies to rapid action. Ada had quickened them, where under Anne they had lain dormant but the quickening had been corrupt. It came from Ada, poisoned at the source, and took to poisonous ways.

They had touched bottom now and reached essentials. "Sam," she said, "I was joking like when I said a man's not rational when he's in love. But it was a true word spoken in jest. You're not rational or you wouldn't be doing these things and making a byword of the name of Branstone, and the reason you're not rational is Ada. If you were in love with a good woman, you could no more do dishonourable things than fly. But you're in love with a bad woman and it leads to bad results. Sam, do you think I like to tell you that you've made a mistake? And do you think I don't know? Lad, lad, I love you, and I've never reckoned myself a fool. Choose now, I'm not the sort of fool to be jealous just because you get wed. I'd none be jealous of the right lass, Sam. I'd take her and welcome her and know she had a better right to you than me. But Ada Struggles has no right: she's mean and grasping and she's small in every way there is. She's——"

"Stop, mother. Don't forget that I am marrying Ada."

"And nothing that I say will alter you? Sam, she'll go on as she's begun by sending you to this." She put her hand on the lurid polemics of the *Sunday Judge*. "She'll drive you down and down. You may make money and you may be rich, but there'll be a curse on your riches and on all you do, and Ada Struggles is the name of the curse."

Sam attempted a small levity. "That will be all right," he said. "She's going to change her name." Anne shook her head. "A change of name'ull none change Ada's nature. It's the best part of your life that's before you, and life with Ada spells ruin. I'm not telling you what I think. It's what I know, and I ask you, Sam, to heed my words."

"I'm heeding them," he said, "but I know you're wrong."

"That's the last you've got to say?"

"I'm sorry we don't agree, mother."

"Agreeing's nowt," she said, "and I'm nowt against your happiness. See, Sam, I'll prove it. There's a thought at the back of your mind that I've nothing against Ada but a grudge because she's come between you and me. I say that girl's no good for you, and I say I'll do anything to force you to see it. There's nowt of myself in this and maybe this will make you believe it."

There was a good fire in the room and she put her hand into it. Sam was alert enough to drag her away before much damage was done, and he had oil on the hand in a moment.

"Don't fuss," said Anne, "but tell me what you think."

"I think," he said, "that you're plumb crazy—with jealousy."

It was not craziness, but fanatic devotion to an idea: and the idea was Sam, Sam's happiness, Sam's future. She put her hand into the fire hoping to convince, and she would have sat on the fire if she had thought the larger act would carry a fuller conviction. But he did not need to be convinced that she objected to Ada; the point was that her objections were unfounded, and, in the face of Ada's sublime and stunning merits, idiotic.

One cannot put a hand into the fire without suffering for it, and Anne was suffering acutely. Her face was drawn with pain and her lips were trembling uncontrollably, but her voice was firm.

"I've done my best to save you, Sam. If you've nothing better to say than that, you and me have come to a parting."

"Then," said Sam, "we've come," and turned his back on her. He thought she would come round, that she would get over her attack of frenzied jealousy. It was idle threat to talk of a parting. Why, she was dependent on him, and in more ways than one. He housed and kept her, but, more than that, she needed him. His presence was the breath of life to her. He knew that, and he let her go!

Of course, he thought she would come back, with a sharp lesson well learnt. She had to learn that he was grown-up, of an age to act for himself and choose and think without her tutelage. Only, she did not come back. She went to Madge and stayed with Madge; and the terms on which she stayed were her terms. "I furnish the room," she said, "and I pay you a rent for it. Also, I pay for what I eat."

She paid. At the age of fifty-two the mother of Sara Branstone, of Branstone and Carter, and the mother-in-law of George Chappie, of the Chappie Window-Cleaning and Bill Posting Company (a smaller affair than its name, but the source of a regular five pounds a week), was a charwoman on three days out of the seven, and it was not lack of offers which limited her to three days, but the fact that she paid her way on three days' result. She kept other people's houses as clean as she had kept her own.

It was suggested to George Chappie that it was hardly decent in him to allow his mother-in-law to go out charring at her age—a prosperous man like him. "I know," he was reported to have replied, "and we've tried all ways we can. But you can't argue with Mrs. Branstone."

"She's one of the old sort, isn't she?" said his gossip, who, perhaps, endured a mother-in-law of another kind.

"All that," said George succinctly.

CHAPTER XIII
THE INTERMITTENT COURTSHIP

ONLY by long service does one become an artist, but one becomes married by a simple ceremony. It is the tragedy of marriage, which is the most difficult of all the arts, that most people come to it without apprenticeship. Perhaps the popularity of widows as brides is due to the fact that the widow is a widow: that she has been broken in to marriage: that she has not everything to learn: that one, at any rate, of the contracting parties, is expert. There is much to be said for the policy of the "trial trip."

Courtship, if intimate enough, may be a fairish substitute, bowdlerized, as it were, for a "trial trip," but when Sam married Ada he knew pitiably little about her.

He thought that she was wonderful. Not only had he to think it, but he actually did think it. He had to think it because only for a prodigy among women could he have treated his mother as he did. He had thought her crazy when she put her hand into the fire, but he knew it was heroic. If she were crazy, it was for love for him, and at the core, he loved her too and felt ashamed of himself, but Ada stood between them, and he was not going to give up Ada. Then he was busy, time wore on, custom blunted the prick of conscience, and it finally became a habit either not to think of Anne at all, or to think comfortably of her as happy enough with Madge.

And he actually thought Ada wonderful because the conditions of his courtship fought for her. He was visibly prospering; he liked prosperity; it was Ada who had initiated his prosperity; and she was glamorous for that. Again, he was very busy in those days with the first steps of his new business, too occupied to play the diligent lover, and saw her very fitfully. So seen, she did not lose the wonder of surprise, but came upon him freshly with each of their meetings, able to parade for each some new attraction from her slender stock of charm. She kept their intercourse egregiously correct, and he thought her mystery was infinite. She hid her shallowness behind affected modesty, knowing that an intimate courtship would discover to him that there was nothing to discover, and attracted by aloofness. It was immensely clever in its short-winded way: a cleverness that lasted the course of courtship, but evaporated when the tape—the altar—was reached. It did not seem necessary to Ada to go on being clever once that ring was on her finger. She was married, she had achieved: she was clever for the spurt, and had no cleverness left, for the Marathon Race. And Sam had many preoccupations in those days which prevented him from thinking too much about Ada.

If he was dull about his courtship, his wits were sharp enough for other matters. He had the satisfaction, almost from the day of its issue, of seeing the pamphlet sell steadily. Very quickly it ceased to be a case of getting his money back, and became merely a question of how many cents per cent he was going to make. His first edition of five thousand (the *soi-disant* thousand) was rapidly exhausted, and the presses of Carter Meadowbank worked overtime to cope with the demand. He cast bread upon the waters by sending copies to every name in the Clergy List and every Member of Parliament; and did not cast in vain. Free advertisement was lavished upon him. Somehow, he had found one of those times when the social conscience is stirred: he published, without knowing it, opportunely, and the diabolic cleverness of Gerald Adams' writing steered him safely past the rocks of the Public Prosecutor. It seemed only to stimulate demand when he raised the price to a shilling.

He had no further trouble with the pamphlet. It sold itself, but sitting still watching the wheels go round did not appeal to Sam, who had a thousand pounds to multiply. He hadn't quite the hardihood to believe that he could multiply his thou sand as rapidly as he had the twenty-five which he paid Adams, but he felt that he was launched as a publisher and had nothing to publish.

His thoughts were diverted from that solecism one day when he went into Carter's printing-office to speed up the foreman. The foreman admitted that the pace could be improved. "But I dunno, sir, that the boss wants it improved. There's nothing in to follow this job of yours. You might say you've been the saving of Mr. Carter."

Sam was thoughtful for a minute. He had not looked upon himself as the saviour of Mr. Carter and did not appreciate that character when it was thrust upon him. He went into Carter's office.

"This little tract of mine," he said ("tract" seemed the light description in that text-hung room), "is selling remarkably well, and the demand increases. Now, I've nothing to say about the past.-I came in here a total stranger and you quoted me accordingly. But it's only fair to warn you that I have gone into prices with other printers and I may find it necessary to make a change."

Carter made no effort to hide his dismay. "I hope you won't do that, Mr. Branstone. At least, give me a chance of revising my price."

"Once bitten," said Sam, "is twice shy, and you don't deny that you bit."

"But surely business," argued Carter, "is business."

"It is," said Sam grimly, "and if you'll answer me a few questions on the understanding that this is a business interview and I'm not being impertinently inquisitive, I shall be obliged."

"I'll do my best," said Carter.

"Thank you. How old are your printing-presses?"

"Twenty years."

"Consequently they are almost hopelessly out of date?"

Carter had a tenderness for those presses. They had been young when he was young, were bought when the world smiled on him and his business had its hedyay. They had kept him and he could not be disloyal now. "I believe that they have printed your tract efficiently, Mr. Branstone," he defended them.

"Oh, there's life in the old dogs yet," said Sam. "I'm not proposing to make scrap-iron of them."

"As they belong to me," said Carter tartly, "it would not make such difference if you did propose it."

"Therefore," said Sam, "I don't propose it—yet. Please remember that I'm talking business. Do you care to tell me what that text cost to produce and what you get for it?"

Carter did not care, but, though he wondered at himself, he told. "And that?" Sam asked, pointing to another; and again Carter told.

"Then," said Sam, "there are two religious papers which you print for the proprietors. What——?"

"Young man," interrupted Carter, "are you proposing to buy my business?"

"No," said Sam coolly, "only to become your partner in it. What profit were you going to tell me you made on the papers?"

Carter told: he was too stupefied to do anything else. "Um," said Sam. "It isn't much."

"They are a good work," said Carter, and Sam looked at him sharply, but the old man was perfectly sincere. It was good work to print religious magazines and he did it for next to nothing.

"Well," said Sam, "thank you. Now I won't mince matters: When I came along with my—tract, I enabled you to postpone filing your petition, but it was only a postponement, and if you'll look facts in the face the one big fact for you is bankruptcy."

"The Lord will provide." Carter had lived from hand to mouth for many months in that belief.

"If you like to look at it that way. He has provided: He has provided me. I will make you a good offer, Mr. Carter. I will introduce five him dred pounds capital into the business for a halfshare in the plant, goodwill and future profits of this concern. That is, the printing business. What I, as publisher, do has nothing to do with you."

"... I must think it over," said Carter; but they both knew that he had already decided to accept.

"The Lord," Carter was thinking, "*has* provided " Sam, on the contrary, was thinking, "I may or may not be a fool to go into this without getting an accountant's report on the books, but I believe in rapid action, and if I'd offered too high a price I'm certain that he's imbecile enough to have told me."

It remained to find something to print, and he wanted Stewart's advice, but, with the idea of being first on the side of the angels, went to see Peter Struggles. The battle which had raged round the pamphlet had left Peter untouched, even though more than one of the clergy who received it from Sam had thought it their duty to write to Peter's bishop. The bishop failed to see a case for disciplinary measures: Peter might have been sinned against but he had not sinned. And the *Sunday Judge* was read by neither Peter nor his bishop. (The Church is notoriously out of touch with modern life, but, after all, it is hardly reasonable to expect the Church to compliment its rival, the *Sunday Press*, by reading it.)

Nevertheless, Peter had, on reflection, felt some wavering doubts about the pamphlet. His intermittent shrewdness threw a flickering light through the haze of his charity and gave him moments of discomfort.

Sam's attitude during this call was admirably calculated to resolve his doubt. He wanted, with an eye to the future, to make sure of Peter, whose name he might require another day, and was ready, even if it were not immediately profitable, to placate Peter now. He explained that he had joined forces with Mr. Carter, and at once acquired merit in Peter's eyes.

Carter was irreproachable. He did not explain by what means he had been able to join Carter and it did not occur to Peter to ask. Sam was not going to tell Peter, who would tell Ada, of his legacy. If she found out, as Anne had found out, he could not help it, but, meantime, it was his secret. Ada, like Anne, belonged to the sex which had no understanding of business.

"And the point," said Sam, "with a business like Mr. Carter's, is to use it for good. I take it that the texts do good, but perhaps they are only for the simple-minded. I hope I don't despise people for their simplicity, but my own taste runs rather to books and I think you will agree with me."

Peter agreed, with a quotation which rather dashed Sam; he had an idea that poetry did not sell.

"'Poets are the trumpets which sing to battle. Poets are the unacknowledged legislators of the world.'"

"Yes," said Sam. "Quite so. But isn't poetry going to the opposite extreme? I had the thought of something more direct. Good prose with a good moral."

"Excellent," said Peter, off again.

"'Were not God's laws,
His gospel laws, In olden time held forth
By types, shadows and metaphors?'"

"Of course they were," said Sam, wondering when Peter would close his mental dictionary of quotations and come down to business, "and that quotation is very apt because I was thinking of classics. English classics, you know," he explained hurriedly, "and classics because they are not copyright."

"And have stood the test of time," said Peter.

"Yes. Do you think you could propose a list? I should like to know that the first books I publish had been selected by you. I don't think they ought to be exactly theological, but they must be good in every sense of the word."

"Why not begin with the book from whose in traduction I just quoted?"

"Why not indeed?" said Sam, who hadn't the faintest idea of the source of the quotation.

"Very well," said Peter. "Suppose you put that down for one."

Same made vague scratches on paper. He had a bookish reputation to sustain and he was not going to betray ignorance prematurely. "Then," said Feter, "there is Law's 'Serious Call to a Devout and Holy Life.'"

"I'm letting myself in for something," thought Sam, but he wrote it down.

"'The Imitation of Christ,' and 'The Little Flowers of St. Francis,'" Peter went on.

"I think those should be enough to begin with," said Sam hurriedly.

"Four, isn't it?" said Peter, recapitulating.

"The 'Pilgrim's Progress '" — —("Thank God," thought Sam, "I needn't give myself away.")

"Yes, four," he interrupted, reading the now completed list. "And I am very much obliged to you."

He wasn't, though, quite sure about it. He had "nobbled" Peter, but he feared those books would be a millstone round his neck. There might be a steady sale for the "Pilgrim's Progress" as a prize, but the others— —! Still, he need not print many copies of them, and—consoling thought—they would be good window-dressing tor his list. He hoped it would include other, very different, books.

"I'm sorry Ada is out," Peter was saying, and Sam was rather startled to realize that he had not missed her. But he was sure of his position with her: it was his position for her which he had to consolidate. He proceeded to consolidate it by going in search of Stewart, and found him where he expected to find him, in a bar.

"I want your advice," said Sam.

"Whisky for the gentleman, Flora," said Stewart. "That's my advice and you'll get no other till you've taken this."

Sam took it. Business is business and, beyond that, his thrifty prejudices were less necessary now.

"You're not unteachable," said Stewart. "It's a point in your favour. The proper thing when you've drunk that is to ask me if I will have another. My reply will be in the affirmative and we shall then retire, with sustaining refreshment, into that corner, where I will advise you for as long as you can continue to buy whisky for me and drink level. I hate a shirker."

Sam told him of his partnership with Carter. "I'm always troubled about you," said Stewart. "I can never make up my mind whether you're too clever to live or whether you were born with luck instead of brain. Obviously, you will publish novels."

"There are so many kinds," said Sam.

"No. Only two. Mine and the rest. But I suffer from honesty. Therefore I tell you that my novel has been refused by every publisher in London. It is waiting," he said hopefully, "for a man with courage. The difference between it and the Yellow Book is that my book *is* yellow."

"I see," said Sam. "But I have gone into the publishing trade to make my living."

"On the whole," decided Stewart, "you are more knave than fool. And you would call it the publishing trade. It's a benighted world, but there are still some publishers who aren't in trade—beyond the midriff. Do you seriously come to me to ask what sort of novels to publish?"

"Yes."

"The sort," he said, "that is written for nursemaids by people who ought to be nursemaids."

"That's jealousy," said Sam. "They get published and you don't."

"Perhaps you're right," said Stewart. "But I've always heard that seeing is believing. Do you ever go to the theatre?"

"Not often."

"It's a pity, because if you did, I've a tragedy in blank verse that you might care to publish. It is great art and will never be produced. Still, I'm a philanthropist to-night and you will come to the theatre with me. I happen to be going for the *Warden*."

"Are you a dramatic critic for the *Warden?*" asked Sam, rather awed.

"I'm a reporter, old son. This isn't the kind of play they waste a critic on. Drink up, and we'll go."

Sam found, to his relief, that he was able to go and decided he had a strong head. The theatre was crowded when they reached it and Stewart was young enough to sit self-consciously in one of the two seats kept for the *Manchester Warden*. Dramatic criticism was taken seriously on that journal; at least two of the paper's regular critics were men of genius, and Stewart hoped that he might be mistaken for one of them. But the audience that night was not the kind which interests itself in the lions of the higher journalism; rather it justified the contemptuous reference to drama as the "art of the mob." It would have made a sincere democrat weep for his convictions. "Behold them," said Stewart. "The Public."

Sam beheld them more than he beheld the play. He reminded himself that he was there on business, to be shown something which Stewart wanted him to see, and if he had not the gift of detachment, he assumed it.

When Adams had read his paper to the Concentrics, Sam had listened but kept his eyes on the audience. In a darkened theatre, the audience was more difficult to watch, but he could feel its quick response to the play, could hear its ready laughter and its quite eager ears. Emphatically, here was a play which seized its audience, gripped them, tickled them, beslavered them, throttled them, did with them what it liked and when it liked; all to their immense and vociferous delight. He tried to keep his aloofness, to see how it was done, to tear the heart out of this mystery. Here was something which the public wanted; he had only to diagnose it, and the Open Sesame to fortune was his.

He couldn't do it. Detachment slipped from him, never to return till the curtain fell. He wasn't a superman, immune from other men's emotions. The play took hold of him and swayed him with the rest. He tried resistance, vainly; told himself that he was here, not, as these others were, for pleasure, but to learn, to learn; and the play gripped him the harder for his attempt to take it coldly.

At the end, Sam was applauding wildly while Stewart watched him with cynical amusement. "Caught you all right," he said, "and by way of a confession I'll own that the damned thing nearly got me once. Rum place, the theatre, isn't it? But," he grew more serious, "I've to write about that, write without being libellous about that maudlin, sentimental, erotic, religious trash. It's enough to make a man give up journalism and take to something honest, like coal-heaving. But I'm forgetting. I brought you here to teach you something. Have you learnt it? That's a play, but the same thing applies to a novel. You find novels with 'The Sign of the Cross' in them, my boy. Queasy sentimentality to sicken a bee, and, for the rest, don't forget that Jesus died for you to make money out of novels. This play makes me blasphemous, but I'm doing the devil's advocate to you to-night, so it's all in the picture. When I've finished my notice I think I'll try a 'short' on 'The Tradesman Publisher' or 'The Dignity of Letters.' It will be good for my conscience."

"I wish you would," said Sam. "I'll reply to it, with a list of the classics I am going to publish."

"Sometimes," said Stewart, "you rather sicken me. I am speaking of the *Manchester Warden*, not the *Sunday Judge*. Good-night."

But the vacillations of a journalist with a foot in two camps and an idealistic standard which he hardly pretended to take seriously himself left Sam unimpressed. The play and Stewart's description of its essence had given him furiously to think. He imagined that he knew the sort of novel he wanted and he was not troubled by Stewart's disease of dual standards.

Sam had one standard, the success standard; and anything else was muddle-headedness. At the same time he felt most grateful to Stewart who had advertised the pamphlet and now presented him with a policy.

It was a policy, but not one for immediate application. *Festina lente* was his watchword for the moment, and he devoted himself to putting new life into the sales of texts and to the issue of the "Branstone Classics." They were, one might note in passing, the Branstone Classics: his name loomed large and the names of their authors, the insignificants like à Kempis and Bunyan, were properly small; and he put the sign of the cross between the Branstone and the Classics. He intended it to be his trade-mark, and if it were his trade-mark, why not use it? It infringed nobody's copyright.

Amongst it all, he had little enough time for Ada, and she knew how much she gained by being a luxury instead of a habit. But Sam was not engaged for the sake of being engaged, and as soon as he knew he had made no mistake in his business venture was eager to be married. There were no objections from Ada. This intermittent courtship, in which his duties as a lover took second place to his activities as a business man, suited Ada well, but marriage, finality, the bond suited her better.

Even to the end of that engagement it was things for Ada which preoccupied him, rather than Ada herself, and he took the matter of furnishing seriously—from a business point of view, interested less in the furniture he bought than in the discounts he might, by this means or that, secure. He suffered the usual surprise at the cost of mattresses and kitchen equipment, but, to Ada, he appeared royally lavish. Ada did not know of his legacy: she knew that Anne had told her on the top of a fantastic tram-car that Sam had earned two pounds ten a week with Travers, and the scale of this furnishing did not square with what a man could save out of two pounds ten a week. It followed in Ada's mind that Anne had lied to her, malignantly misrepresenting Sam's position to frighten her; and the breach between Anne and Ada, which never had much chance of closing, was permanently open.

One does not have old connections with an estate agency without being able to rent a good house cheaply. She was going to be mistress of a house which fell little short of the dreams of her boarding-school days. It was certainly "stylish"; she was not sure that it was not positively "smart."

Madge wept on the night before her wedding. Ada did not weep. She was too busy hugging herself because she had surmounted the perils of courtship. She had accomplished her aim in life. She was going to be married.

CHAPTER XIV
HONEYMOONERS

ADA was married in white satin, though Peter sold books to do it and her trousseau lacked essentials. It depends, though, on one's point of view. Ada thought white satin essential, while another might have put underclothing first. But it is fitting to wear a crown at a coronation and, when the object of one's life has been to get married, to celebrate in satin the attaining of one's aim.

It also reminded the congregation that the bride is the central figure at a wedding. People might otherwise have remembered that they did not come because Ada was Ada, but because she was Peter's daughter.

She entered with *réclame* into the state of being Mrs. Samuel Branstone, resenting a little the tweeds of Stewart, Sam's best man, but liking his manners and liking, too, the way in which Sam took it for granted that the day was hers, not his. He did not even obtrude a family.

George was, in fact, obscurely there, hidden among the congregation. He was there in the spirit of schoolboy, playing truant from Anne, who was at home with Madge. Ada thought that the conspicuous absence of Branstones added lustre to her satin. None but the necessary Sam was there.

They went to London, where neither of them had been before, and since it is a bitter thing to have to look back to a boring honeymoon, the choice of place had great discretion. There was so much besides themselves to see in London that they postponed looking at each other till they came home. They saw sights and went to theatres, but though they slept together and rose together and saw the sights (all but one) together there was no realization of "togetherness," no birth of a new life in which they were not Sam and Ada, but these two in one. They were furiously modest about things which no honeymooner has any right to be modest about. If they are modest about them, they have no right to be honeymooners. It may have been in their case something both worse and better than modesty. It may have been downright shame. Perhaps subconsciously they knew that this was not a marriage, not the coming together of two fit mates. It had no passion in it. There was self when they should have been ecstatically selfless. They were two when they should have been most one.

But Sam, if he fell immensely short of ecstasy, was still too much under her spell to be critical. He wondered a little at the frank delight in being married which she displayed in public, at her flaunting of her new wedding ring, at her advertisement that this was a honeymoon, and contrasted this outward relish with her intimate frigidity; but even this seemed a disloyalty, and he told himself that Ada in a hotel was one person and at home would be another. Ada would "settle down," and meantime they were in London, and London was waiting to be explored with her.

They explored chiefly the London which Londoners do not know, the London of the guide-books, and felt tremendously metropolitan because they went to the Tower, the British Museum and the National Gallery. The shops seared Ada. Their windows fascinated but their doors repelled. Probably Sam would have held her back by main force had she attempted to go in, but, as it was, she had the same satisfaction in identifying them that social snobs find in recognizing, at a distance, famous people. These were the authentic shops which advertised in the papers and they had a game called "hunting the Harrod" or "looking for Barkers," which led to a lot of fun with 'buses after they had quartered Oxford Street and Regent Street. It was all very gay, and gayer, almost naughtily gay, to go one night to a place called the Coliseum—a music-hall; a thing to do audaciously, not to be spoken of at home; and yet the place was very full of really most respectable people. They marvelled at the emancipation of the Londoner.

On his honeymoon, Sam became possessed of an ambition. It was not an extraordinarily fine ambition, but he came to care about, it greatly and it repaid his care a thousandfold. The way to sanity is to desire very keenly something which it is just possible one may get, and Sam's ambition kept him sane in the days when he knew that Ada had failed him.

Struggles had suggested to our debater of the Concentrics that he ought to see the House of Commons at debate, and had written to their local Member for a pass to the Gallery. The result was the most thrilling experience of Sam's honeymoon! It was, for one thing, unique that Ada could not be with him: these were the first hours since he married her that they spent apart and perhaps that, all unconsciously, had gilded them for Sam. They had almost a tiff before she let him go: not quite, but she resented his desertion of her and considered it his fault that she was not allowed to sit with him to hear the legislators who made laws for her as for him. Not that Ada cared who made her laws, nor cared to watch the makers at their work, but she managed to put enough snap into her resentment at his going to lend the added quality of a stolen pleasure to his experience.

That gallery, with its foreshortened view of the dingy cock-pit, is not the first choice of the connoisseur in thrills, but on Sam its effect was amazing. He must have had some gift, quite undisclosed till now, of veneration, for it is almost beyond belief that the reality of the House of Commons can impress. But the idea can and perhaps (to be just) the reality is more impressive than that of any other Chamber on earth. Imagination helping him, it caught and held his mind.

A small stout man of undistinguished appearance was speaking in a conversational tone not easy to hear from the Gallery, but presently the orator warmed to his subject and poured out living words in a spate of real emotion. He was one of those rare men, and this one of those rare speeches, that really convert an opponent: and Sam's ambition to speak as this politician spoke, and from those benches, came instantly to birth.

Not only did he want to be a Member of Parliament, but a Liberal Member, because this man of words was Liberal. Up to this time, Sam had not been a political animal although he had voted, and voted Tory because that was in general the line of Mr. Travers and the property-owning class he represented. Now with a swift enthusiasm he was Liberal, knowing nothing of either side, but caught by sudden hero-worship for a little, pudgy, snubnosed politician who spoke in sentences of prodigious length and never lost his way in them.

In a twinkling he acquired the bias of the politician: his hero's opponent was palpably a fool; he had no gifts, no argument. Yes, Sam was doubly right to be a Liberal. They had so obviously all the brains, they were so undeniably the winning side. He did not understand the technique of a division and was surprised when he looked at the paper next day to find that the Liberals were outvoted. It gave him pause, but did not shake him. When the Liberals came back to power, as with their superiority in brain they were certain to do, he, Sam Branstone, would come with them. Let it be only a year or two and he would be ready. He too would loll upon those padded benches, and catch the Speaker's eye, and be an orator.

He walked along the Embankment towards his hotel, and it came into his mind that he had spent four hours in the Gallery and had not thought of Ada. Nor could he, though he tried, think of her now.

Sky-signs still flashed across the river, and as he paused and leaned against the parapet a young policeman kept a wary eye on him. But Sam was meditating life, not death. The lights of London gleamed upon the Thames and made it magical for him. He conquered London in his reverie, and stepped, a member, from the House to his automobile. His home, he supposed, was somewhere in Park Lane.

He thought back now to the theatre where he had seen *The Sign of the Cross*. It was different from the London Theatres he had seen where audiences seemed afraid of emotion. Or was it that the plays had not been right? That was it: they had not the note: they weren't—what was Stewart's phrase?—erotic religious plays. He wanted to move audiences as that play had moved its audience. Power! The power of the spoken word. That was the thing, and since he could not write a play he must rely upon himself, his oratory, his single voice. He saw himself on platforms facing crowded halls, gripping his hearers, leading them where he would, taming the mob till it made an idol of its master. As to where he would lead, why, he would lead and that was what mattered. Branstone was Prime Minister that night.

It was one o'clock before the young policeman felt at liberty to resume his beat, and Sam left the enchanted river for his little hotel in Norfolk Street. Ada had her back to him and apparently she slept. Actually she was wide awake; she was wondering whether it had happened to any other woman to be treated so abominably on her honeymoon.

She brushed her hair nest morning with a notable viciousness. Hair has uses beyond those of mere adornment. It is an admirable veil through which one can watch without being seen to watch. Ada was watching Sam and she was also listening to him.

She listened not because his enthusiasm for the House of Commons interested her, but because she was waiting for some word of apology. It did not come. He was full of regret, but only because this was their last day in town and he could not go to the House again.

"What time is our train?" she asked.

He told her.

"Then I have time to do some shopping first."

"Shopping?" he asked, but unsuspiciously.

She nodded. Sam was going to pay for his pleasures. Those blouses she had seen at Peter Robinson's no longer seemed impossibly expensive. If Sam chose to enjoy himself in his own way, without her, she would enjoy herself in hers—with Sam to pay the piper.

Shopping is a loose term; one shops when one buys a kipper or a diamond tiara. Ada was putting her hair up and he imagined her to mean that she wanted a packet of hair-pins. "Oh, yes," he said pensively. "And while you go, I think I will just slip down to the House of Parliament again."

The House would not be sitting and he could not get in. He knew that, but he wanted to gaze, to look at the frame which was some day to contain him. He wanted to be certain that it was still there.

"I think," she said, "that you will come with me to the shop. I shall want you there to pay."

Sam paused in the act of fastening his collar. "To pay?" he asked, not unsuspiciously now.

"Are your selfish pleasures all you think about?" Ada wanted to know. "Isn't it a privilege to be allowed to buy me nice clothes?"

He had not looked upon it in that light. In budgeting for their future he had indeed assumed that a trousseau lasted a bride for her first year. "I see," he said gloomily; then remembering that he was in love with her, "of course," he added with a smile which might count to him for heroism. "But we must not forget the fares, and after I have paid the bill here I shall not have more than two pounds left to spend."

"Then I spend two pounds on blouses," she said.

He made a monosyllabic noise which might have been "Yes." It might also have been "Damn."

The truth was that he had deliberately kept those two pounds back, intending to spend some, but not, he hoped, all of it, on a present for Ada He had thought of a hand-bag, had imagined her gasp of delight when he audaciously entered with her one of those forbiddingly inviting shops, her appreciation of his generosity.

Last night had driven the thought entirely from his mind, and he was annoyed now not only at his forgetfulness, but at Ada. She did not ask, she demanded. A night in the Gallery may be regarded as dissipation, but at least it is not a crime. It is even patriotic, and he was asked to foot a bill for two pounds as the price of his patriotism. Ambition, he thought, would be an expensive luxury if he had to pay in clothes for Ada every time he went to a political meeting. For that, plainly, was her attitude: she demanded a *quid pro quo*: she announced a policy of retaliation.

There is a queer perverted pleasure in scratching an open wound, in cutting off one's nose to spite one's face. He had meant to be generous and he wanted still to be generous, but the money he had laid aside for generosity was now hypothecated to meet her claim. He would give her her pound of flesh, but wanted very badly to roast it for her with coals of fire.

Gloom lifted from him suddenly. He took off the old tie which he had put on as being good enough to travel in, and fastened very carefully one which he had bought "for London."

"I'll do it," he was thinking. "It is—almost—a stroke."

At breakfast he was positively gay, so that Ada wondered furtively what he was up to, and whether the way to raise his spirits would always be to demand new clothes of him. It did not seem likely, but she proposed at any rate to experiment freely in that direction.

He divided his attention between her, breakfast, and the Parliamentary report of the *Times*. He felt that he had virtually participated in that debate, and even the shock of reading that the division had gone against his hero did not spoil the pleasure he found in reading of it. He read with a prophetic eye. He, too, would be reported in the *Times* some day.

He called the waiter. "Marmalade, sir?" asked the man.

"No, thanks. Bring me the directory."

"The directory," protested the waiter, "is in the reading-room."

"And I," said Sam superbly, "am in the coffee-room."

The waiter brought him the directory.

Sam smiled broadly. He was testing his form, and decided that if it were equal to coercing a waiter into carrying a directory to his breakfast-table, it would probably not fail him in what he proposed to do. He consulted the book and noted an address which was not, he observed, in Park Lane. His respect for Sir William Gatenby suffered a slight decline.

Half an hour later he rang the bell of that gentleman's house. Gatenby was the local member, to whom Peter Struggles had written for Sam's pass to the Gallery.

"Sir William in?" he asked.

"Yes, but——" A trained eye observed his clothes. They were not cut in Savile Row.

"He will see me," said Sam serenely. Some people are at their best in the early morning.

His card was accepted from him, and he was shown into a library of severe Blue Books, possibly qualified by a reproduction of Millais' portrait of Gladstone. Ordinarily, Sam would have been met in the library by a secretary who earned his salary by his talent for administering polite snubs to unwanted callers. The secretary was not earning his salary to-day, but, probably, spending it. It was Derby Day.

After all, a vote is a vote, and Sir William came in with a show of geniality. "Good morning, Mr. Branstone," he said, reading Sam's card. "From the old town. I see."

"Is that all you remember about me?" asked Sam.

"At the moment," confessed Sir William warily. His majority was not large.

"Well," said Sam, "the Reverend Mr. Struggles is my father-in-law."

"Sit down," said Sir William. "I am very glad you called. How is Mr. Struggles?"

"I left him well, thank you. Perhaps you remember that he wrote to you to ask you for a pass to the Gallery for me."

"I was happy to be lucky in the ballot," said the Member.

"Yes," said Sam, "I went last night. But I mentioned that to establish my identity. My object in calling upon you is to ask you to lend me five pounds."

Sir William thought of his secretary, who should have saved him this. Thinking of his secretary, he thought of Derby Day and the probable intentions of a man who chooses that day to ask for a loan. "My dear sir!" he said.

"Quite," agreed Sam. "Life would be unbearable to you if every constituent who came to London tried to borrow money off you. But I am Branstone. I run the Branstone Press and the Branstone Classics. I published the 'Social Evil' pamphlet and sent you a copy which, I regret to say, you did not acknowledge." Sir William thought again of his secretary, and unkindly. "This," said Sam, "is merely to indicate that I am a man of substance."

Sir William Gatenby wore side-whiskers. He was an old man and there was little left of him besides pomposity and a determination to hold his seat. He looked, what at this moment he felt, some one in a farce. He was quite sure that Sam was some one in a farce. They were both in a farce, and of course five-pound notes fly in farces like gnats in August. It did not seem to him that there was anything to do but to produce a five-pound note.

"Thank you," said Sam, and sat at a desk. "I will give you my cheque for this."

It staggered Sir William. He nearly warned Sam of the danger of issuing a cheque which was not likely to be honoured, but refrained in time. "Then," he said, "there was really no need for you to come to me at all?"

"Only," said Sam, "that I wanted you to remember me."

"I think I shall do that," said Sir William.

"Thank you," said Sam calmly. "I wanted to know you because I intend to go into politics."

"The Cause," said Sir William solemnly, "demands his best from every earnest worker."

"I will work for the Cause," said Sam. Neither of them attempted to define the Cause, and Sam left without further remark, but his call had this result: that on finding the cheque honoured Sir William wrote to his agent to tell him of "a queer fish called Samuel Branstone who called on me the other day, and offered to work for the Cause. A young man whom I think you should encourage. He is the son-in-law of Mr. Struggles, and the Church, alas, is so tepid towards our great Principles that we must not neglect a promising recruit from that fold."

CHAPTER XV
OTHER THINGS BESIDE MARRIAGE

DEBT appeals to some people. They feel that when they are in debt they have had more out of life than life owes to them. Sam had given Gatenby his cheque and was therefore not in debt to him, but he proceeded to spend the five pounds as recklessly as if it had been borrowed money.

He meant to astonish Ada, and succeeded, but the surprise he sprang did not work quite as he anticipated. For a moment, indeed, as he bought her hats and blouses she glowed with unaffected gratitude, and he tasted with her the joy of headstrong acquisition. But Ada's glow was quick to pass.

She had time in the train to forget the splendour of his presents and the dash that she would cut next Sunday, and to remember that he had spent a lot of money; he who denied that he had more than two pounds to spend had spent seven. Obviously, he had lied to her.

It was true, she thought, that he had repented of his lie and of his meanness, and bought handsomely: the more handsome the purchase, the more demonstrable the lie.

She recalled her dreadful interview with Anne, Anne's statements of his means, and how little they conformed to the scale of Sam's furnishing. She pondered Sam's open-handedness in the blouse-shop, and concluded that the Branstones were congenital liars about money.

In the future she would know how to act. Sam had plenty.

"So you had money up your sleeve all the time," she said.

Sam winked facetiously. "There are a lot of funny things up my sleeve," he said.

"I'm learning that," said Ada. Which he took for a compliment; and grinned.

He had long since made up his mind that the way with women was to mystify them, to treat them like children at a conjuring entertainment, to surprise them with results, but never to explain. He nearly choked with pride over his exploit with Sir William Gatenby. But for the hat-box and the blouses up there on the rack, what he had done was too good to be true, and certainly it was too good to be told to a woman. They did not understand business; no woman could appreciate the daring spirit of his feat.

If he told Ada that he had borrowed from Gatenby, she would simply say "Oh, yes," and treat his unexampled audacity as a matter of course. It was inspiration, brilliantly conceived and brilliantly executed, and its bright memory was not to be tarnished by a woman's dull acceptance of it as something not in the least extraordinary.

He grinned and did not tell, and what did not occur to him was that if he offered no explanation she would supply one of her own. It is idiotic to tell a wife everything, but wise to tell nearly everything; especially when it is open to her to draw a false conclusion.

Sam did not think a false conclusion open to her, because he still believed the best of Ada, because he was still in love. But falling out of love is desperately easy.

"As a walled town," says Touchstone, "is worthier than a village, so is the forehead of a married man more honourable than the bare brow of a bachelor," and Sam was married. He could lay that flattering unction to his soul, could hold his head higher, because he was a ratepayer and bore responsibilities, and went home at night to a house with a garden. He did all that, and it was empty honour because success in marriage, as in all else, is not to be had ready-made, but depends upon the will to make adjustments.

The will can come best from passion, and there was no passion here to tide them over the awkward age of marriage, the first difficult year when the adjustments must, if ever, be made. Granted passion, a man can love a woman whom he knows to be a murderess; let passion lack, and he can fall out of love because the woman snores or is untidy. Sam's marriage was not made in heaven, but by Ada in Heaton Park, and with a marriage so made it is as easy to fall out of love as off a house. Little things count more than big when there is no passion to create its life-long mirage.

If you cannot have the mirage of passion there is a useful substitute called common sense, another name for compromise, and Ada refused to compromise. She was for self, unmitigated and supreme. Ada left the adjustments to Sam, and relaxed in nothing from her perfect selfishness.

The little thing which counted heavily against her, almost at once, was simply that Ada was untidy. She did not invent places for things, or, if she did, they were never used. She left her clothes downstairs after she had been out, and the piano is not the place for a hat or the sofa for an umbrella.

It annoyed Sam to distraction to find her clothes distributed about their bedroom, slung carelessly over chair backs, pitched on the floor.

Men are not the untidy sex: the virtue of tidiness, like most others, is evenly distributed. Sam was tidy by nature, and habit is stronger still. Ada's misfortune was that he was used to Anne, that Anne was neat and Ada a slut. Sam did not know until he missed it how much he appreciated Anne's tidiness, how much he needed it and how much he hated untidiness until he lived with it in Ada. In London, in the hotel, he had excused what he saw of it, because it was in an hotel; which was also why there had been little to see, by reason of a good chambermaid.

At home, it hurt him and he could do nothing. Ada did nothing, either. She had not married for love, and one does not change a habit without strong motive. His hints appeared to Ada peevish and unreasonable. She thought he made mountains out of molehills and despised him for small-mindedness; he thought a woman who could not put a petticoat into a drawer when he asked her was wilfully provoking him.

She was not wilful of set purpose. She simply refused to disturb her habits, to accommodate herself to him, to make a sacrifice to love. She had no love to which to sacrifice.

And presently he found out that he, too, did not love. But that was all. Then and afterwards that was, damnably, all. He did not love, but neither did he hate. He had never loved her deeply enough to hate her. That was the tragedy of Sam's marriage: indifference, the deadliest sin.

He was indifferent to her, to her untidiness and even to her extravagance. She could not treat clothes reasonably, she did not know how to wear them when she had them, but she lusted madly to possess them. She was grossly, inexcusably extravagant, and he was indifferent. He was indifferent because he was growing rich, and wanted his energies for the purpose of growing richer, not of quarrelling with her.

That was another tragedy. They never quarrelled. They never cleared the air, they never flushed the drain. They did not make adjustments, but left things where they were, in a bad place. On honeymoon, they turned from looking at each other to look at London, and at home, after one experience of revelation, they did not seek another, but rebounded and looked anywhere but at themselves.

But Peter was looking, and Anne, through the eyes of George, was looking, and it seemed to her that things were happening as she had expected they would happen. She had said the girl was no good and what George told her in his fumbling way gave her to see that the girl turned wife was equally no good. Anne tightened her lips grimly and went on with her efficient charring. She thought her time would come.

Peter looked for the coming of love to bless this marriage to which he had consented in the belief that his God of love would sanctify. He had trusted to the strength of Sam, and to the hope that Sam's strength would turn to sweetness; and it only turned to business. It did not lead Ada from materialism, but drew Peter himself, unwittingly at first, towards it. Peter found himself selecting texts for Sam's "Church Child's Calendar," a labour of love, which nevertheless had nothing to do with Ada, except in the most indirect way, and nothing to do with the Sam and Ada situation.

It was the fact that, to them, there seemed to be no situation which distressed Peter. They simply let things be, and things let be obey the law of gravity. He hoped, ardently, for children. Children blessed marriage in the physical sense, and from that blessing the other, the spiritual blessing, might arise.

There was at one time hope that Ada might have a child... and then the hope was blighted, and the doctor told them not to hope again. Ada would never be a mother.

"I could have told them that," said Anne. "You'd only to look at the girl to see it." Which may only have been wisdom after the event, but certainly did not imply that Anne was disappointed; though Peter was, and bitterly.

Sam, too, had wanted a son, but not, as Peter thought, by Ada and for Ada. He wanted an heir for dynastic reasons. He was the Branstone Publishing Company, its parent and original, and wanted flesh of his flesh to publish after him. He dreamed of a young Sam in the cap of the Grammar School, who should go to the University to which he had not gone and have the chances he had missed. He built many castles in Spain for the son who was never born.

Ada got up from bed and flashed greedily into new clothes. If the measure of her buying was the measure of her grief, she had been deeply touched. Perhaps she was touched, for she had aimed at marriage, which is incomplete without a child. But in the shops, the fashion papers, her clothes and the clothes of other women she found distraction and an occupation. She passed a milestone and went on her way. Ada was no stoic, no hider of her grief, and since she did not complain she must have thought her childlessness was nothing to complain about. When she set her heart on marriage, she hadn't, perhaps, looked further than the ring, the ceremony and the honourable state of being Mrs. Branstone.

She plunged to shops and spending money, Sam to business and making it; and some, at any rate, of the now thwarted love he had been storing for his son passed to the business. Somewhere at the back of his mind he knew his business was not lovable; that it was pitch; that one cannot touch pitch without being defiled. But neither can one deal successfully in pitch without arriving at faith in the virtues of pitch. At intimate moments he was aware that the "Social Evil" pamphlet was pernicious, but Sam Branstone, inducing a bookseller to stock it, was more than an advocate who believes temporarily in his brief: he was a missionary with faith in his mission. So, too, with the texts. He sold them with the conviction that it was good for people to have texts on their walls. He counterfeited sincerity until he came to be sincere, or, at all events, to forget that he was insincere.

Further and further into the unsearched recesses of his mind he pressed the thought that he sold texts because their sales were good for him, and with his working, everyday, non-introspective mind he had a sincerity about his wares, convenient but none the less authentic,-which was invaluable both to his self-respect and as a first aid to success in salesmanship. He never, in the old days, praised a house with the ringing voice of absolute conviction which he used about Law's "Serious Call." He had not read Law, but the sales hung fire till he became persuaded of Law's tremendous worth.

He had a serious call of his own, a call to sell good books at good profits, and the call expressed itself in his clothes and his appearance. He seemed older, graver, took his frock-coat into daily wear, used only black in ties and socks, and had the air of one, who, if not a clergyman, was often in their company, though as a fact he was more frequently with commercial travellers, and in the hotels at night his repertoire of smoke-room stories came no less gaily from his tongue than of old.

And about this time his moustache began to droop like a curtain over his resolute mouth.

Stewart came into the office one day with a parcel under his arm. He had seen neither Sam nor his office lately, and stared wide-eyed at both. Carter, partner in the printing business, still occupied the dilapidated office where Sam had found him, but the Branstone Publishing Company had ampler premises next door, in a building which Sam rented as warehouse for his stock. Gilt lettering on its windows called the attention of the passer-by to the Branstone Classics.

Sam still looked after detail, and when Stewart came in was correcting proofs of a tear-off calendar with a Bible at his elbow.

"I suppose," said Stewart, "that you *are* Branstone, but why disguise yourself as a Scottish Elder?"

"I am in my usual clothes," said Sam, rather huffed.

"If the clothes are the man, this is no place for me. Do you often use the Bible in your business hours?"

He often did, not only to check with a quite beautiful precision the texts on his calendars by the Authorised Version, but in another way, and one which seemed to show, if it showed anything, that he looked upon the Bible with intimate familiarity. Perhaps one mascot was the vellum-bound copy of the "Social Evil" pamphlet and the other the Bible. At any rate, his price code used in the office was made up this way:

M Y F A T H E R G O D

1 2 3 4 5 6 7 8 9 10 20

New clerks initiated into that code used to wonder at it for a day. Then they got used to it.

"I'm correcting the proofs of this calendar," Sam explained. "You see, it's a shaving calendar. You hang this up by your shaving-mirror and study the text for the day while you shave."

"I don't," said Stewart. "I go to the barber's. My hand's unsteady in the morning. But I see the idea. First read the text, then wipe your razor on it."

"That is not the idea. See." He pointed to the card of the calendar, and read solemnly:

"A text a day
Drives care away."

"It wouldn't drive my sort of care away," said Stewart. "Mine's serious."

"There can be no trouble too serious for you to find consolation in this calendar."

"But suppose I have toothache on quarter-day, and the consolation you offer for that date is consolation to a man who can't pay his rent? Seriously, Branstone, am I behind the scenes in this office, or do you never drop the showman? I admit you're in the pi-market, and you've dressed the pi-man's part and you've got his patter, too, but I don't know that you need exercise it on me. This stock of yours looks dire," he commented, strolling round the office. "I suppose it's the stuff that sells?"

"My business," said Sam, "is founded on a rock."

"I came in here to sell you a fortune," said Stewart. "If you're going to talk cant at me, I'll take the fortune to a London publisher. Your business may be founded on a rock, but the name of the rock is the 'Social Evil.'"

"The word rock," said Sam, with a twinkle in his eye, "is also used for a kind of toffee."

"Well, now that I know you're sane, I'll talk to you. And I'll talk toffee, too I didn't think in the days of my earnest youth that I should come to this, but you never know what debt will do to a man. I've written a novel. At least, it isn't a novel, it's an outrage on decency. It's a violent assault on the emotions. It's the sort of thing I deserve shooting for writing. Treacle is bitter compared with it, and it does not contain one word of literature. It is a cast-iron certainty."

"I must read it," said Sam.

"You're growing distrustful," said Stewart sadly.

"I don't buy pigs in pokes, even when they're yours," said Sam. "Come along in a couple of days."

He read the novel, and was ready for Stewart when he came.

"I have taken the liberty," he said, "of marking some passages in this manuscript which you may care to alter."

"Oh? I know it's mawkish, but I don't believe there is a limit to what they'll stand—and like."

"I refer particularly to the character you have called Hetaera."

"But only once. After that she's called Hetty."

"Hetty," said Sam severely, "will have to be cut out. She is an impure woman."

"Even the most popular of novels should bear some relationship to life."

"If you wish me to publish this one, Hetty must go. Branstones have a reputation to sustain."

"Good God!" said Stewart. "Hetty is the one oasis of truth in a desert of sloppy sentimentality. She's true because I happen to know her."

"That is nothing to your credit, Stewart."

Stewart stared. "Are you pulling my leg, Sam, or is this really serious?"

"Why should you doubt my seriousness when I ask that fiction should be devoid of offence?"

"Don't you mean devoid of truth?" He recovered his temper and his perspective. After all, he was very short of money. "All right, Sam," he said. "Edit me. Censor me. I thought I knew things, but there are deeps below the lowest depths, and you have reached them. I surrender. What are the terms?"

Sam offered terms which were quite generous. He might want Stewart again.

The novel was purged of Hetty and published. The three-page prayer of the distressed heroine was used, in paraphrase, from quite a number of nonconformist pulpits, and the book was a huge success. It was the first of that series—Branstone's Happy Novels for Healthy Homes—which carried the strength of the literary emetic to a point of concentrated sweetness undreamt of before, and discovered somewhere a public stomach which did not reject its nauseating jam, but revelled in it.

CHAPTER XVI
THE POLITICAL ANIMAL

IF only Ada had had the courage of what ought to have been her convictions, things would have been very different. But she hadn't the pluck or the zest in life to be anything at all except an almost perfect negative, and a man will fight for a wife for many reasons, but not for the reason that she is a full-stop.

Ada, as Peter knew when he consented to the marriage, could be led: with even surer hope of good result she could be driven, and if Sam had cared to drive, to play Petruchio with Ada, he could have turned her negative into a comparative, if not into a positive.

Unhappily, his driving powers were otherwise engaged, and his objectives were on the battlefield, his office, rather than in the dormitory which he might have turned into a home. And since Ada had all that she was conscious of wanting, she had a dull contentment. Two servants and credit at the shops were good enough for Ada, and good enough, too, for Sam, because they advertised success. If Ada had been actively vicious, if she had drunk, if men or a man had obsessed her, if indeed she had been anything that was bad perceptibly, Sam would have abandoned his indifference and taken a strong and effective line with her. It might, at first, have been only because a positively vicious Ada would have been bad for the Branstone Classics, but it would have ended by being good for Ada and for Sam: it would have been the beginning of Ada *and* Sam, of their dual life which had not yet come to birth. But, as it was, he saw nothing to fight. There was a superficial rightness; therefore all was right, he could forget Ada and turn to the things which were vital to him, business for its own sake, and business considered as a stepping-stone to politics.

He was content for some time to leave his political ambitions alone, because it seemed to him that money, quite a lot of money, was needed for politics. In truth, he was rather awed by his ambition: the House of Commons seemed a tremendous distance from his office in Manchester, and he thought a great deal of money would be needed for the fare. Fundamentally, he was modest and rarely overrated his abilities, but he believed that he had luck, and thought money a good first aid to more luck. Well as he was doing in business, he could not afford to divert his energies from moneymaking to politics, wherein he did not mean to begin at the bottom.

He was not ready yet to make political opportunities for himself, but if political opportunities came to him, that was another matter. And they did come. When he interviewed Sir William Gatenby, he threw a pebble into a pool whose wave was to wash him to high places.

It washed him into the knowledge of Mr. Charles Wattercouch, who was agent for the Division. Wattercouch read Gatenby's letter about Sam with some surprise, as one of his recruiting grounds for voluntary workers was the Concentrics, and he thought he recalled hearing Sam speak for the other faction, but he catalogued the name for future reference on his list of earnest young men.

Wattercouch, like Sam, was in no hurry. He preferred men to come to him, not to go in search of them, but Sam did not come, and a letter from Gatenby was not to be neglected. Though Gatenby had probably dismissed the subject from his mind, he paid half of Wattercouch's salary, and he might inquire about Sam some day. So the agent called on Sam at the office.

He was a square-built, square-faced man of forty, with a pink, eupeptic complexion, and light hair which bristled hardily. Your organizer of victory, like your editor, is apt to be cynical about the politics he is paid to profess, but Wattercouch kept his perfect faith in Liberalism, in spite of the fact that he served the Liberal Party, a feat in the accommodation of blameless principle with unscrupulous opportunism, which he accomplished with entire sincerity. One can be sincere and Jesuitical, in fact one can hardly be Jesuitical without being sincere, and to Mr. Wattercouch the most egregiously illiberal acts of the Liberal Party were justified because they were the acts of that party, and must, however improbable it seemed, be means to the end which was Liberalism.

This is not to suggest that Mr. Wattercouch was complex, for he was indeed quite simple, as witness the man's relish in his grotesque name. He knew the value of being ridiculed when one can turn ridicule into respect, and much of his popularity resulted from the genial way in which he took jokes about his name. He made an asset of what might, to a less good-natured man, have been a handicap. "Indeed," says Ben Jonson, "there is a woundy luck in names, sir," and Wattercouch turned doubtful luck to good account.

Sam had the gift of the gab, which means that he knew both how and when to speak, and how and when to be silent. He was silent while Mr. Wattercouch spoke of the valuable work to be done by an earnest labourer in connection with the annual revision of the register. The point of the work was to see that all possible known Liberals were on the register, and all possible objection taken to any known Conservatives, and, complicated as the work was by the removal habit amongst electors, it was no light undertaking. Certainly no agent could have carried it through without the aid of industrious volunteers.

But Sam did not see himself in the character of an industrious volunteer, and he was silent for two reasons. The first was that his silence was causing Mr. Wattercouch visible embarrassment, and Sam liked the other man to be embarrassed; the second was that he was considering how to make Mr. Wattercouch see that his suggestion was an absurdity, if not an insult.

He smiled with quite polite superiority. "But I think, Mr. Wattercouch, that you are making a mistake," he said, as one who apologizes for having to be blunt.

"Well," admitted Wattercouch, "I had my doubts, because I fancied I'd heard you support Stephen Verity at the Concentrics."

"That," said Sam, "is not the mistake to which I allude. I am aware that I have supported Verity at the Concentrics. And I am aware that the way to learn how to cut a man's hair is to practise on a sheep's head. Verity was my sheep's head."

"I'm afraid I hardly follow," said Wattercouch, who was indeed rather scandalized by such an allusion to Mr. Verity, who, if a Conservative, was an alderman and a noted figure in local politics.

"I will make it easier for you by admitting that even I had to learn," said Sam.

"Ah! I see. You have now seen the error of your ways. You realize the grandeur of Liberalism, the — —"

"I always did," Sam asserted. "When I supported Verity, I was teaching myself to speak. I was practising on Toryism that I might become perfect in Liberalism. Those days when I made a convenience of Toryism were the days of my apprenticeship to the art of speaking. Would you have had me speak badly for such a cause as Liberalism? No. But if I spoke badly for Toryism, I damaged nothing. Toryism *is* nothing unless, as I said, it is a sheep's head for Liberals to practise on when they are novices, and the mistake you made is to suppose that I am still a novice, when, as a matter of fact — —" He paused elaborately and hoped that Mr. Wattercouch would fill in the blank intelligently. "But it is premature to speak of that," he said. "As to the registration, I can send you one of my clerks." He made a gesture dismissing as an affair of pygmies that chief event of an agent's year.

"I see... I see," said Wattercouch, trying hard to believe that he had so far been looking at Sam through the wrong end of a telescope. "And you yourself, Mr. Branstone?"

It tempted Sam, that tone of quite startled respect which Wattercouch adopted now. The misfortune of Sam's imaginative flights was that he never knew when to stop. All that he cared about, at the moment, was to give Wattercouch the impression that Sam Branstone was too important to be asked to drudge at registration work. He was in no hurry about politics, but when he began it would not be as a volunteer clerk.

"I?" he replied. "Two things. One a fact and the other a prophecy. The fact is that I am an orator, and the prophecy is that Sir William Gatenby will not live long and that I shall take his place as member for the Division. Have you a cold?" he added, as Wattercouch choked with irresistible stupefaction.

He had not a cold, neither had he powers of speech just then, and the silence grew emphatic without in the least disconcerting Sam. Once launched on the sea of bluff, Sam was a hardy navigator, and he had the moral support of knowing that his whole purpose just now was to avoid being a clerk. To avoid being a clerk it is justifiable to do more than to romance: it is justifiable to commit most of the crimes in the Newgate Calendar. Sam was hardly asked to do that, but Wattercouch's cough was a challenge, and a bluff half bluffed is worse than no bluff at all. It became a matter of pride to convince this unbeliever.

"I intend," said Sam with aplomb, "to do a good deal of platform for the Party. If an election comes soon, so much the better. I shall take the opportunity to make myself more popular with the electors than Sir William Gatenby is. That is easy. He quotes Latin in election speeches, and I'm a man of the people. After that, I expect to contest a by-election for a seat which the Party regards as a forlorn hope. If it is possible to win that seat for our Great Cause, I shall win it. If not, I shall trust to two things, the senile decay of Sir William Gatenby and the discretion of the Whip's office."

Wattercouch was adapting himself painfully to the new perspective. He granted that Sam had plausibility, and an assurance which nearly lent conviction to his astonishing statement.

"You are in touch with the Whips!" he gasped.

Sam remembered and varied an old formula. "Do you suppose," he asked indignantly, "that I should be speaking to you like this if I were not?"

Wattercouch did not suppose it. For one thing he was acquainted with the devious ways of Whips, and nothing that those secretive autocrats did could surprise him: for another, he wished to believe what Sam wished him to believe. He saw in Sam the way out of a dilemma.

His dilemma was a common one. A death had caused a vacancy in the Town Council, and the local Liberal caucus was almost pathetically embarrassed as to its choice of a candidate. There were at least three veteran workers for the Cause who expected, with justice, to be approached and none of the three could be selected without offence being given to interests which it was impolitic to offend.

It was all very well for the caucus: they left it to Wattercouch, the general handy man, to make suggestions, and as he listened to Sam he thought he had found a candidate who, simply because he was politically unknown, could offend nobody. If the obvious men were wrong, he must rely on the rightness of the unexpected, and, after all, Sam might be speaking the truth. One never knew where one was with Whips, and here was his chance to propitiate Sam and at the same time to solve the problem which troubled the caucus. Sam was a dark horse and he wished he knew more about him; it was startling to come in search of a voluntary clerk and to find a candidate; but, finally, he saw it as a legitimate case for taking a risk.

"I don't know, sir," he said, with a very pretty respect in his voice, "whether municipal politics will appeal to a man of your calibre, but there is a vacancy in St. Mary's Ward, and I hardly think there will be any difficulty about your adoption as candidate if you cared to stand."

Sam pretended to reflect. The truth was that the prospect of an immediate seat in the Council made his heart beat fiercely. He had meant for a while longer to put business before politics, but this sort of politics was business. The Council took up one's time, but conferred a prestige on Branstone and the Branstone Publications which would more than compensate for the waste of time.

And it was deliciously unexpected. He had not studied to impress Wattercouch, but had talked exaltedly simply to excuse himself from the unseen, thankless drudgery of organization: yet it seemed he had impressed. Virtually, he was offered a seat, He was, this soon, to sit where Travers had sat, to be a City Father before he was thirty-five. He had romanced glibly about a bird in the bush, and found himself grasping a bird in hand, and no contemptible fowl either.

"We must despise nothing," he said, "which makes for Liberalism." Wattercouch nodded with enthusiasm. "Of course," Sam went on, "strictly between ourselves, the Council is small beer. But it is for the Cause, and if I were asked to stand, you may take it that I should not allow the larger view I have of my ultimate activities to interfere with my acceptance. I take pleasure in duty and I see it as my duty, even if it involves the postponement of my Parliamentary ambitions, to throw myself wholeheartedly into this conflict." He was wonderfully pious.

Wattercouch was less emotional. He had heard too many speeches from prospective candidates to be carried away by Sam's. "Quite probably there will be no contest," he said dryly. "It's a safe Liberal seat."

"I should have preferred a fight," Sam lied wistfully. "But I put duty first."

As a fact, there was no contest, and if each of the three veteran workers thought himself aggrieved, he had the consolation of knowing that the other two shared his grievance. Wattercouch was discreetly mysterious about Sam in the inner councils of the local Party, used Gatenby's name freely and managed to convey that Branstone was something much bigger than he appeared to be. He had, at least, got them out of their quandary.

Nor did Sam discredit his sponsor either at the private meeting he addressed or at the public one which followed. He had said he was an orator, Wattercouch had repeated it indefatigably, and Sam's audience believed it implicitly. He was not quite an orator, but was coming along nicely under the tuition of an old actor who had failed on the stage and now called himself a professor of elocution.

He became Mr. Councillor Branstone, and happy little references to the event began to appear in the papers. The *Sunday Judge*, for instance, had "no doubt that Mr. Branstone will live to look back upon his unopposed return to the Council as a minor episode of his political career, and we speak by the book. Branstone will go far, but, meantime, it is something even for him to know that he is the most popular man in St. Mary's Ward. We had almost written in the whole city, but that would be to anticipate. How is it done? How is such popularity achieved? How, in other words, did merit become recognized? Mr. Branstone himself only smiled when we asked him, but his smile is half of his secret and his rousing, earnest oratory the other half. They are indeed an open smile and an open secret. But there are other secrets less open. All we shall say now is, 'Watch Branstone. He will not disappoint you.'"

There was a low evening paper, run in the Conservative interest, which fastened on the phrase "other secrets less open" and published the scurrilous statement that one of the less open secrets was the fact that Mr. Councillor Branstone's mother was a charwoman, but the paragraph appeared only in the early edition and unaccountably disappeared from later issues. It did no harm, as first editions are not published for politicians, but for sportsmen, and, in any case, there was a brief, but dignified, eulogy of Mr. Branstone in the *Manchester Warden* next day. That paper happened, fortunately, to be Liberal in politics, and indeed to be, on just occasion, a valiant log-roller. It rolled a log for Sam; the popularity of Branstone was established, hall-marked by the Press; and it was about this time that Stewart's second potboiler was accepted for inclusion in Branstone's Novels. The terms were even more favourable to the author than before.

CHAPTER XVII
THE VERITY AFFAIR

THE curse of the Wandering Jew is upon the advertiser: he must move perpetually. Not that Sam would have been in any case content to sit idly on a seat in the Council Chamber. He hadn't the sedentary gifts, nor was he of the breed of Ada, who, the state of matrimony once achieved, existed in contemplation of a glory which was even more vegetable than animal.

He had to do something to justify a paper reputation for popularity and he had even to convince himself that he would not soon wake up to find it all a dream. It had happened too easily to be true, or, at least, safe. Wattercouch had hinted that things were expected of him.

They were, of course, expected of him as a Liberal, and Sam was not, in fact, a Liberal but a Conservative. A Conservative is a man who conserves, who says "Aye" to the words of Giovanni Malatesta.

"What I have snared, in that I set my teeth
And lose with agony."

Sam had snared, he proposed to go on snaring and never to lose what he had snared. Whereas a Liberal is a Conservative weakened by sentimental compassion for the dispossessed. He is not the opposite of a Conservative, but a Conservative who is weak-minded, or timid or scrupulous enough to think himself a robber and to propose to give the poor some five per cent of his plunder. The opposite of a Conservative is an anarchist.

Politically he was a Liberal because he thought the Liberals certain to come in for a long innings at the next election, and if there was any feeling about it at all (beyond a desire to be on the winning side), it was for the pudgy orator whose tremendous sentences had caught his imagination when he visited the House of Commons.

What he did became known as the Verity affair. It might with equal and perhaps superior justice have been called the Branstone affair but for that malicious impulse which causes people to refer to a scandal by the name of the exposed rather than the exposer. It is like the odium which we attach to a man who has been in prison, where he had already had his punishment. Mankind is resolute against letting sleeping dogs lie.

Mr. Alderman Verity was an elder statesman of the Council and a Conservative of the honest, unyielding type who thought that to approve of Tory Democracy was to be either a rogue or a fool, and Sam objected to him not because he was a Conservative, but for deeper reasons. Verity was the landlord of Sam's offices. Every tenant objects to every landlord.

One calls Verity an honest Conservative because he made no concessions, not because he was himself a fount of honour. He had no sympathy with the modern mawkishness about pampering the people. He admitted that one had to make promises, that the way to win elections was to tickle the elector as if he were a trout, but as an Alderman he sat above the cockpit of electioneering and frowned upon the Liberal attitudes to which younger Conservatives descended to catch a vote. And their view that the Council existed for the people honestly revolted him: it was so patently the other way about.

The particular instance was Baths in Hulme. He saw no sense in Baths in Hulme. He was quite sincere in his belief that to build Baths in Hulme was to cast pearls before swine. Hulme had not asked for Baths and did not want Baths. Baths were opportunities for cleanliness and Hulme did not want to be clean. Hulme would not be Hulme if it were clean.

The uncleanliness of Hulme was an institution. Conservatives conserve institutions, and the only thing which could remove his Conservative and Aldermanic objection to Baths in Hulme was self-interest.

Self-interest is the greatest institution of them all.

He continued to oppose the young bloods of his Party because for a long time he did not see where his self-interest came in. He even opposed them publicly. He said in public that Baths in Hulme were a nasty, pandering, Liberal idea and that no decent-minded Conservative could think of it without nausea. And then, suddenly and silently, he was found to be with those who proposed that Hulme should bathe if it wanted to. His change of mind coincided with the discovery that there was no open space in Hulme where Baths could be erected. Something would have to come down that the Baths might go up, and what would come down, and why, was the secret of Mr. Alderman Verity and one or two others of the Old Gang who had the habit of standing loyally by each other when a little simple jobbery was in question. Really, it was too simple to be reprehensible. If a Town Council can by one and the same resolution clear away a slum, and confer Baths, who benefits, and doubly, but the Town? Naturally, the slum owner has to be compensated, though adequate compensation can hardly be put high enough. Slums are so profitable.

Wattercouch had many preoccupations just now, but his vigilance was a habit, and he was struck by the change in Mr. Alderman Verity's attitude. The silence which succeeded his eloquence seemed pregnant with something, and Wattercouch wondered with what. It was an error of judgment in the Alderman not to be ill at this time, but he had covered his tracks and the affair was prejudged, settled before it ever came before the Council. Verity had neither conscience nor fears about it, and the Conservative Party, with a prescient eye on the imminent General Election, was going to use its majority in the Council that it might figure as the Party which bestowed cleanliness on Hulme.

Wattercouch wondered why it was Simpson's Buildings which those benefactors of mankind proposed to buy and demolish so as to clear a site for their Baths.

"This might be your opportunity, Branstone," he said.

"Isn't it asking a good deal of the junior member of the Council to suggest that he tackle an old hand like Alderman Verity?" asked Sam, leaning back in his chair with his thumbs in his waistcoat armholes.

"We all expect great things of you," flattered Wattercouch, who had still to justify his selection of Sam to the Liberal caucus.

"I don't intend to fail you, either. But I can't oppose these Baths. As a Liberal I am in favour of them."

"So are we all. But we are not in favour of Alderman Verity's being in favour of them."

"It's David and Goliath to pit me against Verity, Wattercouch."

"David won."

"And Samuel will win. But he will make a condition. The condition is a free hand. I want no help and no advice and I undertake on that condition to pulverize Verity."

"But you'll tell me what you propose to do?"

"I said a free hand, Wattercouch. Leave this to me and I'll settle it."

It seemed to Wattercouch that every time he had dealings with Sam he was asked to take a gambling chance, but he had no plan of action, and the man without a plan is always at a disadvantage against the man who, with or without a plan, looks confident. He left it to Sam and there was, as it happened, nobody to whom he could have left it better.

Wattercouch had no inside information and only vague suspicions that Verity's change of mind was rooted in the same earth as Verity's self-interest.

But Sam knew something and was not boasting idly when he undertook to "pulverize" Verity.

What he knew, rightly used at the right moment, was dynamic enough, but he lacked evidence and he did not see how to get evidence. The Council meeting was at hand and he was finding it each day more difficult to grin with cheerful assurance at the mutely questioning Wattercouch. He felt distinctly unassured.

The facts were clear enough to him. Verity now approved of the Baths because they were to be erected on the site of Simpson's Buildings, and Verity owned that dilapidated pile. He did not own it publicly because respectable aldermen do not own slum property; he owned it in the name of Mr. Sylvester Lamputt, Verity's second cousin, a man of straw; and Sam knew that he owned it because he had a good memory, he remembered a conversation between Lamputt and Mr. Travers, which he had overheard, and all the present circumstances pointed to the relations of Lamputt with Verity being as they had been when Sam was in the estate agent's office.

Verity was aware that retail profits are higher than wholesale, and small retail than large retail; that when, for instance, a poor woman buys an ounce of tea she pays a higher rate for it than when a rich woman buys a pound or ten pounds, and similarly that when a family rents a room in a slum property it pays immensely more for it proportionately than when a cotton king rents a warehouse in the centre of the city. But it is dignified to let a warehouse to a cotton king, and disreputable to let single rooms in Hulme, so second cousin Lamputt was the putative owner of Simpson's Buildings. Sam smiled at the ludicrous thought of the burly alderman sheltering behind the shrivelled form of his second cousin Lamputt. It was like trying to hide a bull behind a weasel.

But he did not smile often in those days. He paid a visit, at dusk, to Simpson's Buildings, and breathed softly lest Simpson's Buildings should collapse upon him. Obviously, the alderman was finding his market in the nick of time. It eliminated doubt, but did not provide proof.

He knew that in the matter of Simpson's Buildings, Lamputt was identical with Verity, but he wanted evidence, and to get evidence he must rely upon the dullness of Mr. Lamputt, and did not think that he was dull. The totem of Lamputt was certainly a ferret, and Sam credited the ferret tribe with nimble wit. He had to be more nimble, then.

He rejected the idea of making Mr. Lamputt gloriously drunk because it seemed impossible to associate glory, even the glory of intoxication, with Mr. Lamputt's feeble body. It was a case, as usual with Sam, of taking chances.

He did nothing at all until the morning of the meeting which was to decide if Hulme might bathe, and, even then, left his office only a little before his usual time for going to the Town Hall. He turned into a back street, ran up many stairs to the attic office whose door bore the name of Sylvester Lamputt, Agent (more sins are committed in the name of agency than of charity), and flung panting into the single room.

He won the first throw in his game. Sylvester was in.

He sat on a high office stool writing on the malodorous page of an enormous ledger, looking for all the world like a diminutive office boy on whom some one has fitted, in cruel jest, a hoary head. If the calendars on his walls were trustworthy witnesses, he was agent for half the insurance companies in the British Isles. Autolycus was Sylvester's other name.

He reverenced his ledger as other men reverence the Bible. He kept no other diary, for the ledger was his book of life, and when Sam burst upon him he was absorbed in his records. He closed the book mechanically through pure secretive habit, and closed into it just enough of his wits to put him at a disadvantage with Sam.

Sam gave no quarter. "Mr. Verity," he gasped before he was fairly in the room. "Simpson's Buildings... the title-deeds... here, or has Mr. Verity got them?"

It succeeded. Lamputt took him for an urgent special messenger from Verity. "If Mr. Verity's memory is going," he said with dignity, "mine is not. The title-deeds are in the third drawer of his safe in his office."

"In his name?" asked Sam quickly.

"Of course," said Lamputt, and then, too late, became suspicious. "I say," he began, "what — — —-?"

But Sam had gone, and though Mr. Lamputt reached his hat and the door in one bound and careered down his familiar stairs like the office boy his figure aped, Sam had turned a corner and was lost to sight. Lamputt raced to Verity's office, only to find that the alderman was then attending a Council meeting. Lamputt could do no more, indeed for a man with a weak heart he had already done too much: but he had a strong foreknowledge of the wrath of Alderman Verity, and goes, an unhappy, shrinking figure, out of this story to an unknown fate.

Sam went to the Town Hall with his bomb-shell, and they disapprove of bombs at Council meetings, so he was sedulous to spare their feelings. He supported that part of the resolution which referred to the erection of Baths, but proposed that it should stand alone and that the naming of a site should be deferred. Curiously, his proposal made the Conservative majority very angry: the resolution was one and indivisible. Sam regretted that in order to vote against the misuse of a particular site, he was forced to vote against the Baths, but standing as he did for purity in civic life, detesting the very shadow of jobbery, he had no alternative but to move that the resolution be rejected. Here was a proposal which, however innocent its wording, did in fact imply that ratepayers' money was to be handed over to a prominent member of the party opposite, to a gentleman in whose safe, at whose office, in the third drawer of the safe, were deposited at that moment the title-deeds of the property whose acquisition by the city was suggested. He abhorred personalities, he shrank from mentioning a name, and if the second part of the resolution were withdrawn, he— —

It was too much for a young, impetuous innocent opposite. "You dare not mention a name. You lie."

Sam hoped the Council would absolve him of causing a scene.

"Prove your words," cried the rash gentleman.

"I suggest," said Sam blandly, "that we avoid unpleasantness. I have made a statement and I am asked to prove it. If a deputation of three will go with me and Mr. Alderman Verity to his office, the title-deeds of Simpson's Buildings will be found in the place I have indicated."

It was the sort of drama which appealed more to the readers of the evening papers than to the Council. Mr. Mayor, in the chair, was speechless in embarrassed distress. Sam had the calm of imperishable rock in wind-tossed surf. In the midst of a breathless excitement, Mr. Alderman Verity was seen to totter to his feet. "I own the property," he said, collapsed into his seat and graced that seat no more.

Impossible even for a Conservative paper to uphold Verity, impossible to do more than to suggest that Sam's manners were deplorable: while his own papers made a hero of him, found his manners a model of consideration and his triumph as graceful as it was complete.

All Sam cared to know was that he was on the crest of a wave of popularity and a general election was at hand. Night after night he spoke, and the tritest platitudes, with Sam's smile behind them, shone like new-found truth. He was *persona gratissima* before he opened his mouth: it gave him confidence, and confidence is half the speaker's battle. He coined some of those ugly, smart, journal-easy catch-words which help to win elections, and are quoted in the papers and blossom on the placards. And, with it all, he became what he had prematurely called himself, an orator.

He had the satisfaction of watching audiences sit through the boredom of Gatenby that they might hear Branstone, and of being himself the "star" speaker at outlying meetings. Gatenby was returned by a record majority and it was Bran-stone for whom the mob yelled outside the Town Hall.

The election was an early one, and Sam was called to speak in other constituencies. He had wires, not only from agents in quite distant divisions, but actually from Headquarters. He was in touch with the Whips! Less than a year after he had lied to Wattercouch, the lie turned true. He was in touch with the Whips, a wanted speaker, a man of reputation, a name to be applauded when it was announced on a platform, for all the world like people applaud when the number of a star performer goes up on the announcement board of a music-hall. He was not of the Great Unwanted, but of the few who were wanted.

Someone discovered at this time the old canard which had once appeared in the first edition of an evening paper, that his mother was a charwoman. He did not deny it, but used it as Wattercouch his name, making an asset of a handicap. He was of the people, blood of their blood, a democrat by birth, knowing their aspirations and their needs because he, too, had needed and aspired. In the heat of that election he became egregiously a Radical. It told, it "went" with the audiences: that was the thing that mattered to Sam. He hadn't so much as the shadow of a principle, he was winning, on the winning side, and pleased himself enormously.

And by the end of the campaign he stood, actually, where he had aimed to stand: amongst prospective candidates who fight, as it were, probationary elections where, they have scarcely a sporting chance, to pay their footing towards the sort of candidature which gives a man his seat. If the Conservatives had offered him a tolerably safe seat, without preliminary fight, he would have ratted eagerly, and the charwoman his mother would have been pressed into service on the other side. It was all one to Sam Branstone.

CHAPTER XVIII
WHEN EFFIE CAME

THEN Effie came with beauty, shattering the life he lived as sunshine breaks the April clouds. At first he did not know what had happened to him: there was a radiance, but he thought it nothing greater than her physical appeal. He was disturbed, moved as nothing had moved him before—not even applause—but did not see that more had come to him than loveliness where all had been unlovely. He did not realize that there were greater things in Effie than her comeliness.

She was the daughter of a doctor who had lived up to every penny of his income and died leaving his widow nothing but a cottage in the country, which had been their week-end haunt. The widow sold the practice and got for it enough to keep herself, with care, in the cottage.

There Mrs. Mannering lived unhappily, resentfully, nourishing a grudge against her poverty, developing a vein of hardy thrift unseen till now. With management, she had enough, but lacked the gift of management. She did not see things in proportion, imagined herself deep sunk in poverty and made unreasoning demands on Effie. On Effie, not on her son who managed a rubber plantation at Penang and followed the spendthrift habits of his father. Father and son, the Mannerings were cursed with a passion for popularity and entertained with open house to all comers. In the East, it cost Rex Mannering more than it had cost his father at home and, granted his habits, he was right in saying that he could do nothing for his mother. He could deny himself nothing.

It left the more for Effie. She who was not trained to work must go into the world and fight not only for her bread but for her mother's luxuries. Augusta Mannering was merciless in her demands. She believed, quite sincerely, that Eflie was gaining riches in the offices of Manchester and withholding a share from her in simple self-indulgence. Was it not by going to offices that Dr. Mannering's rich patients had been able to pay their bills? And hadn't they an army of friends who used to eat their salt?

But the friends, misunderstanding Effie's pride, offered no help of the kind she could accept. She wanted work, not invitations to houses where, with dress and servants' tips, it would cost her more to live than in the rooms she found in Rusholme. She had not the means to be decorative now, and it occurred to nobody that Effie was a clerk, wanting a clerk's place. They could not think of her, that brilliant girl, shackled to a typewriter. They did not offer what she wanted and she was too proud to ask.

Then memories are short, especially of the popular men who buy their popularity across the dining-table and charge high fees to the unwell to procure high feeding for the well; and when the Mannerings disappeared, Augusta to her cottage and Effie to Rusholme, there were few inquiries made.

Some other entertainer stepped into the breach of local hospitality; Effie's net-play became a legend on their tennis lawns; and she herself was deemed to be with her mother in the country, shining on other courts than theirs.

It was not pure callousness, but things are as they are, and one cannot live by money and then lose money without losing more than money.

Effie went into the city unfriended and alone, and her mother lived, a miser, in her cottage. She wrote to Effie that she needed this and that; that Effie must spare of her abundance or her mother must starve, and Effie out of her thirty shillings a week did send, but her mother did not buy. She warmed her hands at a bank-book, wore ancient clothes and watched her credit grow. It was more than a perversion of her old extravagance, it was insanity and Effie knew it. To keep an insane woman moderately happy, she sacrificed necessities. That is why she was shabby when she came into Mr. Branstone's office for the post of typist one bright, revealing afternoon soon after his party had triumphed at the polls and he had made himself a figure on the hustings.

Effie had found companionship in Rusholme, and knew by now the difference between the friendship which is given and the friendship which is bought. She had become expert in friendship, and Sam, from their first encounter, seemed to her more like a friend than an employer. By then, she had experience of employers. That was why she was out of work.

It wasn't, of course, the normal Sam she met, but a Sam exalted, genuinely raised and not merely puffed up, by his electioneering notoriety. He had a new self-confidence; it seemed to him that little was beyond his reach, that he might even hope to come to terms with Effie. Not, that is to say, to such terms as her last employer had proposed. Sam was not, in these matters, the average sensual man. The point was, and it was to his credit, that he discerned something fine in Effie even at this stage, and the mood of confidence gave him to hope that he might not seem commonplace to her. Already, that afternoon, he cared so much. Her opinion mattered.

It mattered so greatly that he went slowly about the business of surprising her: for that, of course, was what he thought he had to do. She might not know things about Branstone which it was good for her to know. He might be any employer who advertised for a typist, and he was not any employer. He was Branstone, of the Classics and the Novels; town councillor; politician; and she must be told about him. She must learn what manner of man he was. He wanted to tell her how much greater he was going to be, but decided that could wait. First she must know what he had done, before it came to telling her what he was going to do, and his record would come better from others than from himself. In the office they knew it all and, even if she asked no questions, there was much which the routine work would tell her of him.

He curbed impatience and left her for some weeks in the general office, where it was supposed that she was picking up some knowledge of the business before beginning to act as his secretary, but what he hoped she was picking up was some knowledge of him. He had the idea that he was popular with his staff, and did not think that they would libel him to her.

All the time he burned to have her sitting with him in the private office. It was for that purpose that he had advertised for a typist-secretary, and to bring her from the general office could excite no comment. On the contrary, to leave her there so long might look strange or at least suggest that Effie was a failure. A failure! Much he cared whether she was efficient at her work. Yet she was splendidly efficient, and still he coquetted with his purpose of having her with him. It seemed to him that to call her in would be a step definite and irrevocable, one which he wanted and even yearned to make, but about which he hesitated sensuously as a bridegroom might hesitate on the threshold of the bridal chamber. He neglected to make two certainly profitable journeys to London at this time because he could not deny himself the pleasure of seeing her neck as she bent over her typewriter when he passed through the office.

And he had hardly spoken to her! But his dreams were vibrant with the music of her voice, swelling like an organ till it filled his life with new harmony. It filled his life not because he refused to think of Ada, but because he could not think of her. Ada wasn't there; she didn't exist. She never had been there, for Sam, in the true sense, so that the step from the custom which is nothingness to complete nothingness was almost imperceptible. She was a ghost from the past fading in the radiance of the present. The sun puts out the candlelight.

He was seeing Effie, of course, with quite grotesquely unperceiving eyes. She might have been, for all he saw of her, the beautiful doll she emphatically was not. Her outside pleased and satisfied his eye, and he took it for granted that the woman within would satisfy him in the same way as the woman without. And so, in the long run, she did, but not till Sam had made a hurdle race of it and come some awkward croppers on the course. The harmony of his organ dream might have been true prophecy; it certainly was not present fact. He wasn't seeing himself as Effie saw him, or the sidelong glances he cast at her pretty neck might have expressed more desire to break than to kiss it.

He seemed to her a jolly monster, quite lovable if trained, but at present as untrained as a badly brought-up dog, and perhaps too old to learn. But it might be amusing to see if he could learn, and from her who was not used to breaking in a mastiff. That made the thing worth while, his bigness and the lovableness she recognized behind the rankness of him. Chance might not come her way, and she thought it unlikely that it would, but if it did, she meant to take it with both hands. Effie, aged twenty-six, proposed to herself to form Sam Bran-stone, who was thirty-five and her employer! She smiled at her preposterous audacity, but the more she saw and the more she heard of him, the more determination bit into her. Droll, officious, absurd—all these her idea was, and she liked it because it was fantastic and because Sam was Sam. In Effie's wise, impertinent eyes fantasy and Sam seemed bound together. And yet he paid her wages; he was a solid man, a member of the Council, and a serious politician! She was impertinent indeed.

But he could not, either for his sake or hers, keep her for ever on the threshold. For all his late-won confidence he was quite pitiably nervous, and held back for days in pure hesitation before the simple action of calling her into his office. He thought of it as initiation, a ritual to which a high solemnity attached. He intended to act up to its solemnity, to usher her into that office with all that was most impressive, to signify to her the importance of being secretary to Branstone; and, instead, he who was wordy fumbled for words, he who was painfully correct dropped two aitches in a sentence, and stood there most comically aghast at his slip.

Of course, the ritual was finished; one cannot be ritualistic and conscious of aitchlessness. Ritual implies the superhuman, the something, at least, which sets the executant above the common clay, and to drop an aitch is human. In the moment of solemnity, in the mouth of the ritualist, it is drolly human. We find incongruity amusing, and the more solemn the occasion the more readily does an impish mirth intrude on light pretext.

Effie giggled. She did not mean to be unkind, but the spectacle of his confusion was too much for her. She hadn't the strength to resist, and though she turned her giggle, quite neatly, into a cough, it was not before he had seen.

This was his great moment, to which he had looked forward, and she giggled at him! He felt himself writ down an ass, and wondered for the fraction of a second whether he would get more satisfaction from smacking her or from kicking himself. Then he saw her looking at him, and nothing seemed to matter. He dropped aitches and she giggled. Very well, then he wasn't a superman, and she wasn't divine. They were human beings, at this moment in the relationship of employer and employed.

"In future, you will sit at the little desk in here, Miss Mannering." He met her eye defiantly as he spoke the "here."

"If you have your notebook you can take this letter down."

He was running away from his ruined situation. To dictate a letter to her had not been in the scheme at all, as he had planned it. It was a refuge, and a safe one, but as he dictated he saw in the letter his opportunity to indicate to her that he forgave the giggle. He was writing to an author about a manuscript, which he intended to publish, but broke off before he reached that decisive point of his letter.

"Wait a bit," he said. "Here is the novel I am writing about. I want your opinion of it to fortify my own before I do anything definite. Will you have a look at it in here? I'm due at a Council meeting and must go."

"Certainly, Mr. Branstone," she said; "but my judgment isn't very reliable."

"We don't know that until you try," he said, escaping from his office to the Town Hall, where he kicked his heels for an hour till the meeting began Nor did he return to business that day. He had a shyness and a feeling of deflation. He needed time before he could expand again.

Effie took her reading of the novel conscientiously rather than seriously, not supposing that her verdict either way would go for anything, but appreciating his hint of confidence, and the fact that, considered as work, novel-reading was pleasant. And not finishing the manuscript at the office, she took it home with her to Rusholme.

In Rusholme the landladies are a little humanized from their primitive Grundyism, partly by the girl clerk, but mainly because few of them have avoided, at one time or another, the theatrical lodger, a valiant tilter at conventionalities; and it is possible for a woman in lodgings to be called upon by a man in the evening without being evicted as a sinner. One must, of course, choose one's landlady with discretion.

Effie, who had not had the opportunity of selecting her parents and had suffered accordingly, chose her landlady with discretion. By now she had her friends, those she had made in Manchester, not those she inherited from her father; there were men amongst them, and they came to see her. Often, in fact, and especially on Sundays, her room was over-crowded; but a bed, in the semi disguise of a travelling rug, holds many callers, and they solved the problem of hospitality by bringing each a contribution to the feast.

To-night she had one caller, Stewart, who, having been brought one Sunday by a man who knew a woman who was a fellow-clerk with Effie at her last-but-one place, had formed the habit of coming as often as he could. He was not at the *Warden* office that night, for the same reason which accounted for his not knowing that she had gone to Branstone's. He was convalescent after influenza, too limp to write the super-journalism of the *Warden*, well enough to come out to take the tonic called Effie.

"I ought not to let you in to-night," she said. "Thank Heaven for that," he said, coming in. "Doing what one ought is the dullest thing I know— unless you're really serious, Effie? In which case I'll go." His hand was on the door-knob.

"I'm really serious," she said with mock impressiveness. "I'm working overtime. Behold!" She threw herself on the bed with the manuscript in hand. "This," she announced, "is Work."

"I can believe it," he said, "because that looks like the typescript of a novel. If it were mine it would be a pleasure to read; but as it is not mine, it is probably work."

"Oh, it's work all right," she said. "Hard labour, too. I'm reading it by order of my new chief. He publishes things like this."

Stewart sat up. "Not Branstone?" he, said. "Don't say you've gone to Sammy!"

"Yes. Do you know him?"

"Know him? I invented him. Bit of a Frankenstein for all that. Better say I know most of him. He can still spring surprises on me, and you in his office are one of'em."

"Why? Don't you like his office?"

"It's an office. So long as you've to be in an office, you could pick worse—easily. Sammy's a stream with a lot of shallows in him, but there are also depths, and I've never fathomed them. There's mud in him, but it's not the nasty sort of mud."

"I've seen that much," she said. "Polluted but curable."

"You're not by any chance thinking of yourself as a Branstone River Conservancy, are you?"

"I rather like him, Dubby," she said.

"Good Lord! You and Sam: I say, old thing, no offence, but you know he's married?"

"I know," said Ellie. "What's she like?"

"Haven't seen her since I was his best man. Wasn't tempted to see more of her."

"It's as bad as that?"

"Oh, rather worse, I believe. Pitch that novel over. I'll tell you in five minutes if it's any use."

"Five minutes isn't very fair to the author," she protested.

"Oh, quite. I'm a reviewer, and reviewing's badly paid. It teaches you to rip the guts out of a novel quickly. Smoke that cigarette and I'll tell you all about it by the time you're through."

He fluttered the pages while she smoked. "Utter," he decided. "Utter."

"I haven't finished it," she said; "but so far I agree with you."

"You'll agree with me to the end. Pluperfect trash. Sam will love it."

"What!"

"You'll see. It's just his line."

"Aren't you trying to prejudice me against him?"

He stared. "I'm trying to save you the trouble of reading the beastly thing. I've given you expert opinion. It's trash and the brand of trash that he likes. Didn't I tell you there, was mud in Sam?"

"You told me you invented him. I don't believe your influence has been for good."

"Don't be hard on a fellow, Effie; I only introduced him to the mud. I didn't know he'd wallow. Anyhow, let's talk of something else."

"You know," she said, "you do influence people, Dubby."

"Of course. That's what I'm paid for. I'm a journalist. Have you never heard of the power of the Press? It means a lot of little journalists like me writing as their editors tell 'em to. But I don't appear to have much influence on you. I asked you to change the subject and you're still thinking about Sam."

"Yes," she agreed, "I'm still thinking of Sam."

"You and Sam!" he repeated, looking incredulously at her.

Effie nodded. "But," she said, "I don't know yet."

He rose to his feet. "You're sure, Effie? You're sure you don't know about him yet?"

"Quite sure."

"Then you do know about me? Effie, I've got to ask. Are you sure about me?"

She met his eyes bravely, knowing that she must hurt. She was sure she did not love Stewart, who was free, and not sure about Branstone, who was married. "I am quite, quite sure, Dubby," she said softly.

"I see," he said. "Well, I'm not the sort that pesters, but if you want me, Effie, if you find you want me, I'll be there. I... I suppose I'd better go now. It will take some doing to change the subject after this."

"Dubby, I'm sorry. You're not well, and——"

She could see him trembling.

"Not that, old thing," he interrupted. "Not pity. That would make me really ill. Love's just a thing that happens along, but one starter doesn't make a race." He held out his hand. "Well, doctor's orders to go to bed early. Good-night."

"Good-night, Dubby," she said, and added hesitatingly: "You'll come on Sunday?"

"Lord, yes," he said. "I don't love and run away. Good-night."

She sat for a long while staring into vacancy, then found that something wet was dropping on her hands. She bathed her eyes and took the novel up again. A proposal occupied, she found, twelve pages of turgid, emotional dialogue; but, of course, her experience might be limited. Certainly it did not confirm the book's verbosity.

She was quite sure that she did not want Dubby Stewart. He did not strike her as humorous at all.

CHAPTER XIX
EFFIE IN LOVE

SEVERAL causes combined to make her think of Sam, too, as not at all humorous when she saw him in the morning. Unlike him, she was not at her best in the early hours of the day, and the strain of arriving at an office by nine a.m. was one from which she did not recover for some time. She hated business, but without that cross of early rising she might have found it almost tolerable.

She woke that day to her landlady's rap more resentfully than usual. The world was disgustingly mismanaged. Why couldn't she love Dubby, who was free? She couldn't, but she hated Sam for being married, he had no right to be married. "Damn Mrs. Sam! Damn her!" she said heartily, by way of a morning prayer, as she ran hairpins viciously into her glorious hair. "But I'll cure him of mud," she added, as she raced downstairs to swallow the tea and toast which she took almost in the same rush that carried her from her bedroom to the tram.

She reached the office and walked into Sam's room to find him already in possession. His obvious briskness at that hour struck her as almost indecent; it was, at any rate, another cause for resentment, and one of which he was himself quite blandly unaware.

He was not stealing a march upon her any more than he habitually stole marches on the rest of the world. He knew that early morning suited him, and used it to advantage. They were certain in town that Branstone had luck rather than brains because he was lazy; but if a man arrives at his office at eight a.m., and puts in two hours of solid work by ten o'clock, he is well ahead of his fellows of the employing class who go down to offices on the 9.21 from home. He can afford to appear lazy.

He liked that uninterrupted hour with the books, opened the letters himself, and had them annotated before the men came, whose business it was to deal with their contents. He planned out the day's work, and saw it in hand before his earliest caller came. After ten, which is the first hour when it is etiquette for a salesman to call, Sam was never too busy to talk of matters which were not strictly business—with the right, the gainful caller.

It was known that one could kill time pleasantly with Branstone. Branstone was a lazy fellow, and his office a good place to sit in on a wet afternoon, when there was no point in going to Old Trafford.

He came this morning even earlier than usual, to be ready for Effie when she came at nine. He had slept off his embarrassment, and was ready in his early morning ebullience to pooh-pooh it. It was stupid to be so extraordinarily sensitive about an aitch. Accent had always troubled him, but he need not overrate its importance, and especially now that he wore the political badge of a democrat, and had acknowledged publicly that his mother was a charwoman.

So he was here, installed in his chair with the back of his morning's work broken, waiting for her when she came.

No, she decided, not at all humorous to-day: formidable, in fact. He had all the advantages; he was seated; he was first upon the ground, and that ground his own, and he was abominably awake. He might have run away yesterday, but this was the morning of retrieval.

"Good morning," he said, assuming an attitude of leisure.

"Good morning," she said, then saw that he was looking quizzically at the parcel she carried, as if, she thought, he mistook it for her lunch. "I took the novel home to finish," she explained nervously, and called herself a fool for giving him this readymade chance to open the subject which of all things she wanted to delay until her suaver hour had come. She might be able to cure him of mud, but a doctor should have a bedside manner, and she distrusted her manners until the landlady's knock had ceased ringing in her ears.

If she had not given him the chance, he would have made it. He gave no quarter to bad starters. Had he known of her weakness, he might have spared her. He might, because she was Effie; but it wasn't his habit to indulge the weaknesses of others, especially a weakness which he did not share, did not understand, and denied to be anything but sloth.

"Yes," he said encouragingly. "And the verdict?"

"Does my verdict matter, Mr. Branstone?" she asked. He hadn't given her time to get her jacket off!

"What? Certainly it matters. I wasn't asking you to waste your time when I gave you the manuscript to read. The question is whether we ought to publish it, and the answer depends on your opinion."

"Is that quite fair—to the author, I mean? My opinions of novels are inexpert."

"That author can take care of himself very well," he assured her. "He won't starve if we refuse his novel."

"I'm afraid my opinions are also intolerant," she said.

"Still," he smiled, "I should like to hear them."

"They might infuriate you, and—well, I'd rather not be sacked if I can help it."

"We will forget that it is in my power to sack you. Does that satisfy you?"

Oh, how she loathed people who could be magnanimous at nine a.m.! "You are being very kind," she said.

"And you are not giving me your opinion. Come, Miss Mannering, you've read it. What do you think of it?"

Later in the day she might have put it more gently. Just now she could manage nothing more kindly than: "I think it's appalling. It's false from start to finish," and she rejoiced to see how much her vehement candour disconcerted him. "I've drawn first blood," she thought; but bleeding as a curative process is discredited.

"But," he said, "it is very like others of my series. I made sure it would be popular."

"I'm not a judge of that. It's possible enough. And now"—she smiled a little wryly—"I'm afraid you know my opinion of the series. I warned you," she added hastily, "that my opinions were intolerant. I imagine you will not ask for them again." She turned resolutely to the typewriter and took its cover off. She thought she had closed the discussion, and was suiting action to her word, and sitting at her desk when he motioned her back to the chair opposite his. It was not the sort of motion one ignored.

"I may ask for them again or I may not," he said; "but in the meantime I have certainly not given you anything to do at that machine, and we were trying to forget that you are my typist."

"I thought after what I've said that it might be time to remember it," she suggested.

"Not at all," he assured her. "I get to the bottom of things, and, if you please, we'll have this out."

"Of course, if this is part of your secretary's work——" she began.

He cut her short. "It is. Now, you find my novel series appalling?"

Effie was growing angry. *In vino veritas* — and in anger. "I could go even further," she said. "I find it degrading."

He thumped the desk. "But it sells, Miss Mannering, it sells. Did you know that?" He leant back in his chair in one of the attitudes he took when he was scoring heavily, thumbs in his waistcoat arm-holes.

"It's the most popular series of cheap novels on the market. See any bookstall, if you doubt me." He paused for her apology.

Effie did not apologize. "That does not alter my opinion of it," she said coolly. "A public danger isn't less dangerous because it's large. I'm afraid I can believe that there are no depths to which it is impossible to degrade the public taste, but that does not make me like any the better a series which degrades it."

Now a child is a child. It may be deformed, and its begetter may in clairvoyant moments have acknowledged the deformity to himself, but he resents its being pointed out to him. Sam was the father of his series.

"I say!" he protested. "That's nasty."

"It's a nasty series," she said hardily. "You are proud of it because it sells when you ought to be ashamed of it because it's bad." Somehow she had to say it. She couldn't hedge from what she saw as truth, even though she expected truth to hurt him and to be hurt in return. But Sam wonderfully controlled himself. Emphatically, he was forgetting that she was a typist. He remembered that she was Effie.

He addressed the ceiling. "The fact is," he mourned, "that women do not understand business. Even business women don't. Even you don't."

Mentally she thanked him for his "even you." It seemed to her a good place to end the matter for that morning. She still distrusted her manners, and not, she thought, without reason.

"Consequently," she told him quietly, "my opinion cannot matter," and moved as if to go to her typewriter.

He held her to her seat. "That is to beg the question," he replied, "and we were to have it out."

"But," she tried, "you have told me that I do not understand business."

"And you did not believe me."

He challenged her, in fact. Well, she must pick up his gage. "I do not understand this about business, Mr. Branstone. What is it about business which makes a man like you content to be a confectioner selling people wares that give them mental indigestion? Business! It's the name for half the meanness and nine-tenths of the ugliness in the world. You see, women do know something about business to-day. It isn't their fault that they are not still sitting cosily at home, hugging the old belief that business is a dignified, majestic thing to which only the masculine intellect can rise. It's your fault, the men's. You wanted cheap clerks, and you raised the veil so that women have seen business at close quarters, and the only thing they do not understand is how men continued for so long to magnify its low chicane and its infinite humbug into a cult which deceived them."

Sam came to the conclusion that Effie was not perfect. She suffered from hysteria, but she must be answered. "Well," he said, "you don't think much of business. But you came into it."

"I needed money," she defended that.

"So did I," he said dryly. "We're birds of a feather."

"You hate it, too?" she asked hopefully.

"Honestly," he said, "I like it. But," he went on with mischief in his eye, "I can tell you something that will please you. You dislike the novel series. You think they degrade. You don't think the Classics degrade?"

"No."

"I would much rather that the Classics sold largely than the novels."

"Why?" She was eager now. "Because they are great literature?"

"No. That would be being sentimental about business, and it can't be done. Because they are not copyright, and it saves book-keeping." He grinned at her discomfiture. "Business," he defined, "is money-getting." He was feeling tremendously pleased with himself, her master in argument. He gave her rope indulgently, for she was Effie; then crushed her utterly, for he was Sam.

"Isn't it better," she asked, "to win a little money decently than to gain a great deal by trading in poison? Whether you know it or not, these books are poisonous."

"I don't know it," he said brusquely. "They give pleasure."

"So, I suppose, does opium. There are lots of pleasant poisons. Would you keep an opium den if it paid? If you were a milkman, would you adulterate milk and poison babies? You adulterate books and poison minds. For money! Oh, yes; I, too, needed money, and I, too, came to business. But we are not birds of a feather. I do not like business. I don't like having to get money. I don't like money, but I need it. I've things to do with it."

"My case again," he capped her. "I've things to do with it." He saw that she was looking at him curiously, and that she took him to mean that he wanted money for Ada. Incidentally he did, but essentially he did not. "Politics," he added. "Power! Power!" He repeated the word ecstatically, not only because he was admitting her to the intimacy of his private thought, not only because he felt it an ecstatic idea, but because he had so thoroughly defeated her in argument. She sat there staring speechlessly, and he exulted to perceive that she was mute before his slashing common sense.

Only, that was not the reason of her silence. She thought that, for a first attempt, she had gone far enough, and had the hope that something of what she had said would remain in his mind, perhaps stingingly. She could only hope. Heaven knew it had been a queer enough interview between an employer and his typist, and her prayer, as she sat there permitting his exultation, was for an interruption.

Her prayer was answered. Just as she thought him on the brink of seeing that her silence was not entirely acquiescent, the office-boy brought in the name of a caller he must see, and Effie rose with huge relief. She hadn't it in her to keep silent much longer, and felt that if she then let go all that was firing her, she would say more than he could stand. True, he had stood a good deal, but then she had said little of what she had to say! She wanted to say it gradually, to lead him, not to spur him, to her point of view. Already she was taking a more modern view of the virtues of bleeding her patient.

She thought, too, that his was the easier part.

She had ideals for her Sam, but when she attempted to define them, they seemed nebulous, indeed, against his simple practice of expediency. He had his theory that what was expedient was just, and she—what was her theory except that his was not good enough for him? And his was in possession everywhere, established, honoured, received of all but a trivial minority. He thought with the mass and she thought mass-thinking was not good enough for him. It was difficult to explain. He wasn't a criminal, he wasn't even individual in thought or method; he played the common game, playing perhaps a little more astutely than the average, but keeping honestly within the rules. He followed the crowd, and she wanted him to follow the gleam. A gleam is indefinable, but she thought she had a chance because she was so much more grown-up than Sam. Business was a game of marbles, and girls do not play with marbles, but with dolls.

He was not to remain for long with the delusion that he had silenced her in their first talk. There followed many other talks, although she was coming to the conclusion that talking would not do the business for her. It helped, it made a preparation of the ground, but it was stubborn clay in which he had his roots. Talking did not dig deep enough; she must uproot, she must transplant.

"Politics," he had said to pulverize her argument.

"Another thing," she told him, "which is not quite the mystery for women that it was. Politics, but—why?"

And he replied with the word which had raised him to ecstasy. "Power,"; he said.

"Yes?" she questioned. "Business leads you to money, money to politics, and politics to power. And after that? You want power—for what?"

"Why," he cried, "power is power."

"An end in itself?"

"At least, it's an ambition," he replied.

It was, and so had Ada had her ambition to be married, an end, *the* end. He did not think of Ada, but he found it difficult to justify himself. He could not even tell her that he was a Liberal, because he had a decent hatred of a Tory; he wasn't in politics for a faith which enabled him to endure their artifice; he relished the artifice, he was in with an axe to grind, but with no clear idea of the use he wished to make of his axe when it was sharp. Ambition, purpose narrowed to two letters—M.P. He wanted to be M.P. for Branstone, that Bran-stone might hear the voice of Branstone speaking in the House of Commons.

She watched him slyly, and thought her leaven worked. "Of course," she said casually, "it would be useful for your business if you were an M.P."

"Enormously," he agreed, marching blindly into her little trap. "It gives prestige to any business."

"And completes the vicious circle," she said. "Business takes you to politics and politics brings you back to business."

He remembered an appointment hastily, and went to keep it. Sam Branstone stumped for a reply was an unusual phenomenon, and she con gratulated herself again that it worked. It worked, but slowly. She was not impatient, but he was still doing unchanged the things she hated to see him do, and she wanted the change to come. She doubted that it would ever come by talk alone. One did not convert by conversation.

She had intended to say so much, to keep a steady pressure on him, and she couldn't do it, partly because her point of view was difficult of definition, partly because she thought no talk, no matter how inspired, could change him of itself. She did not know of Anne, who had talked and kept the pres sure up, and put sacrifice behind the talk even to the point of thrusting her hand into the fire; but Effie, too, had sacrifice in mind. Anne's sacrifice had failed. It wasn't, perhaps, the right sacrifice: it was, at any rate, the immortal commonplace, the sacrifice of the older generation to the younger, of the mother to the son, of age to youth. Spectacular, heroic as it was, it was yet in the scheme of things, and it is the sacrifice of youth to youth which can surprise by unexpectedness.

For some it is a sacrifice to cease talking even when they are convinced that talk is futile. If Effie was one of these, she made that little sacrifice at once. She never told him that his life was mean and ugly and despicable, his triumphs worthless, his success a failure, his highest ambition to know that people grovelled to him, his money and his power. She did not say these things, but neither did she yield an inch of her attitude which implied them.

"I'll win," she told herself, "I'll win."

By now she was crusading for the soul of Sammy Branstone, and all the while her passion grew, fed as much by that in him which irritated her as by what attracted. She accepted the fact that he was married and discounted it. It was one with the other irritants, mattering less to her, for it was irremovable. She could neglect the wife: what mattered was the man. She must bring beauty to his life.

They have tamed many wild things in a world growm standardized; they have tried for centuries to bridle love and make it run in harness; but love refuses to be tamed and standardized by the marriage service. You don't scare love away by the bogey-sign, "Trespassers will be prosecuted." Love's wild, it's free, blind to the handcuffs which Church and State pathetically try to rivet on a given pair, lawless because it knows no law, timeless because it know's no time. Sometimes it lasts while a butterfly could suck a flower's honey, sometimes the space of a man's life, and they have tried to regulate this love, this volatility, to pretend that because it sometimes does not evaporate, it never evaporates till death. They sought to link love with property, and to control the uncontrollable. They make laws round love, which is like enclosing an eagle in a cobweb; and we suffer for their laws. We keep the law and suffer; break it and we suffer.

She knew that she would suffer, but she would bring beauty to Sam. He hadn't capitulated to her talk, and she thought that he had no chance in Manchester. Perhaps her Sam was with her in his dreams, but each dawn brought him to accustomed ugliness, and habit clogged his days with mud. He couldn't escape, he wanted wings, and she was there to bring them him. He did not know there was another side to life, but she would show it him. He should see her beauty, and, through that, the beauty of the other side.

She was presumptuous, but presumption is a quality of faith. She interfered, but there are three inevitable interferences in life—birth, love and death—and hers was one of these. It was them all: it was love and the birth of the new Sam, and the death of the old. She interfered, where she had right to interfere. She loved.

Time passed between the day when she came to her decision and the day when they acted upon it, and she never knew how long it was nor how she spent it. She belonged to a living fact, and there were shadows in the world, such as her work, her mother, the silly detail of arranging to go away, and Stewart, a haunting shadow of one Sunday afternoon, but these were unrealities and only her idea was real. She never remembered how she put it to Sam, nor what he said, though she had a hazy memory that he was desperately shocked and more profoundly humorous than ever before. But she thought that he was only shocked as the right thing shocks by rightness, not as the wrong by wrongness: and she knew that difficulties melted: and they came.

They came to the Marbeck Inn and entered into their kingdom of a week.

CHAPTER XX
THE MARBECK INN

SAM was vilely dull about it all at first: his comprehension, stuck in the mud, failed utterly to rise to the occasion, but before long; he was looking back with horror on his turgid mental processes when she told him that they would come away together.

He had a shadow, not more than a shadow of excuse for his preposterous misunderstanding of her ease. Sam followed the crowd, accepted readymade their principles and their lack of principles, their morality and their immorality, and to the crowd he followed the theory was faithfulness and the practice as much licence as they could take without being found out. They made a boast rather than a secret of their affairs with a shopgirl or a typist, he had never had an affair and was flattered to think that he was to have one now.

He thought that an affair was rather a manly thing to have.

When Effie spoke, he had a great surprise, then cheapened her insultingly. He decided that he had been wrong about her. After all, she was nothing more than a pretty typist with whom he was going to have his first affair, who was going to give him the opportunity to join in that sly boasting in hotel smoke-rooms which was the habit of his crowd. He, too, would rank amongst the sportsmen.

But, even at his worst, he had the grace to doubt that this was of the same kind as those other affairs. It had a lowest common measure with them, but—Effie! Cheapen her as he would, he could not think of her as cheap enough for that. When others did this thing it was, surely, that they were giving rein to grossness: it was at least charitable to assume that the women of their amours were of coarser grain than their wives, and Effie's was not the coarser grain. He drifted, acquiescing and puzzled, through the fog of his perplexity.

Illumination came to him, not in the crowded railway carriage, but in the trap which drove them from the station to the Inn. It came, he thought, miraculously, but perhaps the miracle was nothing more than that a man sees clearly in Westmoreland, and sees through dirt in Manchester. He worshipped Effie who was sacrificing all to him, and with abasement at the thought that he had meant, with his pitiful achievements, to surprise her.

He, shepherded to joy at the Marbeck Inn had set out to surprise Effie! That was what made it, from the first dawn of understanding, a perfect wonder-tale. He had not calculated this; it happened, like a dream, in the air, unrooted in prevision. But that was all it had, except its rapt intensity, of the quality of dream. It was dreamlike because it was more vivid than his experience of life, but it was life. Only, he had not known these things about life before. He had underestimated life.

The Inn lay in a saucer of the hills at the end of a road which led to nowhere. As a road, it finished at the Inn and went on only as a rough cart-track which dwindled and divided into two trails across the passes. The fells came down in grandeur to the Inn—it wasn't a place from which one looked at distant hills, but one where the hills were intimately there—and half a mile away there was the Lake.

They were twelve miles from a station, at the end of the world, alone with happiness. Of course, there were other people at the Inn, but Sam and Effie were alone: they two with the heather and the bracken and the pines: they two with love.

The crowd has not discovered Marbeck. The Inn, the Church, the Vicarage, down by the Lake the Hall, a farmhouse or two along the road, and that is all. Six miles away there is a post-office.

He had followed the crowd on his rare holidays. He knew Blackpool Promenade and Morecambe and the things to do at Douglas. Here, one did not do those things. One walked and climbed and lay extended on the heather or in the perfect isolation of high bracken, and bathed in the Lake or the streams or the tarns, haphazard, naked, where one liked and when one liked; and all the time one breathed the air.

It needed no thunderous knocking on the door to get her out of bed into the Marbeck air. Sam would go for an early dip in the pool below the Inn where two streams cascaded into a swimmable basin, and when he returned she would be up or ready to get up that he might brush her hair, or not up that she might play at being peevish and be lifted out of bed by him.

And the food, the good rough plenty of the Marbeck Inn! They ate of it prodigiously and carried to the hills parcels of sandwiches and cakes and cheese, shamelessly large, which they emptied to the last crumb, and eked out in the woods with raspberries and nuts.

She took him on the Lake, with a rod borrowed from the Inn, and showed him how to fish. He relished it amazingly, catching little but the spirit of the thing, happy because of the green reflection of the woods in the water and because of her. His restlessness found pause in a boat with Effie and she noted with a keen delight that he did not envy the expert basket of the postman who cycled to Marbeck in the mornings and fished till he cycled away with the letters in the afternoon. She registered as a happy gain that he did not want to shine, or try to beat that seasoned fisher at his game. Nor did the posts distract them. They had no letters there.

They bathed continually, for it was hot, and here again he made no effort to excel, but let it be admitted that she was the better swimmer. How much the better she did not let him know. She knew that he found the water here a purer element than in the old Blackfriars Baths where he had learnt when he was at school, and she tired less rapidly than he did. But he was wondrously content to own inferiority.

She had a deep symbolic faith in bathing. They were here to wash his mud away, and water was cleaner than talk. Talk, indeed, was but a surface pattern of their time. They hardly needed it, except as levity to mitigate a deep communion which sometimes grew almost intolerably sweet.

It was Blea Tarn, one of the many of that name, which they made peculiarly theirs, their favourite bathing-place, their best lunch-room. Effie stretched herself luxuriously on the close-cropped turf, at peace in mind and body.

"Sam," she asked, "have you noticed that Frump at the Inn? She sits behind me at dinner."

"No," said Sam truthfully. "When I'm with you I notice nobody else. And I don't know how you saw her if she sits behind you."

"Eyes in the back of my head," she explained. "You have them when you're a woman. Do you mind if I give her a shock?"

"You would if she could see you now," he said. "Yes, but she doesn't deserve it," said Effie complacently. She surveyed herself and Sam did the same. She pleased them both, taking her sun-bath there on the mossy turf. "But I may shock her?"

"You may do anything," he said.

"Thank God for that," said Effie joyously, and something glittered in the sun and fell with a splash far into the tarn. "Too deep to dive for it," she decided. "Bang goes a shilling and I'm glad. I never liked pretence."

"I say!" Sam protested, and then fell silent comprehendingly.

She looked at him and greeted his silence with a nod. "I shan't catch cold," she said, holding up her finger where the wedding ring had been. "I feel better now I'm rid of that."

The remarkable fact was that Sam understood. His education had progressed and he knew that it was not for the Frump at the Inn that she shed the imitation wedding ring which for form's sake he had suggested she should wear: it was for him. The ring was counterfeit, it was a false symbol of something which was not true: it had no place in the Marbeck scheme.

She curled up happily like a stroked cat, partly in sheer physical well-being, partly in gladness at her scheme's success. "And to think," she crooned, "that I am a wicked woman!"

"Effie," he pleaded, taking her hand. "Don't."

"As if I care," she said, rolling over on to her back and taking his hand with her to shade her eyes. "I might have been doing this all my life." Indeed, in her perfect absence of embarrassment, she might. "Wicked!" She shied a stone after the wedding ring into the tarn and laughed at a world well lost. "The Frump won't understand, my dear, but I think you do."

"I think I do," said Sam, but the fullness of understanding had not come to him yet.

Something, indeed, of her fineness he did perceive, but not its whole, its utter selflessness. He saw, roughly, what she was after: that it was here, in Westmoreland when she made her sacrifice, here when she lay beside him in the sun that she expressed in deed what she had been baffled to express in Manchester. She had brought him away from the murk and the fog and the place where they rather like dirt than otherwise because dirt means money, to where nature was beautiful. She had shown him beauty there, her beauty and the beauty of sacrifice and the beauty of things. She had taught him that there was beauty in the world. "We'll never go back," he cried.

"No. Not back," she said. "But we will go to Manchester."

"No. No. We'll build a tabernacle here."

"Here? No. We've been lawless here. We'll go to Manchester."

It rang in his ears like the trump of doom. So far they had marched in thought together, and he imagined that in her scheme they were to be together to the end. He thought her purpose was that they two were to work together to give shape to beauty—and no bad exercise in perception, either, for Sam Branstone.

That was her purpose, but, as she saw it, they were not to work together in the sense he meant. Her spirit was to go on with him, but she herself would stand aside, denying herself the right and the joy of sharing his work with him in physical partnership. She would have done her share at Marbeck: she was a sign-post whose direction he was to follow but which he left behind, not a guide to go with him on his way: and she thought she was content with that.

She renounced and she imagined that of the two of them it was she who was the realist and he who was romantic, he was romantic because he wanted her with him and she the realist because she remembered Ada. She was not jealous of Ada no'; if she could not bless Ada, neither did she damn her. Ada had never held him as Effie held him now. She thought it satisfied her to know that she held him, and to let the days slip past uncounted. Nothing is infinite except our human capacity for self-deception.

For the present, for the Marbeck heyday, it did satisfy her, and she went about the business of her tutelage with the unruffled serenity of fulfilled purpose, almost involuntarily now, thinking little, feeling everything in the passionate intensity of her sacramental love. It would end and she would suffer: meantime there were only so many days and it was no use impairing finite days with regrets that they were not infinite.

Thought was for before and afterwards, not for now when she crusaded for the soul of Sammy Branstone with the mystic rapture of a trance, joyful like the other sorts of true religion. She would wake up, but she would have taught Sam his lesson; she would have given him his gleam; and she was selfless after that....

Of course she may have deceived herself. There is spiritual love, but Effie was flesh and blood.

Sam, at any rate, was not etherealizing things. He did not appreciate the happiness of renouncing happiness. He wanted it to last, to go on with the gay days on the hills when she put health into his body and health into his mind, when it was all a high-spirited riot without an undertow. For hours on end, they lived their lives unclouded by a thought... rude, rough, exhilarating exercise on the glamorous fells like that illustrious day when they climbed the Pike and lost themselves in mist and found themselves again just where they wished to be, on the downward trail by Corner Tarn to Yorkdale: then on the steamer down the Lake, and the lonely moonlight walk across the Moor to Branley, where the trap from the Inn met them and took them, comfortably tired, to Marbeck and a giant's feast. And there were other days, more leisured, on their Lake or in the woods when more seemed to happen in his soul and less in his body; and their day of Bathes, in five well separated tarns, with a makeweight bathe in the Marsland Beck for luck. He wanted it to last. He had intoxication of the hills, of her, of everything.

He had not seen, he would not and he could not, see the possibility of her leaving him. He did not know that leaving him was as fundamental a part of her plan as coming to him.

"We'll go hack to Manchester," she said, and it seemed to him that he was ordered hack to hell. "That's where your business is," she added, a little wickedly.

Business! Hadn't she shown him the ugliness of his business, and the beauty of Marbeck? Why should they ever leave the hills? He had all the extremity of a convert.

Effie would say no more, and now, as the end of their time grew near, the magic seemed to him less magical, because he had to leave it, because she would not stay for ever in that lonely place, but wanted him to go where other men lived, in an ugly town, where he had a business she had taught him to despise, and responsibilities, and Ada.

He plunged to gloom. What was the use of knowing that there was light if he must go back to darkness? Was it not treachery in her to come so far with him, then leave him to himself?

"Effie!" he pleaded, and she consented to make things clear.

"Don't you see, Sam? We've done what we came here to do. You've seen, you know, and you will not slide back. I won't allow you to."

"You won't allow! Then you'll be there?"

"I hope my spirit will be always there," she said. "Do you doubt that?"

"Spirit?" he said. "You're overrating me. You're asking more than I can give. I cannot give what isn't there."

"I've put it there," she said. "You cannot fail. You can't forget."

* "I'd not forget, but I should fail. It's we, my dear. Not I alone, but you and I. Without you I am lost."

She made a great concession. "Then, if you're sure— —"

"Quite sure," he said, and she decided to indulge his weakness.

"Then don't dismiss your secretary. Then I'll be there."

"As secretary?"

"Of, of course." She spoke impatiently. All else was at the end.

That only made it more impossible than ever. She was to be there—and not to be there. There, in his office where he would see her every day, where he had only to stretch out his hand to touch her, and where he was not to touch, where he was to forget that he had ever touched. He wanted her, all of her, the touch, the glow, the life of her, and she offered—what? A sexless wraith, a spiritual guide, her presence in asceticism.

"No," he said. "No. I'd rather die than that."

"Oh, death is a good arrangement, Sam, but well be brave."

"There are limits even to bravery."

"No," said the realist. "There are none."

So she sent him, though he did not know that the suggestion came from her, to gather strength in the peace of the everlasting hills. She sent him to Hartle Pike to think, to see that she was right. He would remember Ada there.

He did remember Ada, but it seemed to him, when he tried to sum up his recollections, that Ada was not the woman who counted in his life. The women who counted were before Ada and after Ada. They were Anne and Effie.

In the gathering dusk on Hartle Pike he tried to be cool about it and to see things in proportion. Effie had the supreme advantage of immediacy. It wasn't easy, whilst he lived encircled by her glamour, to see Ada at all.

But he had been Ada's husband for ten years, a long time, more than a quarter of his life. In all those years there must be something which he could positively remember of her, some definite characteristic; something, at any rate, which was individual to her. He searched and found nothing. She had less individuality in his mind than his sideboard. He supposed that she kept house, or did she? Didn't he recall that the cook's wages went up one year, and that the cook became cook-housekeeper? In that case, and he felt certain of it now, Ada did nothing. He was equally certain that she was nothing. Since he had grown accustomed to her demands for money, she was not even an irritant. She was a standing charge, like the warehouse rent.

Quite suddenly, as he lingered over that definition of his wife, "a standing charge," he saw that it was double-edged. It cut at him, and shrewdly.

Ada, like Effie, was a woman, and he knew from Effie what a woman could be. There must, at least, have been possibilities in Ada. Dear God, what had he done with them if she was nothing now? That was the charge— that he had married her and that she was nothing: that he had permitted her to become nothing. He could summon no witness for his defence, he remembered no occasion when he had fought for Ada, as Effie had fought for him. And as to sacrifice— —! Yet he was supposed to have loved Ada.

He could have howled for very shame, he could not, in fairness, think that Ada had given him anything, but writhed that he had thought just now of Anne and Effie as the two women who counted in his life. They were the women who gave. Was he to take all from women and render nothing to a woman in return? If he could say of Ada, his wife these last ten years, that she did not count, then he was very much to blame and the path was clear before him. He saw to where the gleam that Effie gave him pointed. To Ada. It annoyed him desperately that it should point to Ada.

He began to descend the hill in a cold fury. The world was hideous, Marbeck an illusion, Effie a fool. No: Effie was right. One could not run away from facts and hide one's head amongst the hills, and say there were no facts. She had not brought him there to obscure facts, but to reveal them.

It remained to face them, to return to Manchester with new knowledge and new courage. It needed courage to turn his back on Marbeck, to go away from happiness to Ada.

He stamped upon that thought, as on a snake. It was disloyalty to Effie who had sacrificed to him and shown him all the beauty of her sacrifice. He, too, would sacrifice and find a beauty in it.

He found it extraordinarily difficult to meet Effie, and spent an unnecessarily long time with the landlord of the Inn. Then he went in to her.

"I'm leaving," he stammered. "I couldn't stay another night. By driving fifteen miles I can catch the South Mail at midnight. I've arranged for you to come to-morrow."

He jerked each sentence out painfully.

Effie met his eyes with her serene gaze. "That's infinitely best," she said. "I'm proud of you."

He had seen! It was her victory, complete and unequivocal, and she was proud of him and of herself. He had got rid of mud and he had seen beauty. Now he was facing the facts as she would have him face them, clear-eyed, without romance. Like her, he was a realist, and she was glad... glad.

But when he went up to their room to pack his bag, Effie left the Inn quickly and walked hard. She must put space between them: space, that she might cry unheard. It seemed to her that if he heard her crying he would not go, and she wanted him to go. She was a realist. She was... stifling her sobs amongst the heather; triumphing in victory on Marbeck Ridge.

She won, as she had said that she would win. But there were limits to her bravery.

CHAPTER XXI
SATAN'S SMILE

THE theory that Satan is a subtle devil is one which will not bear examination. He is a crude fellow, theatrical, Mephistophelean. It may, of course, be only because his experience of human nature has made a cynic of him, and certainly his interferences do not as a rule lack success because they want delicacy. He attacked Sam with a blatant effrontery which suggested that he thought Sam's a contemptuously easy case.

Sam reached Manchester very early in the morning, and spent the rest of his broken night in a lugubrious hotel near the station. Manchester hotels rarely make for gaiety, but it is wonderful what even a short night will do in the way of altering a point of view.

He expected to be depressed at the very air of Manchester, and, instead, he sniffed at it as Mr. Minnifie had once relished the odours of Greenheys, with an exile's greed. He knew that he ought to feel a loathing of the office, but found that he opened the letters with more than his usual zest. He knew that it was wrong, all wrong, and checked his itching fingers.

There have been prisoners who, when offered freedom, have pleaded to remain in the familiar cell.

Was it like that with him, he wondered, as had as that, the jail-fever so ineradically in him that he must breathe the tainted air to live? But, was he offered freedom? He had to go to Ada, who was a mill-stone and implied the other mill-stones. Unless she was not a mill-stone, unless he could alter her. In the meantime, at all events, she was not altered, she wanted the things which she had always wanted; and the office was their source. It seemed to him that he was still in prison, with the difference that he now knew that it was prison. He found little comfort in the knowledge.

His gaze returned to the pile of correspondence. There seemed nothing else for it to do, and he saw an envelope, addressed not to the firm, but to himself, which sent the blood whirling to his head in simple premonition of its contents. From the postmark (S.W.—Satan's Work?) he saw that it had only come that morning and had not been waiting his arrival. He thought of that as of a portent. Suppose he had stayed another day at Marbeck! He might have been too late.

It was a careful letter, but the facts were that, owing to the sudden death of Sir Almeric Pannifer, the seat tor the Sandyford Division of Marlshire was vacated. Mr. Morphew, who had reduced Sir Almeric's majority in that agricultural constituency to three hundred was, for private reasons, unable to stand again ("I know these private reasons," thought Sam. "Morphew considers he has earned a walkover next time"), but Headquarters were of opinion that a resolute candidate of strong personality, etc....

In short, he was offered the opportunity to be the figurehead in a demonstration for the Liberal Party. It was no more than that. Morphew had doubtless nursed the constituency like a mother, and if at the landslide of the last election he had done no better than to come within three hundred of his opponents' votes, the chances of a stranger's capturing the seat were negative. But it was the stepping-stone, the *liaison* between obscurity and the House of Commons. It was what he had aimed at.

He tried to believe that the letter did not exhilarate him as it would have done a fortnight earlier, and Satan, the connoisseur of good resolutions, smiled his age-long smile.

He looked across at Effie's chair. "My spirit will be always with you," she had said; he wondered if it were there now, and tried to see her. Surely now, if ever, was her time; now when he had so lately left her, when her scent was in his nostrils and her voice in his ears. Her voice *was* in his ears. He heard it clearly. She spoke one word, "Renounce."

"Yes, but, my dear," he argued, "I have renounced. I've renounced you. I've come back here and I'm going to Ada, to plumb the depths of her, to find the good in her, and drag it to the top. I'm going to dive for pearls," he grew almost picturesque as he cited his intentions towards Ada in his defence, "and I shall grow short of breath. I'm not doubting that the pearls are there, because Ada's a woman, and so are you, but I know that they lie deep and I want breath for such a dive as that. I've renounced you, and I'm going to make a woman of her; don't I deserve some recompense to make amends? It's here beneath my hand, and I have only to say 'Yes.' Effie," he pleaded, "if you knew what this meant to me, you wouldn't frown. It's not backsliding." He denied that it was backsliding, well knowing that it was. "It's politics, I know, and you don't like politics. You told me women knew about politics now. Oh, but you don't know, you don't. Smile at me, Effie, smile as I have seen women smile when men talked of golf. I know we men are babies, and so do you. Give me my game. It's nothing but a hobby, like golf, but this is mine, and I want it so much. Ada is my work and this is my play, and just as necessary. It will not be a hindrance to what I have to do for Ada, it will be a help. Effie, tell me that I may have my help."

He tried to blarney a consenting smile out of the figure of Eflie he imagined sitting in her chair. He had no difficulty in imagining her there; he saw her, too easily, too really to imagine a false Effie. He could not imagine, try as he would, that he had won consent from her. He was too near the real Effie for that. And Effie said "Renounce."

Then his cashier came into the office and routine swallowed him for the day. A score of little points had arisen in his absence and must be discussed and settled. The thought occurred to him that if he telegraphed to London in the morning, Headquarters would hear from him as soon as if he wrote to-day. They might expect a wire to-day; well, they would not get it. He crammed the letter into his pocket and decided that he would sleep upon it before he sent them his reply.

And if Satan still smiled it was wistfully, as if he regretted his lost subtlety; but there was still Ada, the married woman.

If Ada was nothing else, she was a married woman; in a world where many fail, she had succeeded; she had got married, and, like other people who have reached their earthly paradise, she did not know what to do when she got there, and did nothing. She stopped growing when she married.

The emptiness of her life was a thing to marvel at. She slept and ate and shopped. She was spared the ordinary duties of running a house, and the trials of servants, because the cook, an elderly, reliable woman, took (it seemed) a fancy to Sam and became a fixture first and a housekeeper second, taking from Ada's shoulders the burden of engaging her underling. She had two "At homes" a week, and went to other people's "At homes." On Sunday, she went to church, where one can display new clothes to a larger audience than at the largest private "at home." She killed the evenings somehow, in company with a friend, or with the fashion papers.

Evenings interested her little; they were the time when Sam was often, but not too often, at home. He was not, strictly, a nuisance, because he never asked her, after a first experiment, to entertain a business acquaintance, and did that at hotels. Nor did he ask her to entertain him. Usually, he read a manuscript, or worked out costs or did something which made no demand on Ada, except that she be reasonably quiet. She was very quiet with Sam, for the reason that she had nothing to say.

She did not go out much in the evenings and told her friends that this was because she liked to be at home with her husband. They were supposed to deduce an idyll of conjugal bliss where proximity was perfect happiness. The real reasons were, first, pure laziness and, second, her shoulders. Other married women might expose their shoulders in low-cut dresses, but not Ada. It wasn't modest. Her shoulders were ugly.

She never went to see Peter, who had given her offence by suggesting the blessedness of work. He had dared to lecture her, a married woman, and she let fly at him in such fashion that he never tried again, he deplored his weakness, but he gave her up. The cobbler's child is the worst shod, and something analogous often happens with the daughters of the clergy: Ada was, perhaps, the worst of Peter's flock. He knew and, knowing the hopes he had had of this marriage, suffered at its failure, but silently, confessing impotence. There were always books in which he could forget, and the peace which had come to his house since Ada left it. It is not easy to be saintly all the time, and her outrageous attack had been, humanly speaking, unpardonable.

"There must be something in her," he told himself, as he left the office, "and I've to find it."

The day had, naturally, after an absence, been unusually busy, and had given him no time to think. He was bursting with intention, but it was vague, unformed, though urgent and doubly urgent because of the letter in his pocket. If he could make a woman of Ada, if that evening he could make a fair start, perhaps he could conjure up the figure of Effie, his ghostly counsellor, with a smile on her face consenting to his standing for the seat.

"Oh," Ada greeted him, "I thought you were not coming back till Saturday."

"I wasn't," he said. "Something changed my plan a little. I wanted to get home."

She looked at him resentfully. There was no reason why he should not change his plan and come home two days before she expected him, but she resented the unexpected. And there was something about him which appeared strange.

"Tell me you are glad to see me," he said.

"Well, it wasn't to be till Saturday," she repeated stupidly.

"Are you thinking of dinner?" he asked. "Kate will manage something."

She was not thinking of dinner, and no doubt Kate would manage something. It was Kate's business.

"You're wearing funny clothes," she said.

"Country clothes," he explained. "You see, I've been in the country."

"Oh." She was not curious.

"Yes. In the country. It was rather beautiful, Ada."

"I nearly went with Mrs. Grandage to the 'Métropole,' at Blackpool, but I don't like dressing for dinner."

"Blackpool's not beautiful," he said. "Ada, I want to talk to you, and I hardly know how to begin, except that I want you to understand that I'm in earnest. It's a serious matter."

"Money?" said Ada, sitting up sharply in her chair.

"Not money. We've both been wrong about money, I think. We've both taken it too seriously."

"If you're going to tell me that something has gone wrong with your money, it's very serious indeed."

"It hasn't. No. This is a larger thing than money. I want, if I can, to alter things between us, Ada. How can I put it? There's your father— —"

"I never want to hear his name again," she interrupted. "He insulted me."

"You go to church, you know; you listen to him there."

"People would talk if I didn't go. I needn't listen to him when I am in church."

"He's a good old man. I'm sorry we have drifted from him. But I'll not press that now. If the rest comes right, that will come right with it. It might even come so right as to include my mother."

"My word!" she said, "you *are* digging up the past. I don't see how you could call things right when they include me with a charwoman."

"Ada!" he protested.

"It's what she is."

"By her own choice. But please forget that, Ada. Yes, it's true that I am digging in the past. I want to go back to see where we went wrong."

"Went wrong? When who went wrong?"

"Why, you and I."

"I didn't know we had gone wrong." She looked at him. "You look well," she decided, "but you can't be."

"I am better than I've ever been," he said, "and stronger, and if need be I shall use my strength, but I hope the need won't come for that. Ada, can you tell me this? Can you tell me what it is you want?"

"You're sure it's all right about your money?" she asked anxiously.

"Yes, of course it's right," he said impatiently.

"Then I don't know that I want anything. I could do with more, naturally. Who couldn't?"

"More money. Not more beauty? Not a new purpose? Not something to live for?"

"I don't know what you're talking about, Sam. You're very strange to-night."

"I hardly know myself," he confessed. "I know it's all confused, and I ought to have got things out of the tangle before I spoke to you. But I thought you might have seen and so be able to help me out. No: that's all right, Ada," he went on as she glared at him indignantly. "I'm blaming no one but myself. It's my responsibility. You don't see it yet, and I must make you see."

"If a thing's there, I can see it."

"Oh, it's there," he said. "We can both see that. It's only the cure for it that isn't plain."

"What's there?"

"The failure of our marriage, if I must put it into words."

"Failure! But we *are* married. What do you mean?" What Ada meant was that the ring was on her finger and the marriage certificate in her desk. Failure in marriage, if it meant anything to her, meant failure to get married, a broken engagement, and since their engagement had not been broken, since they had been formally and legally married in church, there could be no failure.

"We didn't exult in marriage," he tried.

"Exult? I'm sure I was the proudest woman in the parish the day I married you." It was true. "But afterwards, afterwards!"

"Oh," she cried, "are you throwing it in my teeth that I didn't have a baby? Was that my fault?"

"No, no. But it might have saved us, all the same, and when the baby did not come we made no effort to save ourselves. There's a light somewhere in every one of us and you and I have quenched our lights. They may be small, they may not be a great light like your father's, or... or the light which I have seen in the country, they may be nothing but a feeble glow, and we can only give our best. You and I have not given ours. We have not tried to find our light, but now—now that we have discovered what has been wrong with us all this while—we can try, and together. We can all of us give something to the world, not children in our case, but the something else which we were made to give. We don't know what it is that you can give and I can give, and we've left it late to begin to find out, but it is not too late, is it, Ada? Ada," he pleaded, "it is not too late?"

She looked at the clock. "If you want to wash your hands before dinner you'd better do it now," she said, "or you will be late." She rose, but before she left him, she had a moment of illumination. She thought she saw what he was driving at, that he must have seen some happy family while he was away and came back with the cry of the child less man on his lips. "I suppose this means," she said, "that you want me to adopt a child. That's what you mean by giving. Well, I won't do it, Sam. I've something else to do with my time than to look after another woman's brat."

"What have you to do?" he asked. "What is it that you want to do?"

"To eat my dinner," she said. She had a healthy appetite. Perhaps that was why she wanted nothing else.

He stood by the door when she had gone, and his hand strayed to his pocket as though it sought a talisman. He felt the letter crinkle, then tore his hand away. Ada was work for a man. There wasn't room for Ada and for politics. "Deeply regret private reasons compel total withdrawal from politics." Yes, that was the wording of the telegram which he would send: it was best to be thorough, and, plainly, the man who had Ada in hand had no time to spare on a hobby or an ambition or whatever it was that politics represented for him. He had other work to do in the world.

He stamped upon the ruins of a hope which came to birth ten years ago, and which he had carried with him in his heart of hearts and, as the letter in his pocket proved, not a fool's hope either. Yes, he had loved that hope which was born on his honeymoon.

It occurred to him that in all he had said, or tried to say, to Ada he had not mentioned love. It had not seemed the right word for use in a conversation with Ada, but, he reflected savagely, he had loved his hope of politics from the time of the honeymoon onwards: and from that time he had not loved Ada.

Was that true? Had he neglected the substance for the shadow, used love upon his hope and not upon his wife? If he had his talk with her again, could he honestly begin it in another way? Could he begin with love? He knew that he could not, and squared his shoulders to the fact. It was a case, then, for the more courage. What was it Effie had said? "There are no limits to bravery." He wondered, but he meant to see.

And Satan's smile had faded. There is more joy amongst the devils over one sinner who back-slideth.... But not this time, Mephistopheles! Effie was winning still.

CHAPTER XXII
THE OLD CAMPAIGNER

EFFIE and Sam knew that they ought to be happy in the weeks which followed, because to be good is, theoretically, to be happy: but they were not happy. Sam, indeed, was less unhappy than Effie because he had sunk into one of those leaden, numbed moods of his which he knew of old as the stage preliminary to his brightest inspirations, and he could wait resignedly if not happily for the inspiration to emerge.

Decidedly, he thought, he needed inspiration, He had to discover Ada, to search for her reality, and, having found it, to drag it out and set it in the forefront of her being. A big task: one whose success he must not jeopardize again by rushing at her prematurely without distinct plan. He had only made her suspicious of him by his first impulsive attempt, and time must undo the mischief before a return to the attack was either discreet or opportune.

He waited, but he did not savour life. When he had quickened Ada, life would, no doubt, be worth the living, but, meantime, it dragged. He told himself that he was too young yet at this new business of giving to feel the joy of it. Certainly, he was not joyful, but he was resolute. There was a grim tightening of the lips and a dogged look in the eyes which proclaimed that this was Samuel, the son of Anne. In this mood he could eat Dead Sea apples and feel they were a proper diet. Politics had gone, and with them any interest in the Council. And he did not know what to do about his business. He wanted to ask Effie, and Effie was not there to be asked.

It was not that she did not want to be there or that she did not suffer for her absence. Effie was not numb, and she suffered keenly, but she thought her absence strengthened Sam. When he came down from Hartle Pike with his resolution formed she took it that her scheme, as she had planned it, was complete and that she could forget her weak concession to return to the office. She was to be there in spirit, and spirit is strong though flesh is weak. Effie at the office in the flesh would have wanted to hug Sam and to kiss him, things which it is unbefitting to do in well-conducted offices. And, of course, she suffered. She had always known that she would suffer, but not that it would be as bad as this.

The office was a temptation every day: to go there was to be with him, it was to find alleviation for her fever, it was to be at peace: but it was also to fling away hard-won success, and she resisted. That resistance engrossed her. It was all that she was capable of doing; it demanded all her strength.

The obvious, the practical thing, if she was not to go to Sam's office, was to go to someone else's, to work, both as an antidote and as a means of livelihood, and she could not rouse herself to do it. She pawned some of the jewellery which remained to her, memorials of her father's lavish past, sent the weekly dole to her mother and lived upon the rest. She had sunk to this, Effie the crusader, Effie the advocate of courage! With Mélisande, she told herself she was not happy. She was not happy, she was not well, and she wanted, wanted Sam. She stayed at home lest she should go to him and ruin all that she had done. It could not last and she knew it could not last, but neither did she see the end of it.

Then began the game of consequences: the moves of two pieces, one a pawn, the other the knight called Dubby Stewart.

It is a frumpish world, a world where the Frumps, of one or other sex or of neither sex, in one or other of their manifestations, have a great deal to do with the ordering of things. That is why it is politic, for one's ease, never to ignore the Frumps and never, never to challenge them by an act of gallant defiance such as shying an imitation wedding ring into the waters of Blea Tarn.

Effie held, of course, that since she was in any case defying the Frumps it was honest to defy them in form as well as in substance, but it is only certain kinds of honesty which are the best policy.

The Frump who sat behind Effie at meals at the Inn (her name was Miss Entwistle) had doubted the genuineness of that ring, and when it disappeared her doubts went with it. The hussy, she saw, had realized that her ring deceived nobody, and was brazening it out in the shameless way of hussies.

Women are wicked, but men are only weak; so that, though Miss Entwistle faced Sam at dinner from the next table, it was some days before she could spare her attention from the back of the greater sinner and transfer it to the face of the lesser. She could stare to her heart's content; it did not matter to Sam, who had only eyes for Effie: and the stare of Miss Entwistle was very persistent indeed. It was rude, but it was also pensive. It seemed to be looking for something it could not find.

She could not place him and was annoyed because she felt certain she had seen him before. She got up early more than once to read the names on the morning's letters, but did not find one which she could associate with Sam, and came home to Manchester a disappointed woman. Her failure to identify him spoiled her holiday.

But all things come to her who waits, especially, as the world is made, to Frumps, and Miss Entwistle came by the knowledge she craved one afternoon when her friend Mrs. Grandage took her to Ada Branstone's "At Home."

The two photographs of Sam in Ada's drawing-room were intended to sustain her reputation for perfect domesticity. She couldn't live without him; she drew her very breath from him when he was there, and from his photographs when he was not. And since one was full-face and the other profile, they supplied Miss Entwistle with reliable identification of the sinner of Marbeck.

It was heavenly. Hers was the power and the glory of initiating a scandal, of exploding a bomb—which would certainly disturb the peace of quite a number of people, of figuring in a maelstrom of backbiting tea-parties as the one authentic eyewitness. It was irresistible, besides plain duty to her injured hostess.

The drop of gall in her brimming honey-pot was that she did not know Ada well enough to tell her the secret by herself, but must share the excitement of that first surprise with Mrs. Grandage. She whispered with her friend for some close-packed, hectic moments, and the two ladies stubbornly outstayed the rest of the callers.

They told Ada with a wonderful tenderness, watching her the while as cats watch mice, and Ada did not disappoint them. She cast no doubt on Miss Entwistle's story; she did not tell her that she knew Sam was in London at the time because she had had letters from him. Though she had nothing in the world but her marriage, she made no effort to protect its reputation. She exhibited herself to them in all the fury of her jealous rage, so that naturally, seeing her instant belief in what they told her, the ladies formed their own conclusion.

"It is not the first time," is what the eyes of Mrs. Grandage said, and the eyes of the spinster looked back at her sepulchrally and said, "It never is."

Ada was married. She had the title of wife, and unfaithfulness on her part was as far removed from her imagination as from her opportunity. She was married to Sam; she was the woman in possession, with the title-deeds in her desk and the seal upon her finger, and this was flagrant outrage. It struck at the roots of her complacency, and complacency was life. Yet she hadn't the wits to confound these iconoclasts with one little uninventive lie. It needed only that to abash Miss Entwistle—men's faces are often alike, she knew perfectly well that he was in London: anything would have done, anything would have been better than this abject, immediate betrayal of her citadel. She struck her flag without firing a shot, and lapsed into a slough of inarticulate anger.

"What shall I do? What shall I do?" she wailed as soon as she was able to speak coherently.

"That," said Miss Entwistle, "that, you poor dear, is your business."

She had announced the glad tidings, she had found a titillating pleasure in watching Ada's reception of them and now she was eager to be off, to spread the news, to be the first that ever burst into her friends' drawing-rooms with word of a glorious scandal. She pleaded another call and escaped to her orgy.

"I'll make him pay for this," said Ada viciously.

"My dear," advised Mrs. Grandage, who had a husband of her own, "I hope you will be tactful."

"Tactful:" blazed Ada. "Tactful, when—oh! oh!" She screamed her sense of Sam's enormity.

"Yes, but you know, men will be men."

"It isn't men. It's Sam. After all I've done for him! Oh!" and this was a different "oh" from the others. It made Mrs. Grandage look up sharply. "The beast! The beast! This explains it all. Ethel, that man came home to me and asked me to adopt his child. He had the face. Of course I didn't know it was his own he was speaking of, but I see it now. Ethel, what shall I do?"

They seemed to Mrs. Grandage to be drifting into deeper waters than she had skill to swim in. "I should take advice," she said, meaning nothing except that neither by advising nor anything else was she going to be entangled in this affair.

"A solicitor's?" asked Ada, catching at the phrase. "Yes. Naturally. Sam shall be made to pay to the uttermost farthing." Her idea of legal obligations were, perhaps, not vaguer than other people's.

"Not a solicitor's," said Mrs. Grandage in despair. "At least, my dear, not yet. Your father's."

"Yes. My father made me marry Sam. He brought Sam home and threw him at me. I will go to my father. Of course, in any case, I can't stay here."

Mrs. Grandage made a last rally for wordly-wisdom. "Couldn't you bring yourself to see your husband first?" she asked.

"See him!" said Ada heroically. "I will never see him again as long as I live."

The visitor buttoned her glove. After all, if Ada chose to make a fool of herself it was no business of hers, and she had tried her best, if a resolutely non-committal attempt can be a best. She kissed Ada with real sympathy.

"My dear," she said, "I'd give a great deal to undo this." And by "this" she did not mean the peccadillo of Sam Branstone, but the pruriency of Miss Entwistle. She was an experienced woman, and angry with herself for having listened to the temptress and for aiding and abetting her.

When Mrs. Grandage referred in after years to "that woman," it was understood that she was thinking of Miss Entwistle.

Ada saw her to the door, and went straight to the kitchen.

"Kate," she said to her cook, "Mr. Branstone has disgraced himself, he's been unfaithful. I am going to my father's. Please tell him that I know everything and that I shall not return." She had no reticence.

"Very well, mum," said the Capable cook.

The result was that when Sam went into the drawing-room that night, he found Anne Branstone sitting there, darning his socks, and perhaps it was because she was happy that she did not look a day older than when he saw her last; perhaps charring suited her; or perhaps living for an idea had kept her young. The idea was that, some day, Sam would need her.

It wasn't a miracle: there was nothing more wonderful about it than the fact that Anne was a very good friend of the cook, Kate Earwalker: but Sam stood gaping helplessly. In his own house, at his age, and after all these years he stood before his mother, the intruder, like a schoolboy who knows himself at fault. She lacked nothing of the old ascendancy.

"Well," she said, "you're nobbut happy when you've got folks talking of you. But you don't look thriving on it, neither."

"Mother," he gasped, "what's this?"

"It's you that will tell me that," said Anne.

"Where's Ada?"

"Gone to her father's, and none coming back, she says. Says you're unfaithful and told Kate she knows everything. What is it, Sam? What's everything?"

"Who brought you here?"

"Kate did," said Anne calmly. "Why, Sam, did you think I've lived with nothing better than what George Chappie and the papers told me of you? I'd a fancy for the truth, and it's not a thing to get from men. Kate's been a spy, like."

"Has she!" he cried.

"She has, and you'll bear no grudge for that. You'd have lived in a pig-sty and fed like a pig if I'd none sent Kate to do for you, but I've come myself this time. It looks summat beyond Kate."

"But what's happened? What is it?"

"You know better than me what it is. You've got folks talking of you and they've talked to Ada. Unfaithful, she told Kate, and she's gone home to Peter's."

"She must come back," said Sam.

"And why?" asked Anne. "Because folk talk? To stop their mouths?"

"No. Because I want her here. They're talking, are they? Well, they can."

Anne looked at him. "You don't care if they do?"

"Why should I?"

"And you a politician?"

"Oh, politics!" he said. "That's gone." It had, and, as he saw thankfully, at the right time. He tried to imagine how differently this would have affected him if it had come in the midst of the Sandyford election. Electors postulate respectability in a candidate. But that had gone, and gossip did not matter now. The real things mattered. Ada mattered.

"You've had a move on, then," she said, and neither her look nor tone suggested that she found the move displeasing.

"I daresay," he said carelessly. "But Ada must come back. I've got to get her back."

"Happen she'll come and happen she won't, and I'd have a better chance of knowing which if you'd told me what's upset her."

"What did she say?" he asked. "Unfaithful? Yes, it's true. I've been unfaithful for ten years. I've never been faithful and I've never been fair. I've thought of the business and politics when I ought to have been thinking of her. I worked at them and I didn't work at Ada. Don't blame Ada, mother. I'll not have that. You never liked her, and you prophesied a failure. It's been a failure, but I made it one; I let it drift when I ought to have taken hold. But it isn't going to be a failure now. I've given up the other things and I've come back to my job, the job I neglected, the job I did not see was there at all until— —" He paused.

"Till what?" she asked.

"Till Effie showed it me."

"Effie?" she asked. "Oh! Then there's something in their talk."

"Something? There's everything, and everything that's wrong-headed and abominable. That's where this hurts me, mother. They'll be saying wrong things of her, of Effie." He began to see that gossip mattered.

"What would be the right things to say?" asked Anne dryly. "Who's Effie? And do you mean her when you say you've been unfaithful for ten years?"

"I meant what I said. That I've put other things in front of Ada."

"Including Effie?"

"Effie's a ray from heaven," he said.

"Oh, aye," said Anne sceptically.

"Look here, mother, you're not going to misunderstand?"

"Not if you can make me understand."

"I can try," he said, "and the chances are that I shall fail. The only thing that will make you understand Effie is to see her."

"Try the-other ways first," said Anne grimly.

"She made me see. She gave me everything. She gave me herself. I found myself because of her and I'm only living in the light she gave me." It was difficult to find words for what Effie was and meant to him. "I don't know if I can ever explain," he faltered.

"Go on. You're doing very well." He was—Anne's insight helping her.

"It's like rebirth. It's as if I'd lived till I met her six months ago with crooked eyesight. I didn't see straight, and then, mother— —" He hesitated as a man will hesitate before voicing a profound conviction, afraid lest he be thought absurd. "Then I found salvation, I've been a taker and we're here to give. I took from you— — —"

"Leave that," said Anne curtly. "I know it."

"And I didn't," he replied. "It seems to me that I knew nothing till Effie come."

"Why do you want Ada back?"

"It's time I gave to her."

"Did Effie show you that?"

"Yes."

Anne was silent for a minute. Then: "I'll have a look at Effie," she said. "You can take me to her."

"I can't do that," said Sam. "We're not to meet."

She pondered it, and him. "Kate told me you were looking ill," she said with apparent inconsequence. "Well, if you can't take me to Effie, I must go alone. I'm going, either road. Give me her address and I'll go to-morrow."

He wrote it down. "Effie Mannering," she read. "Aye," she said grimly, "I'll give that young woman a piece of my mind."

"Mother," he said, alarmed, "you'll not be rude to her! You've not misunderstood?"

"Maybe," said Anne, "but I don't think so. I think I understand that you've got your silly heads up in the clouds and it'll do the pair of you a lot of good to have them brought to earth. I'll know for sure when I've set eyes on her."

"You'll see the glory of her, then," he said defiantly.

"Shall I?" she asked. "If you ask me, Sam, there's been a sight too much glorification about this business. It shapes to me," she went on, thwarting the protest which was leaping to his lips. "It shapes to me like a plain case of love. Aye, and love's too rare a thing in this world to be thrown away. I was never one to waste."

So Anne Branstone took control, and Sam sat staring at her helplessly like a man who dreams.

CHAPTER XXIII
THE KNIGHT'S MOVE

IT might very well have occurred to Sam to retort that he and Effle had not "their silly heads in the clouds" any more fantastically than had Anne her self when she retreated to Madge's and watched her loved son only through the eyes of Kate Earwalker. But it did not occur to him and, if it had, Effie at least would have disproved the retort. Effle outstripped them all.

The truth was that as soon as Effle knew what was the matter with her she was not appalled, dismayed, ashamed, or any of the things appropriate to a young lady in her situation, but simply and purely exultant. Unhappiness fell from her like a cloak, and left her radiant with joy. And she had called herself a realist!

She was a realist; she was engrossed with fact, not with the circumstantial detail of her fact. She hardly wanted Sam now, she had him, she was miles and leagues from care, alone in a shining world with her transcendant fact. Courage returned in full flood to her and she brimmed with bravery and pride.

She was out of work and must find work quickly which would pay her well. She was going to suffer, she was going (to put it mildly) to be misunderstood. What did it matter, what did anything matter in comparison with her exultant fact? She was going to be the mother of his child. Marbeck was not a dream; Marbeck was coming true, and the truth and the glory of it swept her to a heaven which only women know.

Perhaps she was a trespasser within the gates, but they had opened to her and they would not close. She might be prosecuted for her trespass. Let them try! You cannot hurt invulnerability. She was a world within a world, self-satisfying, self-complete, not so much derisive of the other world as utterly forgetful of it. Her cloud of glory hid it from her eyes, and if she peeped at all through breaches in the cloud she saw people as one sees them on the road beneath a mountain-top, like crawling ants.

A knock came at her door, and she looked bemused through a gap in the clouds into the eyes of Dubby Stewart, but it was not to look at the world which did not understand. It was to look at Dubby, who loved her.

And Dubby knew. It had not been difficult to know. She had refused him, she had let him see why, and Sam and Effie had been away from Manchester at the same time. It was not precise evidence, but he had written leaderettes on evidence not more exact and did not doubt the facts. They had kept him from her till now, but he could keep away no longer. And before he went into her room he knew all there was to know.

"Effie," he said, "I'm not sure if I'm welcome."

"Oh, but you are," she said. "I ought to have written to you long ago. I've been home weeks from my holiday." It was no use trying to see Dubby as a crawling ant, and she gave her hand in friendship.

"That breaks the ice," he said.

"If there was ice to break."

"Well," he reminded her, "I said I didn't love and run away, and I did more or less run away. I came one Sunday because I said I would, but I couldn't do it again. The trouble with me is that I ought to be a journalist, and after about twelve years of it I'm still human."

"Dubby! I'm sorry!"

"All right, Effie; I didn't come to bleat. That's only an apology for not coming before. And now I'm here— —"

"You'll have tea," she said quickly, going to the bell, but he caught her hand before she pulled.

"Do you want to put a table between us? Do, if you must"—he released her hand—"but I'd hoped it would not come to that. Shall I ring the bell, Miss Mannering?"

"You needn't punish me by calling names. Don't ring." She armed herself with courage, and turned to face him.

"Thanks. Really thanks, Effie. I know I'm a bore, but if the old song has a good tune to it I don't see why I shouldn't sing twice. It *is* a good tune," he went on with a passion which belied his surface flippancy. "It's the best I have in me, which mayn't be saying much, because I've a rotten ear for music, but this tune's got me badly, like the diseases they play on the barrel-organs, and I can't lose it. I get up to it in the morning, and I go to bed to it at night, and it's ringing in my ears all day. Effie, I'm not much of a cove and I've flattered myself that sincerity departed from me when I cut my wisdom teeth. I tried to live up to that belief and it's only half come off. I've tried to make a raree-show of life, to sit outside and watch the puppets play, and life's won. Life's got me down, and I'm inside now. I'm where you've put me, and a good place too: I'm near the radiator and it warms the cockles of my heart. But I never liked radiators. Mind you, I can do with them and I can be grateful for them. If a season ticket for life for a seat near the radiator is all that you can give me, I can keep a stiff upper lip and thank you for what I've got. But I never had a passion for radiators, and I do like fires. There's life in a fire Must it be just the radiator, or can you make it hearth and home for us?"

"Dubby," she said, "I told you before."

"I know. Nothing doing in second thoughts?" She shook her head.

"All right. I only got drunk last time. This time it will need the binge of my life. I'd cherished hopes of this."

"Drunk," she said reproachfully. "With a stiff upper lip?"

"Oh, I dunno," he said. "It takes a stiff upper lip to get me to the dentist's, but I make him use an anæsthetic all the same. Still, if you'd rather I didn't— —"

"I think it would be braver."

"Right. But I'd like to hit something. There's nobody you'd like me to hit, is there?"

"Of course not."

"Sure?" he said. He had it well in mind that somebody ought to hit Sam. "Let's get back to where we were before I made a stump oration—to when I came in and you looked at me like a friend."

"I hope I always shall."

"All right. It's the privilege of a friend to be impertinent, and I'm rather good at impertinence. You see, Effie old thing, you're supposed to be one of the world's workers, and you're not at the office to-day. You haven't been at the office for weeks. I know, because I gave Florrie half a crown." Florrie was the maid. "And it isn't that you've come into money, because Florrie tells me you've been starving yourself."

"I've not." Effie was indignant. She had not starved herself. While all was dreary, food had certainly not attracted her, but neither had anything else; and she expected to take a lively interest in it now. "Really I've not."

"What you say goes," he said. "And Florrie imagined it, but she didn't imagine the part about your not going to the office, and if anything's wrong there, don't forget that I know Branstone pretty well. I can talk to him like a father."

"There's nothing wrong, anywhere," she said, and, indeed, things were not only not wrong but exuberantly right, only she could not tell him why.

"You're sure of that?" he persisted. "There's nothing you can tell a pal? Nothing you can tell me, when you know I'd walk through fire for you? Damn it, I can't pretend. I'm not a friend. I'm a man in love, and I ask you to be fair."

"Dubby," she pleaded, "don't make things too hard for me."

"Is it I who make them hard?" he asked, "oris it Sam?"

She looked at him amazed, and certainly Effie was stupid then, or, at least, too wrapped up in her great preoccupation to be alert. "Oh, don't be petty," she said. "I didn't debit you with jealousy."

"No? No? And yet I have a certain right to be jealous of him. I think you won't deny it."

It wasn't what he said or even the deep bitterness of his tone, it was something in his eyes, like a hurt animal's, which made her quite suddenly, and as a thing apart from his words, see what had happened. But she did not see even now the whole of Dubby's love and the beauty of his knightly move.

"You know!" she said. "Dubby, you knew when you spoke just now. You knew that Sam and I——"

"I told you I had a word with Florrie."

"Florrie?" she asked. "What could Florrie tell you?"

"Nothing," he said, "that she knew she told. Guessing is another of the things I'm good at."

She saw it then, to what perceptiveness his love had brought him, to what high action. It had sped her cloud and she saw, clear-eyed as he, his fine, impeccable fidelity.

"Oh! And I called you petty! I told you you were jealous. Dubby, I didn't know. You'd have done that for me!"

"Well, you see," he apologized, "I'm in love with you."

"Why can't we order love? Why does it come all wrong?" she cried.

"It hasn't come so wrong but I can put it right for you," he said, making his offer again.

"I? I didn't mean myself," she said, wondering. "Love's not come wrong to me. It's you I'm thinking of."

"But is it right for you?" he asked.

"Oh, yes," she smiled. "Terrifically."

"Is it? When Sam has not been near you in weeks?" It was wedged in his mind that Sam was playing the villain. "When you are here alone, do you see him, Effie?"

"No. That's why it's all so right."

He shook his head, perplexed. "It may be good metaphysics, but it sounds bad sense. I'll be quite honest with you. I'm suffering pretty badly from suppressed desire to horsewhip Sam Branstone. I think he deserves it, I know I'd enjoy it and I think you're trying to head me off it. I daresay it's primitive of me, but it will do me good and I don't mind telling you I need good doing to me. Effie, mayn't I go and horsewhip Sam?"

"If anybody's going to horsewhip Sam," said a voice, "it's me. I'm in charge of this job, not you, my lad."

They had not seen Anne come in. They saw her now, a little old woman of the working class in her best clothes, with a bugled cape and cotton gloves, elastic-sided boots and a quaint bonnet tied with ribbon beneath her chin, and, unaccountably, she filled the room. They would have passed her in the street without a second glance as one of the throng, at face value insignificant; but this was not Anne in the street. It was Anne in arms for Sam, and when Effie and Stewart compared notes afterwards they each confessed to having had the same thought: that their eyes were traitors and that what they saw was fantasy and what they felt was real.

"I'm Sam's mother," she introduced herself, "and it's like enough I were overfond of him when he was a lad and didn't thrash enough, but I'm not too old to start again. You'll be Effie? Aye, I've come round here to put things in their places. They've got a bit askew amongst the lot of you, and what I heard when I came in won't help." She looked accusingly at Dubby. "You'll be her brother, I reckon?"

It seemed to him the best way out. Anne had come to "put things in their places," and she reckoned he was Effie's brother, which, now he thought of it, was exactly his place. Brotherhood was thrust upon him, but he thought he had achieved it. Plainly, for all Effie's enigmas, there was nothing else for him, and he let Anne put him in his place.

"Yes," he said, without a glance at Effie, "her brother."

"You're a clean-limbed family," she complimented them, and Dubby stole a look at Effie, half humorous and half defying her to contradict his brotherhood. "Well, I came to see Effie, but I'll none gainsay that her brother has a right to stay and listen, if he'll listen quiet."

"Yes," said Dubby, still challenging Effie, "her brother has a right." And Effie did not deny him. She had her courage, but the unexpectedness of Anne and the force of her, as if for all these years she had been winding up her will, which now came into play like a spring immensely braced in super-tightened coils, caused her to want an ally and she agreed that Dubby had a right if not the one conferred on him by Anne.

"Won't you sit, Mrs. Branstone?" she said.

"I was wondering when I should hear your voice," said Anne. "You're not a talker, lass."

"No," said Effie.

"More of a doer." Effie was wondering whether that was praise or condemnation, when Anne added: "I like you the better for that, though it's a good voice. I haven't heard it much, but I've heard it. I haven't seen you much, but I've seen enough. I'm on your side, Effie." She astonished them both by rising as if to go.

"But," said Dubby, "is that all?"

Anne looked with humorous sympathy at Effie. "That's men all over, isn't it?" she said. "They're fond of calling women talkers, but a man's not happy till a thing's been put in words. Me and your sister understand each other now."

"I'm not quite certain that I do," said Effie.

"Well, maybe you're right," conceded Anne. "It's a fact that I told Sam last night I was coming round here to give you a piece of my mind, and I don't notice that I'm doing it. The need seemed to go when I set eyes on you, and I'm pretty full of a thing I want to do, only I've not quite got the face to ask."

"What is it, Mrs. Branstone?"

"I want to kiss you, lass," said Anne.

Dubby Stewart had for the second time that day the impression that women talked, so to speak, in hieroglyphics.... There seemed to be a kind of feminine shorthand to which only women held the key, and he did not understand the sudden softening of Ellie's face nor her quick response. And he did not know why, when Anne kissed her, Effie said, "No, no," nor why Anne said, "It isn't no. It's yes." A kiss, it seemed, had various meanings.

Anne in effect had conveyed to Effie that she thanked her and, more, she honoured her. Effie denied that she merited honour and Anne maintained that she did.

"Aye," said Anne, "he's had two dips in the lucky-bag and he's drawn a prize this time. It's more than any man deserves, but we'll not grudge it Sam, will we, Effie?" And to Dubby the thing took on a fresh aspect of bewilderment. If that meant anything, it meant that Anne was welcoming a daughter. Didn't the woman know that Sam was married?

"I've grudged him nothing," Effie said.

Anne meditated that, then looked at Effie with a touch of what was, for her, shyness. "You've grudged him nothing," she disagreed, "except your pride in giving up. And you can do it, you can give up, but Sam's nobbut a man, and they're a weak flesh, men. He looks the shadow of himself," she exaggerated resolutely.

"Does he?" said Effie anxiously, and Anne nodded a sombre face. "What do you want me to do, Mrs. Branstone?"

"I want you to give up giving up. Sam said a thing to me last night. He said you'd make him find salvation. Well, happen; but what's certain sure is that you made him find love. He's found it, lass, and he mustn't lose it, and he will if you leave things where they are. He's trying to do a thing that isn't, possible. He's trying to live aside of Ada, loving you. He'll try to love her for the love of you, and kiss her, telling himself he's kissing you, and it will not be you; and the love he tries to bring her will turn to loathing in his heart. And what'll happen then, when love goes sour within him? Eh, lass, you took yon lad to heaven and you're sending him to hell."

It was not fair to Stewart. It was hardly bearable: he was not her brother and he hadn't the feelings of a brother. He saw great happiness in Effie's face, as if two happinesses mingled there, the one of giving up her dream, the other of awakening to a sweet reality. He saw her put out a hand towards Anne, surrendering, consenting, giving all in one swift, heady leap from cloud to earth, and then he saw her sway, and caught her in time to break her fall.

Anne eyed him sharply. "Have you heard of your sister's fainting before, lately?" she asked, busy on her knees with Effie.

"Yes. Florrie told me. Twice. Can I do anything?"

"I'll bring her round," said Anne. "But you can do something. You can go to Sam at his office and tell him he's wanted here. Tell him I want him, and there's news for him. Send Florrie up as you go, and you needn't take that horsewhip with you, neither."

"No. I needn't take it now."

So Dubby, Effie's brother, went out on an embassy for Anne. "Feeling it? Feeling?" he thought, "you God-abandoned devil, what right have you to feel? A journalist. A looker-on. There's a story in this for you. There's the guts of a story given away to you with a cup of tea... on, no, we didn't have the tea; given neat, and you can't be decently grateful. What's the title? 'The Charwoman's Son'? No, damned if it is. Something about brother. Brother! Yes, you blighter, brother... brother, and proud of it. 'Pride of Kin.' That'll do, and God help me to live up to it." He turned into Sam's office and delivered his message in a cold, unemotional voice. It seemed that Effie, brave herself, was the cause of bravery in others.

"Effie! My mother! What have you to do with them?" asked Sam, amazed.

"I've given you a message," said the taciturn herald.

"But what's behind it, Dubby? Is Effie ill?"

Stewart was silent.

"Is she—dead?"

Dubby was tempted to say he didn't know. It; seemed to him that things went too happily with Branstone, that it was fit, if only for the twenty minutes which it would take for him to reach Busholme, to let Sam think that Effie might be dead, to let him taste the flavour of torture. Dubby suffered and would suffer, not for twenty minutes but, he gloomily anticipated, for a lifetime. Let Sam have his minutes of it! Then he remembered he was Effie's brother, and before Sam had his hat and coat on, malice had left him. "It's all right, man," he said. "She's neither ill nor dead. They've got good news for you."

CHAPTER XXIV
THE NEW BOOK OF MARTYRS

IF there was news which Anne must send posthaste to hid him come to hear, and if Effie was neither ill nor dead, he need not overtax his wits to guess it. Yet he had never thought of this very natural sequel to the Marbeck week, and the plain fact is that he did not much want to think of it now.

"I like your Effie," Anne told him. "I like her very well. She's going to make a grandmother of me."

He thought his mother had never been fatuous before: she thought he took the news morosely, and perhaps her expectation had been too high. She assumed that a child was the first consideration of a man's life; which is not true, even, of all women and true of only a minority of men.

Nor was Sam, in fact, morose. He had never been more intensely and silently alive. In itself, this thing was right with a shining exultant rightness which warmed him to the marrow. It crowned and completed Marbeck and it crowned and completed him. He who was childless was to be a father, and by Effie! He had nothing but a thankful emotion for that, and looked with yearning eyes at Effie, giver of all else, who was now to give him this. He had not known her wonder could increase.

He saw that more was expected of him than that he should look at her adoringly. Anne was on tip-toe with anticipation. Her difficulty, if indeed she had acknowledged to herself that there was any, had been to make these visionaries see that love mattered and that Ada did not; and her success with Effie had been complete. She had never doubted of success with Sam, the weaker vessel, for there was love, sufficient in itself; and there was now the added argument of Effie's child. She could not see that he had any choice.

He stood there conscious of the expectancy of their regard, and knew that he was failing them. He thought they took a blinkered view, seeing the child and nothing else. To them, apparently, the child came first: they were hypnotized by what was, really, an afterthought, and there was the greater need for him to keep a steadfast eye upon the truth. As he saw it, the truth was that he had put his hand to another plough; on Hartle Pike he had lighted such a candle by Effie's grace as he trusted would never be put out; and he had gone to Ada. True, Ada had gone from him, but that was temporary and trivial, whereas here was a real distraction and he saw two loyalties before him—to Effie and the idea, and to Effie and her child. It seemed to Sam that the first was the greater of these two.

He had wrestled with an afterthought before, one which hardly yielded in temptation to that which now confronted him, and he had thrown it. He had refused to contest Sandyford because there was not room for politics in a scheme which included Ada, and still less was there room for Effie. He felt faint with discouragement at the thought that Effie, unless appearance belied her, had capitulated to her afterthought, but he stood firmly by their treaty. They had decided that duty came first; he had shouldered duty; and he, at any rate, had no room for afterthoughts.

He was loyal to Effie and the Marbeck pact, duty's bondsman, Ada's husband. He made a gesture of decision, which Anne misinterpreted.

"Aye," she said a little smugly, "this settles it all right. It wasn't common sense in you to part before, but I reckon there'll be no parting now."

"No," said Effie softly, "not now." She stole a look of shy, glad confidence at Sam, and he found it extraordinarily difficult to meet her eye, and still more difficult to say what he must, at any cost, get said.

"I'm not so sure," he said at last, wishing the earth would swallow him.

At that moment he would cheerfully have given a hand to escape having to differ from them. They were Effie and his mother: they were his mother and Effie: the two women to whom he owed everything: more, he loved Effie so that every fibre in him yearned for her, and, even more than that, he was delicately sensitive to Effie in her present case. But it couldn't change him. His loyalty was engaged, to fanaticism, to another Effie, high Effie of the hills, of the crusade and the idea; and this seemed to him somehow, a lower Effie, an Effie who had dipped the flag of her ideal to a coming baby, whilst he was faithful to the old unbending Effie who had thrown an imitation wedding ring away. It almost seemed as if she wanted that ring back, base metal though it was.

A case, perhaps, of splitting hairs, but, at any rate, the case of a man with a faith at one extreme and at the other his miserable conviction that happiness was not for him. He had abandoned happiness when he left Marbeck, and lived now in a place where happiness was barred by Ada.

"I'm not so sure," he repeated drearily. "You see, there's Ada and I have to be fair to her."

"Ada's left you," snapped Anne. A contentious Sam was not going to find her amiable.

He chose to put it in another way. "My wife," he said, "is staying at present with her father. Yes, mother," he went on firmly, "I'm going to be fair to Ada and I've to guard against unfairness all the more because you won't be fair. You won't be ordinarily just. You always hated Ada."

"Yes," she agreed viciously. "I'm a clean woman. I always hated vermin."

Sam turned to Effle immensely heartened by this virulence. "You see!" he appealed, calling to witness the hopeless bias of his mother. It was, he wished to imply, this blind hatred of Anne for Ada which accounted for his mother's attitude, her exalting of—well—the mistress over the wife, her flagrant unmorality. He tried to put all this into his gesture. "And you," he reinforced it, "you sent me to her, Effie."

She bowed her head, admitting it, but Anne was not prepared to let it go at that. "Even Effie," she said "can make a mistake. She would not send you now."

And, looking at Effie, he saw that it was true. He had seen it from the first and it bothered him profoundly. Effie had changed: there was, in all they said, this noticeable stressing of the "now," to differentiate them from the "then." What was it? Anne's arguments, or the baby, or had Effie, uninfluenced by either, really changed her mind about the Marbeck treaty? he couldn't believe that last. Marbeck was infallible and he was dogged in the faith. He responded to the Marbeck creed like the needle of a compass to the meridian, and if with this needle also there was deflection it was corrected by his racial stubbornness. He had his people's queer, infatuated pride in the contemplation of their own tenacity, even when, perhaps mostly when, it hurts to be tenacious.

Whereas Effie had known ever since Dubby Stewart brought her back from cloud-land that Marbeck was very fallible indeed, or, rather, Marbeck was one thing and living up to Marbeck was another. If he had said, instead of only thinking, that she was a lower Effie now, she would not have contradicted him, though she did not want a wedding ring of either metal. She wanted Sam. She was changed from the idealist who thought she could be happy as a sign-post and a spiritual guide. She had come down to Mother Earth where men and women live. At Marbeck they were on an altitude where the air was too rarefied for human lungs, and she wanted to fall with Sam from selflessness to mere humanity.

"No," she agreed again with Anne, "I should not send you now."

"I shall have to think this out," he said. Effie admitted to being earthly, and he was horribly dismayed! "Effie," he cried in pain, "don't you see?" he wanted desperately to be understood by her, if not by Anne.

"I see," she said, and not without pride either. Whatever was fine in him, whatever reacted from an Eflie come to earth, was due to her, and she was proud of him even when, as now, he used her tempered steel against her.

Anne watched with a grim appreciation his anxiety to make a pikestaff plain. "We all see," she said. "You're none so deep and we're none so daft as all that. You've got a maggot in your brain, and I know the shape of it. I've had the same in mine, and if you'll think back ten years, you'll know what I mean. We're the same breed, Sam, and we can both do silly things and stand by then and suffer for them. I flitted from you to Madge, and I didn't set eyes on you from that day till last night. That's what I mean by suffering."

And there, in those few words, the tragedy of ten years stood confessed. Parted from Sam, she lived in exile, suffering, and, of course, he had known it and deliberately forgot it, so that the point of her revelation was not its truth, but the amazing fact that she should speak of it at all. Anne had the pride which suffers silently.

"Mother!" he said, distressed for her.

"Nay, none of that," she bade him harshly. "If I were soft enough to let it hurt me, that's my look out. But here's the point, Sam. There's another woman soft about you, too, and she's not the same as me. I'd had you since I bore you, and I were not young when you and me came to a parting; but she's young, and you'll none make Eflie suffer the road I suffered while there's strength in me to say you nay. I'd have gone to my grave without your knowing this if it hadn't been for Effie. It's not good for a man to know too much. They're easy stuffed with pride."

She pretended, with deep magnanimity, to think that he had not known until she told him, but they both knew very well that he had always known. She dwelt deliberately on it now to inform him, not of her suffering, but of the intensity of her feeling for Effie. It was so intense that she could speak of her own suffering: for Effie's sake she had unveiled, thrown off her stoicism, and flung the spoken truth as a challenge and a revelation at him.

He knew what speaking in this manner cost her, but he was stubborn still in relating all she said to her ungovernable hate of Ada; whereas Anne did not hate Ada ungovernably, but only when Ada hurt Sam.

Again he said "Mother!" and got no further with it.

"I know I'm your mother," she said, "and you can stop thinking of me now and think of Effie."

"I'm trying to," he said.

"Well?" said Anne impatiently. She hadn't imagined an obstinacy which would not yield to what she had said. Surely he knew the sacrifice of pride she made in saying it! And there was Effie, too, who said little and looked the more.

"I don't know," he despaired.

"Then others must know for you," said Anne, and when his lips only tightened at that, "Sam," she pleaded, "surely you'll never go against the pair of us."

But there were two Effies, and he wasn't "going against" them both, while he held Anne to be mesmerized by hate of Ada. For all that, it desolated him to be in opposition to them now, to Anne and Effie, the women who counted, the women who gave. "Still," he had to say, "there's Ada."

He said it, as he hoped to say it, finally. He wanted to get away from these two, to escape from their distracting presence to a place where he could think. After all, Hartle Pike had not settled his problem, and he must try somewhere else—Platt Fields, perhaps. They had a sort of space.

But he could not escape—not, at least, till Anne had played her ace. Anne had not finished yet, though she had hoped ten years in the wilderness had been enough. It seemed that they were not, and she must wander still. Well, she could do what she must.

"Oh, aye," she said dryly, "there's Ada. There's your bad ha'penny, and I reckon summat'll have to be done with her. But if you'll stop worrying, lad, and if worst comes to the worst, I'll take Ada on myself."

Effie started towards her. "No, no," she cried.

"You hold your hush," said Anne. This was Anne's game, not Effie's.

Sam was still staring at her. "You!" he said. "What can you do?"

"I can see you and Effie happy, and I dunno as owt else matters." It did not matter what the cost was to Anne. "When you used to come home to your tea from Mr. Travers' office, what you left was always good enough for me, and I can stomach your leavings still."

It startled Effie, who had thought herself a specialist in sacrifice. This was the very ferocity of self-denial.

So far, tired and overstrained, Effie had found peace in resigning the leadership to Anne, but here was a lead she could not follow. It was not that she mistook Anne's purpose or doubted her capacity. Her faith in Anne was young but adamantine, and she knew that if Anne replaced Sam with Ada, and made herself heir to the Marbeck plan, she would unquestionably do for Ada what Sam had undertaken to do. But the thing was simply not good enough.

"No, Mrs. Branstone, no," she said firmly.

"Get oft' with you," said Anne impolitely. "I can tackle Ada with one hand tied behind my back."

"Of course," Sam agreed, "you could, but you are not going to. Ada's my job."

"I can be pig-headed as well as you, my lad," Anne menaced him.

"It's not that, mother."

"No, it isn't that," said Effie, conceiving perhaps that it was time for her to enter into this tragicomedy of rivalry in self-surrender. "Sam's right. Ada does matter, and it is I who am the failure, I who have broken faith, I who was arrogant. I thought that I could bear a torch, and I can only bear a child. But I know now what I have to do. I can go away. I can disappear."

It seemed to Anne that this was serious because obviously it was a way out; but she thought it a way much more appalling in prospect than the plan she had proposed for herself of "taking Ada on." She took alarm. In another than Effie it might have been heroics, but Effie's was not the stuff that mouths bravado. Anne granted that, and saw a tragic chasm yawn She signalled her alarm to Sam, who answered it with a glance which made appeal to her, whilst yielding nothing of his obstinacy.

"If you go away," he said, "my mother goes with you. I've meant that from the first."

Anne nodded without enthusiasm. Certainly that was a solution and equally not the solution. It gave Sam to Ada, and Effie, it appeared, was not seeing it as a solution at all. There were strange possibilities, Anne thought, in this young woman, and she did not want them to be tested too far. Effie was not a talker, and when she said a thing she did not overstate. There was danger. Well, Anne was forewarned, and addressed herself in her most humorous, common-sense manner to laugh it out of court. One can deal with danger in worse ways than to apply to it the acid—ridicule.

She put her arms akimbo and surveyed Effie and Sam appraisingly. "I dunno," she said, "that there's a pin to choose between the three of us for chuckle-headed foolishness. We're all fancying ourselves as hard as we can for martyrs and arranging Ada's life for her. It hasn't struck any of us yet that Ada's likely to arrange things for herself."

And if Sam's impulse was to say gloomily: "It isn't likely at all," he repressed it when Anne's eye caught his, and said instead, "That's so," without knowing why he said it and without believing it.

The flicker of a smile crossed Effie's face; Sam as conspirator struck her as crudely humorous. Anne saw the smile and understood, but brazened it out. "Of course it's so," she said, defying Effie. "Ada's a poor thing of a woman, but she's none beyond having a mind and speaking it. I was always one to take the short road out of trouble, so I'll go along to Peter Struggles' now."

"Very well," consented Effie, and Anne understood her to mean that the crisis, if one had impended, was postponed. "But," said Effie, "of course, I saw."

Which was, in its way, a challenge; it was, at any rate, to tell Anne that Effie knew what had been suspected of her.

Anne met it as a challenge. "Well?" she said.

"You were quite wrung, Mrs. Branstone," said Effie quietly. "I'm not a coward."

Anne was tying her bonnet-si rings, and found it convenient to look down. She preferred, just then, not to meet Effie's eye. "I know I'm overanxious," she mumbled in apology.

"And there's no need," said Effie, a little cruel in her victory.

To Sam the conversation seemed to have slipped into another dimension. He hadn't the faintest idea what they were talking about.

CHAPTER XXV
WHOM GOD HATH JOINED

PETER Struggles walked into his tobacconist's and put his snuff-box on the counter. There was no need to state his requirements; in fact, he had not stated them for many years. Shopman and customer understood each other very well, and business came first; then if there was inclination, as there usually was, talk followed.

To-day, however, the shopman gaped at Peter in surprise, and made a half-turn of his head, so that he could see his calendar Wednesday was Peter's day for buying snuff with a regularity to which time had given the force of a tradition, and the tobacconist had even the habit of using Peter's visit as a reminder to a fallible memory that he must wind his clock. The calendar continued him in his belief that to-day was Thursday, and he felt sure that Peter had been in as usual on Wednesday.

Peter had. Snuffing, of course, is a wasteful habit in any case, and a shaking hand misses the target more freely than a steady one; but, for all that, Peter, in his mental anguish, had consumed in one night the better part of his week's supply of snuff. The box was indubitably empty. He had not come to replenish it without some conscientious qualms—an allowance is an allowance—but he felt that life which comprised Ada in her present mood and did not comprise snuff, was beyond bearing. Ada was, it seemed, inevitable: he must mitigate Ada.

"The usual, if you please, Thomas," he unusually said.

"Yes, sir," said Thomas, filling the box. "You've had a little accident?"

"An accident? Oh!" Then the fitness of that guess struck him. "Yes, Thomas, a little accident. By the way, do you know anything about divorce?"

"Well, sir, I read the *Sunday Judge*," Thomas replied deprecatingly. "Very human subject, sir, divorce."

"You find it so?"

"I take a lot of satisfaction in reading about my sinful fellow-creatures."

"Quite, quite," said Peter vaguely, and went out of the shop, leaving a puzzled salesman behind him. "Forgot to pay, and all," thought Thomas. "Not that I'd grudge it if he didn't pay, only it's not like him. He looks sadly to day. The old boy's breaking up. Him and divorce! What does he want to worry his head about divorce for?"

Peter did not know that he had mentioned divorce, to his tobacconist. It would have shocked him if he had known. He spoke unconsciously, and listened mechanically to the man's reply, but he was, harrowingly, "worrying his head" about divorce. He took snuff in the street, an unheard-of occurrence, but it did not clear his aching brain of the fateful word "divorce."

Ada had put it there too firmly in her stupid and invincible malignity. She had one aim—to do Sam the greatest injury she could. His offence was rank, and she demanded a proportionate revenge.

She had lived as a spinster for marriage and as a wife by marriage. Marriage was not a duty, but a state of beatitude, and she had walked in the faith of her grotesque illusion that her marriage was singularly blessed. It was childless, and the more blessed for that: there were no intruders on the perfect union of man and wife. It was illusion, and a wilder perversion of the truth than the ordinary self-deceiver can attain; but illusion is the breath of life, and she had fed on her deception till, like a drug-taker, she could not live without it. She had blazoned it abroad in a hundred drawing-rooms. If there were low-voiced colloquies of this or that affair, if it was hinted that men were faithless ever, Ada would grow superior and boast the flawless rectitude of Sam. These were things which happened to other people, who very likely deserved them, and could by no manner of means occur to her. She was not so sunk in imbecility as to deny that they did happen, and to people who were, nominally, married; but they were unsound people, insecurely married. There was a fundamental difference between their marriages and hers. She couldn't explain; it was too obvious for explanation. She was married, and these others, somehow, were married, yet not married. They had, through lack of merit, stopped short of the seventh paradise where nothing could shake consummate bliss. They were not as she was.

And now she had to face the fact that the impossible had happened to her, and not only had it happened, but was known to have happened. That was where the blow struck home. She had publicly elaborated her case of absolute conviction, she had vaunted his faithfulness, the cardinal connubiality of Sam, and Miss Entwistle was spreading the news that she had been a doting fool! And she hadn't. She had not doted on Sam. She had not been infatuated with her husband, but with the idea of her husband which she had created and maintained. If only she had had the gumption to defy Miss Entwistle! If only she had concealed her belief in the story as successfully as she had hidden the fact that Sam had a separate room! She had been taken by surprise, she had admitted everything by default, and, worse, she had assured Mrs. Grandage that she would never see Sam again. She did not doubt, in spite of Mrs. Grandage's good-nature, that this little sequel to the story of Miss Entwistle was in rapid circulation.

She was humiliated publicly, and, as she saw it, the one course open to her was to make Sam suffer a humiliation as drastic and as public as her own. Though it hurt her, he must pay for it; though she died, he must be punished and, sincerely, she expected it to kill her. She lived in a garden of lies, and life without the illusion of her marriage would be as impossible as life without the fragrance of her poisonous flowers to Rappaccini's daughter, but no matter for that. Ada must be revenged, and divorce, though it killed her, would be the greatest injury that she could do a politician and a pietistic publisher. She managed to square the circle, too. She was to die and make a murderer of him; she was to ruin his business and make a bankrupt of him; and at the same time she was to have the compensation of a handsome alimony. But perhaps vengeance is always irrational, and that is why it belongs to God.

She dinned her word into Peter's ears with the merciless reiteration of a hurt and howling child. It was her first word and her last, and appeals based on religion shattered themselves against it as fruitlessly as the appeal to reason. What she had said she had said: and she had said "Divorce." Alternatives did not exist.

For Peter, divorce ranged itself with the abominations of the world, a man-made legal subterfuge to evade the law of God. There might, conceivably, be occasions when divorce was to be condoned as the comparatively little wrong which did a great right, and he tried very honestly to see Ada's as one of those heroic needs. He failed: he could not even see that Ada was hurt in soul, or in anything but pride. She was in a mood, not of spiritual revolt, but of peevish discontent.

Small wonder that he snuffed prodigiously that night. He had his meed of suffering, and overcharged his small account with dreadful self-reproach. He, not Ada, and not Sam, was responsible for her violence and for the cause of it; he and the books upon his shelves; reading, his darling sin. He blamed himself for consenting too readily to their marriage. Sam, he had thought, would lead Ada: on what grounds had he thought it? What had he known of Sam's leadership—a prolix, fluent boy at the Concentrics? He had exchanged his daughter for peaceful, solitary evenings with his books—

"Self-seeker!" he thought—and the exchange was to recoil upon him now. He had abandoned, after one harsh, undaughterly repulse, his attempt to show her that wearing a wedding ring was not the whole duty of woman— "The sin of Pride," he thought—and had returned to browse amongst his books. Sam seemed a good fellow, too. There were those Classics, and the texts, and the prosperous old age of Mr. Carter, who, but for Sam, would certainly have ended his days in the workhouse. But, failing with Ada, he ought to have appealed to Sam.... Yes, he ought to have taken a strong line with Sam, instead of letting Sam's worldly success dazzle him. Sam had seemed too big for Peter Struggles to grapple with—the sin of cowardice.

Now it had come to this! Sam had broken the seventh commandment, and Ada wished to forget the words which Peter had read over them when he joined their right hands together, and said, "Those whom God hath joined together, let no man put asunder." She commanded a divorce, and it was useless for Peter to insist, out of his small store of worldly wisdom, that divorce was not hers to command. Sam had not been "cruel."

Her fury only doubled. Gone, vanished like the snows of long ago, was her painted idyll of domestic bliss.

"Cruel?" she said. "He's never been anything but cruel. I'm black and blue with his atrocities."

Very gently he tried to tell her that he did not believe it. "We must not exaggerate," he said.

"Exaggerate!" she blazed. "Won't you believe me till you see it? I'll go upstairs and strip. Come when I call."

He soothed her down at that, seeing that she was capable of doing herself some signal injury to call in evidence.

"Well, then," she said, "I want my divorce: get me a divorce." That was her simple demand of the priest who married her: it was why Peter took, unrepentantly, as much snuff in a night as he commonly took in a week, and why, with replenished stock, he continued next day to take snuff with a lavish hand.

It irritated Ada, though she had always associated Peter with a snuff-box, and the untidiness of the habit could not offend her, who was never offended by dirt, as any mechanical movement in another will irritate one whose nerves are ill-controlled. They had talked themselves to a standstill, and sat in moody silence, broken only by the deplorable sound of taking snuff.

She looked viciously at him. "If you do that again, I shall leave the room," she said.

"I'm sorry, my dear," he said, although, really, it was a pleasant threat; but when he did it again, it was through pure absent-mindedness, and he was terribly distressed at his selfishness when Ada flung out of the room. He had the feelings of a child put in a corner as a punishment, and to relieve them he took snuff again. She heard him from the stair, and heard him immediately afterwards poking the fire; and she thought the loathsome self-absorption of men and their utter callousness to the anguish of sensitive women were proved beyond the possibility of doubt. She threw herself on the bed in her old room, alone in a friendless world.... The bed had a warm eiderdown.

Peter poked the fire because it needed poking. It often did. The grate was one of those labour-making contrivances which must be periodically cleared of ash if the fire is to burn at all, and it was rarely cleared. The woman who "did for" Peter, did for him badly, and he was at the age when a man needs artificial warmth: a gaunt, shrunk figure as neglected as his house. Small wonder that, apart from his attachment to St. Mary's, he was still a curate. They had considered him for the living when his vicar moved some years ago, they had considered the little circle of rich parishioners who made an oasis of civilization in that savage place, and they had decided that Peter lacked the social graces. They had seen his mittens, his unfinished coat... they had seen him eat an orange: and he remained a curate.

The fire was gone beyond the reach of his unscientific poking. That, too, often happened with a man who had the habit of standing by his bookshelf reading gluttonously, with his austere person frozen into a grotesque attitude, some book which he had not the patience to carry to the fireside: and he was now upon his knees making pathetically clumsy efforts to revitalize the flame when his inefficient housekeeper opened the door and showed Anne into the room.

It eased the situation for them both. Anne indeed, was nervous, so nervous that she had walked three times past the door before she pulled the bell. She had a befitting awe of the priest, and a tremendous respect for the man. At Effie's, because the circumstances there were tense, it had seemed an easy thing to come to Peter's, but she had needed to call on her reserves of courage to keep her place on the doorstep after she had rung the bell.

Now, however, when she came into the room and saw what he was at, she pushed him gently aside, and took the poker from his hand. She nursed the fire skilfully; she was with familiar things which gave her back her confidence.

As to the trouble, she diagnosed it in a moment. "That woman of yours is a slut," she said. "And I'll talk to her before I go. I reckon I've the right, me and you being connections by marriage."

She looked at him over her shoulder, and saw that he did not recognize her. How, indeed, should he? She had avoided Ada's wedding, and she was one of a large flock: a face, perhaps, but not a name to him. "I'm Anne Branstone," she explained. "Sam's mother; and I'll not have you blaming Sam for this."

"For the fire?" asked Peter vaguely, he was rather muddled by her brisk incursion.

"No," said Anne, almost gaily; "for the fat that's in the fire."

She thought she had his measure now—the sort of a man who could live in a dirty room like this, with a choked ash-pan and fire-irons with the rust thick on them. But Peter was greater than that. She judged him by those of his surroundings which had significance for her, and not by books which expressed everything for him and nothing for her.

"Mrs. Branstone!" he said, as if realizing now with whom he had to deal.

"Sam's mother," she repeated, rising from a healthy fire; "and I've told you where not to put the blame. You can, maybe, think yourself of the right place to put it."

"Yes," he surprised her by saying; "on me."

"You! Oh, if you want to go to the back of behind, you can blame Adam and Eve. But that's not what I meant."

"On me," he said again. "I consented to this marriage. I sanctioned it."

"Well," said Anne, "I've not come here to crow, but I've the advantage of you in that. I did not consent," and her eye strayed involuntarily to a scar on her hand, memorial of the form of her dissent. "I didn't consent because I knew they weren't in love. I told Sam I knew it."

"Then," said Peter, "you are worthier than I am, Mrs. Branstone."

"Because I knew love matters? There's nowt so wonderful in knowing that, and nowt so crafty in foreseeing that a marriage where there is no love is marred from start to finish."

"Love matters," he agreed. "It matters all, for God is love."

"We'll come to an agreement, you and me," she said appreciatively. "We've the same mind about the root of things."

"This is a terrible business, Mrs. Branstone."

"I'm none denying it. It's a terrible thing for a man and wife to live together when love's not a lodger in the house; it's wrong, and the worst of wrong is that it won't stay single. Wrong's got to breed. But, there," she finished briskly, "I'm telling you what you know, and when all's said, there's nowt so bad that it's past mending."

"Ada wants a divorce," said Peter, and a sudden glint of triumph came into Anne's eye, only to vanish as quickly as it came. She had said, without believing it, that Ada might make arrangements, and this was to arrange indeed. It unmade the hollow marriage, it was a solution which really solved, it was a clean cut; and she wanted to glorify Ada, who was proving at the eleventh hour that she had the saving grace of common sense.

Peter did a curious thing. He rose and took a book haphazard from his shelf, came back to his chair and opened the book. He did not read it, and he was not being rude, but this was an agitation beyond the reach of snuff. He tried to calm himself by resting his eyes on print.

Anne was not practised in the ways of bookish men, but, by strange insight, understood that Peter had gone to a book much as she went to his grate, to be soothed by its familiarity, and her rejoicing at his words came to an abrupt end. His action brought home to her, more than his horror-struck tone, whose significance she almost missed in her joy at Ada's practical solution, his loathing of divorce: and it seemed to her, quite suddenly, that what mattered most in all this business was that Peter should be happy about it.

It mattered more than Sam and Ada, and even more than Effie, that Peter, who was, so to speak, an old and sleeping partner, should be satisfied by their solution. She did not care if this was to per vert the values: the remnant of Peter Struggles' life was of more importance than the young lives of the active members of the firm. And because she had a practical mind, and believed that one is happy in soul only when one is first happy in body, she was already thinking past their present problem: she was considering how the slut in Peter's kitchen could be replaced by her own housewifely self.

She resolutely consigned that thought to the future, and returned to the question of to-day. Ada, wonderfully, wanted a divorce: but Anne required that Peter should be happy about it, and she perceived the incompatibility. She saw that juxtaposition could hardly be more crude. He was a priest, the priest who married them, and she wanted him to acquiesce contentedly in their divorce.

"Wants a divorce, does she?" she said. "Well, there's more than Ada to be thought of."

"There is, indeed," said Peter, thinking of his church.

"There's you," said Anne, thinking of him. "If she gets one, does she plant herself on you again?"

He supposed so, unable to disguise his depression at the prospect.

"Aye," she rubbed it in, "you were well rid of Ada once. It's not in human nature to want her back again." She was thinking singly of his comfort.

Peter, on his part, took her to imply that if he opposed a divorce it was for interested motives, that he could continue to be "well rid of Ada." He saw with dismay that it was an interpretation which could reasonably be put on any opposition from him. He thought, in his humility, that it was a reasonable interpretation, whereas, Peter being Peter, it was a ludicrously unjust interpretation, and, of course, Anne did not make it. She had only stated as a fact that Ada at home prejudiced her father's comfort: and the comfort of Ada's father had become a matter which touched Anne Branstone nearly.

"And there are other people, too. There's Sam," she went on, "and he is a desperate bad case. He has no love for Ada. He's hoisted his notion of his duty higher than a living love. He wants Ada to come back."

"I'm sorry to say," mourned Peter, "that the more he wants it, the less likely she is to go."

She tried not to exult too openly at that. "And then," she said, "there's Effie."

"Effie!" He spoke in scandalized protest.

"Aye, that's her name, and yon's just the tone of voice I had myself when I first heard of her. I want you to see Effie."

"Never!" said Peter, and for a mild man his bitterness was remarkable.

"Then I must show her to you," said Anne placidly, "and that'll mean going back a bit and showing you other things as well. It'll mean," and she very much regretted it, "showing you this." She held out her hand and pointed to the scar. "When Sam told me he wanted to marry Ada, I came to see her. I saw what I saw, and I told him she'd be the ruin of him. He didn't believe me, and I tried to make him see I meant it. I put my hand into the fire, and I thought to keep it there till he agreed with me, but he's stronger in the arm than me, and he got me away." She spoke without passion, in simple narrative which Peter found impressed him deeply. "So I left him and earned my living, and all that. Sam married her, and the ruin's come, but it's not come suddenly. It's been coming all the time. I'd date it back," she reflected, "to the day when he fooled you about the 'Social Evil' pamphlet. He did that because he wanted a rich husband for Ada."

Peter had nothing to say. If he had not known before that Sam had "fooled" him, he did not doubt it now.

"And it grew from that. He's made money because Ada wanted money, and after that it grew to be a bad habit. He made it then by writing lies about himself in the papers, and I don't know how he's done it since then, except that it has been by more lies. He began to fancy himself at politics. He wanted to be a crowing cock, and it didn't matter if he crowed on a dung-heap so long as he crowed. And Ada didn't care. He gave her money, and she didn't care. She didn't love, and he didn't love, and there's a thing you said just now that I'll remind you of. You said God's love. I'll leave it to you to name what it is when there isn't love.

"And then love came to Sam. Effie came, and you say that God is love. Sam put it to me in another way. He said he'd found salvation. Well, it's a big word, and I dunno. But I do know he found love and it changed him. He's done with politics, and he's done with crowing and with riches, too. Effie did that by the power of love, and there's another thing she did, that's marked yon lass for me as the finest, strangest woman in the width of the world. She gave him up and sent him back to Ada. Well, I've heard of sacrifice before, and I've done a bit that way myself, but give up a man she loved and teach him how to make a woman of his wife, and send him home to do it—it's more than I can rise to. And that is Effie Mannering.

"He went home and he tried, and Ada laughed at him. She couldn't understand: there wasn't the one thing there that could make her understand: there wasn't love. And he gave up his politics that night she laughed at him, to leave himself free to tackle Ada. Now Ada's left him, and there's sum-mat else turned up as well. You can guess." He looked up sharply. "Aye, that's it, and the rum thing is that it surprised them both. Their love's that sort of love, and I reckon there are folk would call it careless of them. I would myself nine cases out of ten, aye, and ninety-nine in a hundred, but not this case. This wasn't a case for care; it was a case of love. But a baby's coming to Effie, and you know' as well as I do that none will ever come to Ada. I've finished telling you about Effie now." There was a long pause and it seemed several times that Peter was about to break it, and each time changed his mind. All that he finally said in comment on Effie was, "A lawless woman," and it might have been deduced from his tone that he did not condemn, if he could not, confessedly, admire.

"Aye, lawless," Anne agreed, "but there's a law of lawless women and she has not obeyed it. She's not a breaker. She's a maker."

Peter bowed his head. Perhaps he did not wish Anne to see what was written in his face. And he lacked conviction when he tried to speak again. "Whom God hath joined—he began.

"But God," Anne said, "is love."

He threw up his hands in a despairing gesture of surrender. "I deserve to be unfrocked for this," he said, but he closed the book on his knee and took snuff violently. It marked the passing of a crisis.

As for Anne, there mingled with her satisfaction at his consent a keen despondency at his unhappiness. She had both lost and won, and Anne took little pleasure in a mixed victory. She had not finished yet with Peter Struggles.

CHAPTER XXVI
SNOW ON THE FELLS

LIFE is still greater than machines. Machines accomplish marvels and very wonderfully continue to accomplish them, but life refuses the mechanical. It was man, and not nature, who invented the wheel, and life does not revolve upon an axle. Life will not repeat itself: and it can excel itself.

They had not thought, when they came back to Marbeck at the turn of the year, that Marbeck could be better than before. They came hoping, they said, to recapture the old emotions, and brought Anne with them to show her their fairyland. They did not recapture the old emotions, because they were young emotions, a ferment like youth itself, and things were settled now. They seemed to look back from their equable security to a wild infancy of their emotion, a fumbling, frenzied, awkward age of love. Of course they looked back happily, from a place where things were happy and serene to one where things were happy and impetuous.

The Dale was full of wonder, with a wonder which now belonged unerringly to fact and had mellowed in reality.

For Anne, it was a pretty place, but "lonesome," and, amazingly to them, she chafed to leave it. Anne did not suffer holidays gladly.

They had extolled Anne, they had not thought it credible that she should fail at anything, and it ruffled them disturbingly to find her fail at this. They had planned eagerly and, indeed, generously to bring her with them to Marbeck—generously, because they wanted to be alone, and even Anne, owe her what they did and be she what she might, was an intruder. But they wanted her to share with them their wonderland. Marbeck was theirs, theirs intimately and alone, their holy place, and they could think of nothing finer, nothing which came more nearly to her deserts of them, than to initiate her to their secret worship.

They made her free of Marbeck, relived their week for her as much as for themselves, showed her where this and that dear folly happened, took her to view-points whence she could see the tops of hills they climbed, using the landscape as the ground-plan of an ecstasy which they invited her to share, and were discomposed to find that Anne, plainly straining enthusiasm in their behalf, could only say of Marbeck, their Marbeck, "I'm sure it's very nice."

She damned with faint praise their enchanted valley in whose every tree they took by now as fierce a joy as if they had created it, and in despair they dragged her, as a last hope, to the very Holy of their holies, the top of Hartle Pike. If she failed them there, if she did not see the beauty and the grace, the penetrating significance and the absolute sanctity of Hartle Pike, then her greatness was lopsided, resulting, like a show chrysanthemum, from the atrophy of other possibilities.

It was a great day for the fells, when a frozen surface crushed elastically underfoot and kept one dryshod anywhere, and they walked in frosty, sun-kissed air, keenly exhilarating yet spicily warm. Snow capped the greater heights and seemed to clarify an atmosphere already clear, but the dales were free of snow and never more fit for walking than now when their boggy surface was dried up and roughened to the tread by crisp, granulated particles of frost.

Anne granted to herself that if one must take a holiday, this generous activity made nearly a venial matter of it. To climb these slopes was almost as satisfying to her body as to wash a long flight of steps, and she reached the top feeling as pleasantly tired as if she had done half a day's charring.

Still, she hadn't charred, and there was in fact nothing which needed charring, nothing but a cleanliness which positively irritated her. She itched to be doing something and there was manifestly nothing to do except to enjoy herself. And if Anne Branstone was not doing a job, she liked, at any rate, to know that her next job was around the corner. She began, for the first time in her life, to feel a friendliness towards dirt. In the midst of this sprawling insolence of triumphant cleanliness, she hankered for a little humanizing soot. She could have loved her life-long enemy, and he did not appear... it was not a bit like Manchester.

Far to the west, beyond a barrier of gleaming snow, she saw a murky cloud of smoke where the foul boot of industrialism stamps on the Lakeland Coast—a message and a call. It spoke, to her of natural dirt in this great waste of unstained purity; it made her sick for home and the thing she had to do.

Effie and Sam stood gazing at the hills, spell-hound by loveliness, and when they tore their dancing eyes away it was to look into each other's. They had no need of words: their eyes exulted in the burnished splendour of the scene, and with a doubled exultation each in the other's joy. Then Sam turned hopefully to Anne and saw that she was looking with a rapt intensity at the west. At last, it seemed, the hills had touched her.

"Where's yon?" she asked, "yon smoke?"

His face fell as he told her, but he saw that this explained Anne's failure. She had not relished Marbeck because she had not seen it. She had not been looking at Marbeck, but all the while at something else.

And why, he questioned, why, now that things had so admirably arranged themselves, must Anne still live in thought in Manchester? There seemed to him to be no law, nothing which could conceivably distract her attention, nothing which had not with genial finality been neatly finished off. Of course they had stupid legal business to come, but that was well ahead and, in any case, was not to worry them.

She could not, surely, be troubling about Ada. It was he who had made the trouble there, insisting that Ada was "his job."

He insisted to the point of almost literally forcing himself upon her in Peter Struggles' house, and remembered now with a twinge that desolating interview, if interview it could be called, and its liberating end; how Ada had looked at him, and answered nothing to his abject and passionate appeals (he wondered how he could have made them, but he was despairingly sincere): how he had pleaded and apologized for the past and supplicated for the future, all in the mastering grip of his Marbeck faith, and how she had kept silent till she turned on Peter and told him she must leave a house which did not shelter her from the deadly insult of this man's presence. He remembered the good woman, Mrs. Grandage, who had carried Ada to a Hydro at Southport, and wrote to Peter that Ada seemed quite happy there, "nursing her grievance like a child," and was looking for a house. He had found something mystifying about the intervention of Mrs. Grandage: good nature fortified by a bad conscience was his attempt to explain her attitude, but what emerged clearly from the letters she wrote to Peter was that Ada had no intention of returning to Manchester: and when he thought of Southport, he realized its quintessential rightness as her home. He had not shirked his job; he had eaten dirt before her in his anxiety to do his job; and he was not allowed. What she was she must remain, and Southport seemed the aptest place for her. "Only," as Mrs. Grandage wrote, "she mast have money."

That was not difficult, and the money might have come in many ways: it came actually in a way which Effie hated and Sam thought exquisitely right. It came through Stewart, that faithful ally of the publishing business in its early days.

Dubby was in Effie's room, "which is where," he said, "your brother has a right to be."

"You keep that up," she smiled.

"Is the poor dog to get none?" he asked.

"He is to have whatever he wants," she said.

"—that's going," he completed her sentence.

"Yes," said Effie, not smiling now, and kissed him very simply to seal his brotherhood.

He stood silent for a moment, then, with a jerk of his head he, so to speak, cut his loss and turned to her with the frank confidence of their settled relationship. "Now we can talk," he said. "Tell me about old Sam. What are you going to do with him? And with his business?"

She evaded his first question. "The business? Oh, he'll sell that."

"Then let me buy."

"You! Oh!"

"Why not?"

"You know what I think of it."

"I'm only the dog, my dear. Do you know any Greek? There's a connection between being a dog and being a cynic. In certain circumstances, I'd have thought with you to the crack of doom, but your brother's a cynic."

"I see," said Effie sadly. "But he will always be my brother, Dubby."

"Thanks, Effie," he said. "That will keep me on the sweeter side of currishness. But a dog wants meat. You'll tell Sam I'm to have the first refusal of that business. I'll scrape a syndicate together in a week."

So the Stewart Publishing Syndicate, which now has dashing offices near Covent Garden, came to birth and Ada got her money. When Sam tried to tell Effie that his investments outside the business were ridiculously small, she had refused to be impressed.

"It's not the means of life that matters, Sam. It's living: it's the quality of life: it's what we do with life," she said, and Ada got the means.

"She'll be married in a year to a man from Liverpool," said Dubby, when he heard.

"Why Liverpool?" asked Sam, and Dubby shrugged his shoulders. He thought Sam's question stupid.

"By the way, Sam," Dubby said, "have you and Effie any plans?"

"No," said Effie, when Sam hesitated, but a brother's curiosity was not to be stifled like that, and Sam's face told her, too, how he had hung on her reply. She resented his anxiety, the proof that he had not dropped his calculating habit. They had not discussed the question of plans because she held there was no question to discuss, and Sam, she thought, deserved a little punishment for thinking otherwise. "I suppose," she went on, "we shall stay in Manchester and face the music."

"Oh!" said Sam blankly.

"Well, we must give Mr. Verity his revenge," she teased.

"But it can't hurt me now I'm out of politics," he said, confessing by his tone that it would hurt him very much.

"It will please him, though," she said.

"I'd... I'd thought of going to America," he ventured.

"America!" scoffed Dubby. "*O sancta simplicitas!* America's not El Dorado, Sam. El Dorado's been found. I'd even say it's been found out."

"There are big things in America," Sam defended his idea.

"As a matter of fact, Dubby," said Effie, silencing him, "we shall go to Marbeek for a little while. It's a good place to begin from."

With that a great contentment came to Sam. They were to go to Marbeek; they were to begin; and he no longer questioned what. He made no hard and fast surrender of his will, but recognized the fact, not for the first time, that when Effie made a decision it had a shining rightness. Perhaps she had retreated from her first decision of Marbeck, but, if so, Anne helping him, he had retreated with her; and they went to Marbeek now, not to end, but to begin, and to begin together.

Reflecting on it all, he could not see the blemish. He couldn't, for the life of him, make out why Anne was not content.

He half explained the valley's failure to enchant her when he perceived that she had not really looked at it. At what, then, could she be looking? And how could she, how in the name of beauty was it possible for anyone to pick out from all that noble amphitheatre of the hills the one smoke-clouded spot?

"Mother," he cried in downright exasperation, "aren't you happy here?",

"I'd be happier in Manchester," she said. "Yon smoke's too far away to taste. Aye, I think I'll leave you here and go to-day."

"But you're not going back to Madge's—to the work in other people's houses, I mean. That's surely over now."

"Maybe."

"Mother, you've done with work."

She eyed him grimly. "Not till I'm dead, my lad," she said.

"Why won't you tell me what you're thinking of?"

"I'm thinking," she said, "of yon slut in Peter Struggles' kitchen. I'll have her out of that tomorrow."

He glanced at Effie, and then looked again. He fancied he had surprised a little smile on Effie's face and looked twice to make sure. And when he looked he found that Effie was looking back at him in the wise, humorous way that he had come to know so well. "Don't you see?" was what she seemed to say.

And he did see. He saw that it was not Manchester, but a man in Manchester; not the woman in Peter Struggles' kitchen, but the man in Peter's parlour who interrupted his mother's vision of the Marbeck hills. She lost their beauty in a greater beauty of her own.

"And don't be incredulous," said Effie's eyes.

She turned to Anne. "We'll go down to the Inn at once," she said, "and you shall catch the train this afternoon."

A quick look passed from Anne to Effie, from which they both excluded Sam. It almost seemed that Anne was asking Effie for support, and that Effie understood and nodded imperceptibly. And if Anne had seriously doubted, her doubts were dissipated by a look which told her that, where she was concerned, Effie believed in the feasibility of anything.

Nothing at Marbeck became Anne Branstone like her leaving it. "Why, mother, how young you look!" he cried when she came downstairs to the trap.

"It's just as well," said Anne, meeting Effie's eye over his shoulder.

Then, after she had gone, and so pat upon her going as to be hardly decent, life flamed for them ungrudgingly. There was something quite impudently callous about the haste of it, as if life pulled a face behind the older generation and turned lightheartedly to burn more ardently for them. But Anne, and they knew it, would not have thanked them to be sorry for her. She had gone to Peter Struggles, who needed her.

They could not now resume the half amphibious life of their autumn days, but the air itself from the snow-clad fells had all the stimulation of a bath. It cleansed and healed by touch and heightened their well-being till they moved in radiant exhilaration, now clamant at the joy of it, now dumb before its wonder.

Happy themselves, they were the cause of happiness in others, not self-contained in joy, but effervescing to the old black-beamed kitchen of the Marbeck Inn.

They had, as Sam cannily observed, the advantages of a private room at an hotel without paying for it—and abrogated them. In the autumn they had isolated their joy from others: now it brimmed from them and affected all the people of the Inn, making the long nights short. Good listeners were a godsend to the Dale in winter, and the shepherds, dropping from heaven knew how far, found a rare satisfaction in telling this attentive audience tales of the fells, of sheep wanderers that strayed as wide afield as Derbyshire, of dogs that ran amok and ravaged the flocks they ought to tend, of the epic Beast of Ennerdale, of the legends of John Peel and all the sagas of the Lakes. It needed little to make these dalesmen happy, nothing beyond a patient ear for a slow, rambling narrative—a long chain strung with pearls of racy episode—or an hour of Effie at the piano, when the dalesmen disappointed her by knowing no ballads, but having, instead, a sound acquaintance with the latest music-hall songs stacked in the cupboard at the Inn. In here, in the smoke room, they were knowing wags, in the kitchen they were themselves, talking shop, and therefore interesting. Effie and Sam preferred them in the kitchen, telling their slowly-moving tales, to seeing them in their smoke-room mood, imitating badly a thing not worth the imitating. But, in either room, they helped them to be happy.

Well coated they would go each night from the tobacco-laden air of the kitchen down the road to the bridge over Marbeck Force. A great peace brooded there. Even the stream ran softly now when all the surface water of its gathering ground was frozen hard.

They stood there on the bridge while the moon rose over Hartle Pike and scattered silver on the snow. Great shadows leaped to instant birth below the Pike whose comely top was one black silhouette against the brightened sky, and the beauty of the valley, seen by day with an almost Alpine harshness, mellowed in the moonlight to a subtle luminosity. Behind them were the lights of the friendly Inn; near by the low church tower saluted God amongst the pines, and all around them spread the lustrous radiance of the moon-flushed Dale.

For the hundredth time he restrained his impulse to repeat his words, "We'll build a tabernacle here," and Effie read his thought.

"We're making the good beginning here," she said. "We're practising and I think we grow."

"We grow in happiness," he said, which he thought good argument for staying at Marbeck.

"Yes. We grow in happiness. We shall have outgrown Marbeck soon. We shall have grown a sturdy happiness that can withstand the towns. It might withstand Manchester and I think it will. To love, to work, to look for other people's strength and not for other people's weaknesses: that is to be happy, Sam. And happiness counts more than all. It roots and then it spreads. It spreads. Infection isn't only of disease, infection is of happiness and youth. There's too much age, too many men and women in the world who have forgotten love. We have to build, and build on happiness." They gazed at the unguessed future through the silent night. God knows that there was work ahead for them to do!